Rafael Sabatini, creator of some of
was born in Italy in 1875 and ed
Switzerland. He eventually settled in
time he was fluent in a total of five languages. He chose to write in
English, claiming that 'all the best stories are written in English'.

His writing career was launched in the 1890s with a collection of
short stories, and it was not until 1902 that his first novel was
published. His fame, however, came with *Scaramouche*, the much-
loved story of the French Revolution, which became an international
bestseller. *Captain Blood* followed soon after which resulted in a
renewed enthusiasm for his earlier work.

For many years a prolific writer, he was forced to abandon writing
in the 1940s through illness and he eventually died in 1950.

Sabatini is best remembered for his heroic characters and high-
spirited novels, many of which have been adapted into classic films,
including *Scaramouche, Captain Blood* and *The Sea Hawk* starring
Errol Flynn.

TITLES BY THE SAME AUTHOR
ALL PUBLISHED BY HOUSE OF STRATUS

FICTION:

ANTHONY WILDING
THE BANNER OF THE BULL
BARDLEYS THE MAGNIFICENT
BELLARION
THE BLACK SWAN
CAPTAIN BLOOD
THE CAROLINIAN
CHIVALRY
THE CHRONICLES OF CAPTAIN BLOOD
COLUMBUS
FORTUNE'S FOOL
THE FORTUNES OF CAPTAIN BLOOD
THE GAMESTER
THE GATES OF DOOM
THE HOUNDS OF GOD
THE LION'S SKIN
THE LOST KING
LOVE AT ARMS
THE MARQUIS OF CARABAS
THE MINION
THE NUPTIALS OF CORBAL
THE ROMANTIC PRINCE
SCARAMOUCHE
SCARAMOUCHE THE KING-MAKER
THE SEA HAWK
THE SHAME OF MOTLEY
THE SNARE
ST MARTIN'S SUMMER
THE STALKING-HORSE
THE STROLLING SAINT
THE SWORD OF ISLAM
THE TAVERN KNIGHT
THE TRAMPLING OF THE LILIES
TURBULENT TALES
VENETIAN MASQUE

NON-FICTION:

HEROIC LIVES
THE HISTORICAL NIGHTS' ENTERTAINMENT
KING IN PRUSSIA
THE LIFE OF CESARE BORGIA
TORQUEMADA AND THE SPANISH INQUISITION

The Justice of the Duke

Rafael Sabatini

HOUSE OF
STRATUS

This edition published in 2001 by House of Stratus, an imprint of Stratus Books Ltd., 21 Beeching Park, Kelly Bray, Cornwall, PL17 8QS, UK. www.houseofstratus.com

Typeset, printed and bound by House of Stratus.

A catalogue record for this book is available from the British Library.

ISBN 07551-154-0-6

TO

LANCELOT AND MARTHA DIXON

THESE PAGES ARE AFFECTIONATELY INSCRIBED

Contents

Chapter 1

THE HONOUR OF VARANO

Cesare Borgia, Duke of Valentinois and Romagna, rose slowly from his chair, and slowly crossed to the window of that spacious chamber in the Rocca of Imola. He stood there in the autumn sunshine gazing down upon the tented meadow and the river beyond, and upon the long ribbon of road, the ancient Via Aemilia, stretching smooth and straight with never a crease until it was lost in the distant hazy pile that was Faenza.

That road which crosses Northern Italy diagonally – a line of almost unwavering straightness for a hundred miles from the ancient Rubicon to Piacenza – may well have been a source of pride to Marcus Aemilius Lepidus, some fifteen hundred years before; to Cesare Borgia, contemplating it upon that autumn day, it was no better than a source of vexation – a way north and south by which to his relief might march the troops he did not dare to summon.

From the road his eyes shifted again to the besieging camp in the meadows by the river. There all was bustle, an incessant movement of men and horses, industrious as a colony of ants. Yonder a group of engineers were mounting a park of artillery with which they hoped to smash a way into his stronghold. Farther off was a great coming-and-going of glittering armed figures about the large green tent that housed the too-daring Venanzio Varano. Away to the west a half-naked swarm of men laboured with picks and spades at a ditch by which to deviate the water from the river and so serve them as a rampart against any sudden sortie of the besieged.

A faint hum of all this business reached the watcher in his eyrie, and he cursed it between contempt and anger; contempt, to think how the mere lifting of his finger would scatter that presumptuous little army, as a flock of sparrows scatters perceiving the hawk poised above them in the blue; anger, to consider that he dared not lift that same finger lest other and greater plans, not yet mature, should suffer by this too-early display of might; contempt again, of this fool Varano, and his petty daring, to conceive that Cesare Borgia was at the end of his resources and a prey for such a handful of mercenaries – the very sweepings of the martial market-place – as Varano had assembled; anger again, that for a day, for an hour, he must allow Varano to continue in that conceit. With what a puffed-up arrogance would not this fool of Camerino be ordering the business of the siege against this Imola that gave no sign, against this brown citadel drowsing unresponsive in the late autumn sunshine under the Borgia banner with its bull device that floated from the Maschio Tower.

A stealthy step in the room behind him went unheeded by the Duke. That it did so, proved the extent of his absorption, for there never lived a man of keener senses; never a man who combined with an intellect superacute such splendid animal faculties as were his. Merely to behold him was to perceive all this. He was in the very flower of his youth; some seven and twenty years of age; tall, straight and lithe as steel. His father, Pope Alexander VI, had been accounted in early life the handsomest man of his day; of a beauty of countenance, it was said, that acted upon women as the lodestone upon iron – which had by no means helped him to the virtuous course that should be looked for in a churchman. That beauty Cesare had inherited, but refined and glorified by the graces of Madonna Vanozza de' Catanei, the Roman lady who had been his mother. If there was sensuality in the full lips of the red mouth, half-hidden by the silky tawny beard, this was corrected by the loftiness of the pale brow; the nose was delicately arched, the nostrils sensitive, and the eyes – who shall describe the glory of those hazel eyes? Who shall read their message, who shall depict the will, the intellect, the dreamy wistfulness, the impassiveness that looks out of them?

He was dressed from head to foot in black; but through the slashings of his velvet doublet gleamed the rich yellow of an undervest of cloth-of-gold; a ruby-studded girdle gripped his loins, and on his hip hung a heavy gold-hilted Pistoja dagger in a golden sheath of cunning workmanship. His tawny head was bare.

Again came never so faintly the creak of that stealthy footstep behind him, and again it went unperceived. Nor yet did Cesare move when another and heavier tread rang on the staircase mounting to his room. Absorbed he continued his survey of Varano's camp.

The door was opened and reclosed. Someone had entered and was approaching him. Still he did not stir; yet without stirring he spoke, addressing the newcomer by name.

"And so, Agabito," said he, "you have sent my summons to Varano?"

To another less accustomed than his secretary, Agabito Gherardi, to Cesare's ways, this might have seemed almost uncanny. But Agabito was familiar with that superacuteness of his master, whose perceptions were keen as a blind man's and who could recognise a step where another would have needed to behold the face.

He bowed as Cesare turned to him. He was a man of middle height, well nourished, with a mobile, humorous mouth and keen dark eyes. His age may have been forty, and, as became his clerkly station, he wore a black surcoat that descended to his knees.

"It has gone, Highness," he answered. "But I doubt the gentleman of Camerino will decline the invitation."

Agabito observed the Duke's glance to stray past and beyond him. Musing and idle seemed his eyes to Agabito – which but serves to show that, intimately though the secretary accounted that he knew his master, yet he had not fathomed the inscrutability of Cesare's glance. For the eyes which looked dreamy were alert and watchful, and the brain behind them was working swiftly to conclusions. The arras over beyond the great carved writing-table was quivering never so faintly. This Cesare was observing – seeming to muse – and he was considering that the air was still and that no draught could account for that phenomenon. Yet when presently he spoke, he betrayed nothing of observation or conclusion.

"Art ever a pessimist, Agabito," said he.

"True-sighted, my lord," amended the secretary, with the easy familiarity Cesare conceded him. "For the rest, what does it matter, whether he comes or not?" And he smiled, a thousand wrinkles gathering about his eyes. "There is always the back door."

"It is your cursed pessimism again to remind me that there is that and naught but that."

Agabito spread his hands, his countenance a grimace of deprecation.

"Who cares to open that back door?" quoth the Duke. "Why, man, if I make the allies aware of its existence, if I so much as lift the latch, the click of it will so scare them that they'll every one escape me. The back door, you say! You are growing old, Agabito. Show me the way to drive off that shallow fool with such means as I dispose of here."

"Alas!" sighed the secretary hopelessly.

"Alas, indeed!" snapped the Duke, and strode past him into the room. There he paced a while, considering the position, Agabito observing him.

To a more vexatious pass than this matters could not have come. It was the season of the league against him formed by the Orsini in alliance with his own revolted captains Vitelli and Baglioni. These rebels stood in arms a full ten thousand strong, determined upon his destruction, having sworn his death. Cunningly they spread their net to hem him in, believing that they had him safe and that his strength was sapped. And he, the better to take them in the toils they were spinning for himself, had indulged them in their conviction that he was powerless and unprepared. Actively had he done so, deliberately dismissing three of his companies of French lances – the very backbone of his army – and putting it about that they had left him of their own accord, led off by their captains with whom he had quarrelled. Thus had it seemed as if his knell had indeed sounded; already the allies accounted him their prey, for, without the French lances, the forces of which he disposed were of no account. But they knew nothing of the Romagnuoli men-at-arms that Naldo had assembled for him, still less of the Swiss foot and the Gascon mercenaries whom his officers held ready for him in Lombardy – nor should they know until the hour was ripe. He had but to lift his finger, and there would sprout up such an army as should make the allies sick with misgivings. Meanwhile he desired that they should bait their trap for him, lulled by their false security. He would walk into it complacently enough; but – by the Host! – what a surprising stir would he not make within it. How the springs of that same trap should take them on the recoil and crush them!

To have planned so well, so precisely to have reckoned the moves that must enable him to cry "Checkmate!" – and to find himself, instead, stalemated by the act of this rash fool of Camerino who sat out there in egregious self-complacency, little recking the volcano that was under him!

For here is what had happened. This Venanzio Varano, one of the dethroned lords of Camerino, impatient at the sluggishness of the allies, and unable to urge them into swifter action, had drawn off and taken matters into his own hands. Gathering together a desperate, out-at-elbow army of discredited mercenaries of all nations, numbering perhaps a thousand strong, he had marched upon Imola, and there laid siege to Cesare in his stronghold – cursed alike by the allies and by Cesare for his interference in the plans of each.

"Perhaps," said Agabito presently, "if the allies observe the success that seems to attend Varano, they will join him here. Then would be your opportunity."

But Cesare waved a hand impatiently. "How can I put a net about them here?" he asked. "I could rout their army; but what of that? It is the brains of it I want – and at one blow. No, no," he ended. "Meanwhile, let us see what answer Varano makes to my invitation, and what comes of it."

"And if nothing comes, you'll strike?" said Agabito, as though he urged it.

Cesare pondered, his face clouding. "Not yet," said he. "I'll wait and hope for some chance. My luck – there is my luck, remember." He turned to the massive, richly wrought writing-table, and took up a packet. "Here is the letter for the Signory of Florence. I have signed it. Contrive to get it hence."

Agabito took the package. "It will tax my ingenuity," said he, and pursed his lips.

"Attend to it," said Cesare, and so dismissed him.

The door closed upon the secretary; his steps receded down the stone staircase, and the sound of them was lost. Then Cesare, standing in mid-apartment, faced the arras which had quivered on Agabito's entrance.

"Come forth, messer the spy," said he quite calmly.

He was prepared to see a man emerge in answer to that summons – and he had some notion of that man's identity – but he was quite unprepared for the manner in which his order was to be obeyed.

The arras was swept aside, and across the intervening space, it seemed to Cesare, was hurled as from a catapult a great, brown human shape with one arm raised to strike. The blow descended. The dagger took Cesare full in the breast, and there snapped suddenly. As the broken blade tinkled on the floor, the Duke's hands closed like manacles about the wrists of his assailant.

The wretch may never have seen Cesare snap a horseshoe in his fingers, nor yet seen Cesare decapitate a bull at one single stroke of a spadoon, but of the awful strength that could accomplish such feats as those he had now the fullest and most painful demonstration. This murderer was a big fellow, of stout thews and sinews, yet in the grip of that lithe young man his strength was all turned to water. He felt as if the iron pressure of Cesare's fingers were crushing his wrists to pulp, were twisting his elbows out of joint. He came howling to his knees, then caught his nether lip in his teeth to repress another howl. His right hand opened and released the hilt and stump of his poniard, which went to rejoin the blade upon the floor. He looked up with fearful eyes into the Duke's face, and found it calm – horribly, terrifically calm – betraying neither anger nor exertion.

"Messer Malipiero," said his Highness, "you should never have chanced a shirt of mail when there was my naked throat to offer you so fair a mark." And he smiled amiably – the very superlative of mockery – into the other's tortured countenance. Then he released him. "Get up!" he said more briskly. "We must talk."

"My lord! My lord!" whimpered the assassin, holding out his maimed wrists. "Forgive! Forgive!"

"Forgive?" echoed Cesare, halting as he moved away. "Forgive what?"

"My – the thing I did but now."

"Oh, that! Why, it is the manliest thing you have done since you came hither. Count it forgiven. But the rest, Malipiero – your offering your sword to me in a time of need, your lies to me, your gaining my confidence, and you the spy of Varano – must I forgive that too?"

"My lord!" groaned the abject Malipiero.

"And even if I forgive you all this, can you forgive yourself – you, a patrician – that you should have come to turn spy and assassin?"

"Not – not assassin, my lord. I had not meant that. It was in self-defence, seeing myself discovered and accounting myself lost. Oh, I was mad! Mad!"

The Duke moved away towards the table. "Well, well," said he, "it is over and done with." He took up a silver whistle, and blew a blast upon it. Malipiero, staggering to his feet, turned if possible a shade paler than he had been. But the Duke's next words reassured him. "And for my own part, since you lay such store by it – I forgive you."

"You forgive me?" Malipiero could not believe his ears.

"Why not? I am a good Christian, I hope; and I practise the Christian virtue of forgiveness; so much indeed, that I deplore most deeply the necessity of hanging you none the less."

Malipiero flung wide his aching arms, and made a sound in his throat, terror staring from his protruding eyes.

"What choice have I?" quoth Cesare, in answer to that incoherent cry. "There are the things you have overheard. It was unfortunate."

"Gesú!" cried the other, and advanced a step towards Cesare. "I swear that I'll be dumb."

"You shall," said Cesare.

Heavy steps approached. Malipiero gulped, then spoke quickly, with fearful earnestness.

"I swear no word of what I heard shall ever cross my lips – I swear it by all my hopes of heaven, by the Blessed Mother of God!"

"You shall not be forsworn," Cesare assured him. Then the door opened, and the officer of the guard stood at attention on the threshold.

Malipiero clutched at his breast, swung about this way and that in the frenzy of his despair, until his glance met Cesare's calm eyes and impassive countenance. Then his tongue was loosened. Imprecations, ordures of speech too horrible for chronicling, poured torrentially from his quivering lips, until a touch upon the shoulder struck him into a shuddering silence. Limply he surrendered himself to the officer who at a sign from Cesare had advanced.

"Let him be confined in solitude," said the Duke, "until I make known my pleasure."

Malipiero looked hopelessly at Cesare. "When – when is it to be?" he asked hoarsely.

"At dawn tomorrow," Cesare answered. "God rest your soul!"

A trumpet blared beneath the walls of Imola, and its brazen voice reached Cesare Borgia in that room in the Maschio Tower. He dropped his pen and lay back in his chair. Conjecturing what might hang upon that trumpet-blast, he smiled pensively at the groined ceiling that was painted blue and flecked with golden stars, and waited.

Presently came Messer Gherardi with news that an ambassador had arrived from Varano's camp, and Cesare ceased to smile.

"An ambassador?" he echoed, his brows knitting. "Does a servant come in response to the invitation I sent the master?"

Agabito's ready smile deprecated this vexation. "Is it really matter for wonder? These Varani are treacherous, bloody men. Venanzio fears that you might deal with him as he with you in the like circumstances. He knows that were he removed his mercenaries would not avenge him, would not stand together for a day. You will see the ambassador, my lord? I can promise that you will find Varano's choice of messenger most interesting."

"How?" quoth Cesare shortly.

But the secretary's answer seemed almost an evasion. "There has been an arrest made since last I was here," said he. "I never trusted Gustavo Malipiero. How came he in this room, Highness?"

"That matters little. What he sought matters rather more. It was my life." And Cesare pointed to the pieces of the broken dagger, still lying where Malipiero had dropped them half-an-hour ago. "Pick it up, Agabito," said he.

On the point of obeying, Agabito checked, a queer smile twisting the corners of his mobile mouth. "You might presently wish that I had left it," said he. "Let it lie there yet a while, my lord."

Cesare's eyes questioned the secretary.

"Shall I introduce the ambassador of Varano?" was Agabito's bland inquiry.

"Why – what has he to do with Malipiero's dagger?" quoth the Duke, perceiving that in Gherardi's mind some connection must exist.

"Perhaps nothing, perhaps much. Be your Highness the judge."

Cesare waved a hand, assenting. Agabito crossed to the door, opened it and called; then leisurely returned to take his stand by the table at Cesare's elbow. Steps ascended the stairs. Two men-at-arms in morion and corselet clattered in and flanked the doorway, and between them entered, with clank of scabbard and ring of spurs, an elderly man of middle height, very splendid in purple velvet. In mid-apartment he checked with military abruptness, and bowed stiffly, yet profoundly, to the Duke. Then he came upright again, and out of a vulture face a pair of shifty eyes met Cesare's stern glance.

Whilst a man might count a dozen there was utter silence in the chamber, the ambassador waiting for the Duke to address him, the Duke seeming in no haste, but staring at the man and understanding what had been in Gherardi's mind when he had begged that the dagger should be let lie a while.

A bee sailed through the window and the hum of its wings was the only sound that disturbed a stillness that was becoming unnatural. At last Cesare spoke to the ambassador of Varano, to the father of the man who half-an-hour ago had sought to murder him.

"It is thou, Malipiero, eh?" said he, his face impassive as a mask, his brain a whorl of speculation of considering and connecting.

The man bowed again. "Your servant always, Highness."

"Art the servant of the Lord of Camerino?" the Duke amended. "Art the fox that waits upon the wolf?" And the evenness of his tones was marred by the faintest suspicion of a sneer. "I bade your master attend me that we might arrange the terms upon which he will consent to raise this siege. He sends you in his place. It is an affront – tell him – which I shall lay to his already very heavy score. Let him flout me while the little fleeting chance is his. But let him not cry out hereafter when I call the reckoning."

"My lord was afraid to come, Magnificent."

Cesare laughed shortly. "I nothing doubt it. But you – you, Malipiero?" And he leant forward, his tone of a sudden invested with a deadly menace. "Were you not afraid to take his place?"

Malipiero started, his natural pallor deepened, and the corners of his mouth were perceived by Agabito to quiver slightly. But before he could answer, the Duke had sunk back into his chair again, and asked in normal tones: "Why have you come?"

"To treat in my lord's name."

Cesare considered him a moment in silence. "For that and nothing else?" he inquired.

"What else, indeed, Highness?"

" 'Tis what I asked thee," said Cesare shortly.

"My lord," the other cried in quaking protest, "I come as an ambassador."

"Why, true. I was forgetting. Discharge your embassy. You know the thing that I would buy. Tell me the price this trader of Camerino asks."

Malipiero the elder drew himself erect, and formally performed his errand. As he spoke his eyes strayed to the broken dagger lying almost at his feet, the gold hilt gleaming in a shaft of sunlight; but the weapon told him nothing, it was plain, for he never checked or faltered in the delivery of his message.

"My lord of Camerino," he announced, "will raise this siege and withdraw his army in return for your signed undertaking to recall your troops from Camerino, reinstating him in his lordship and leaving him to enjoy it unmolested."

Cesare stared in amazement at the effrontery of the demand. "Was he drunk, this lout of Camerino, when he sent that message?"

Malipiero quailed under the scorn of the Duke's eyes. "Magnificent," he said, "it may be that my Lord Venanzio seems arrogant to you. But you will find him firm in his resolve. He has you, he swears, in the hollow of his hand."

"Has he so? Body of God! Then he shall find that I am made of gunpowder, and when I burst that same hand of his shall be blown to rags. Go tell him so."

"You'll not accept his terms?"

"Sooner will I sit in Imola until the Resurrection of the Flesh."

Malipiero paused a moment like a man undecided. His glance shifted to the shaven, humorous face of Agabito Gherardi; but he saw nothing there to embolden him. Nevertheless like a good ambassador, he said what else he had been bidden say.

"Vitellozzo, the Orsini and the Baglioni are coalescing."

"Do you give me news? And how shall that serve Varano? His subjects of Camerino loathe him for a bloody tyrant, and being once rid of him they'll never suffer his return."

"I am not sure…" began Malipiero.

"I know thou'rt not. But I, who am, tell thee." He pushed back his chair on that, and rose. "Agabito, let this ambassador of Varano be reconducted, and with courteous treatment."

And with that, as if dismissing the entire matter from his mind, he sauntered across the room, past Malipiero, towards the window; and as he went he drew from his pocket a little comfit-box in gold and blue enamel.

Agabito experienced a pang of disappointment. Not so, by much, had he pictured the conclusion of this interview. And yet, perhaps Cesare in his cunning and unfailing calculation counted upon something more. Even as he thought of it he saw in Malipiero's attitude that it was so, indeed. For the ambassador made no shift to go. He stood there shuffling uneasily, his foxy old eyes roaming from the secretary to the young duke, and betraying the labour of his mind.

"Highness," he said at last, "may I speak with you alone?"

"We are alone," said Cesare over his shoulder. "What else have you to add?"

"Something that will make for the advancement of your interests."

Cesare turned his back to the window, and his beautiful eyes grew very narrow as they surveyed the bowing Malipiero. Then a faint smile hovered round his lips. He made a sign to the men-at-arms standing by the door. They turned and clattered out.

"Agabito remains. I have no secrets from my secretary. Speak out."

"Highness..." began the ambassador, and halted there. Then, under Cesare's impatient eye, "My Lord Varano is in earnest," he concluded lamely.

Cesare shrugged and raised the lid of his comfit-box. "So I had understood from you already. Is there nothing more?"

"You were pleased to correct me, Highness, when upon entering here I announced myself your servant."

"By what tortuous ways do you travel to your goal? Well, well! You were my servant once; now you are his. Would you be mine again? Is that your meaning?"

Malipiero bowed eloquently. The Duke considered him, shot a glance at Agabito, then with deliberation picked a coriander-seed.

"The lord of Camerino's fortunes, then, do not wear so very prosperous a look?" said he, between question and conclusion, and thereby set Malipiero infernally ill at ease.

The ambassador had looked for some eagerness on Cesare's part. This calm, half-mocking indifference chilled him. At last he took his courage in both hands. "It was I," he announced, "who made Varano afraid to come – to the end that he might send me."

The lid of the comfit-box snapped down. His Magnificence of Valentinois was interested at last, it seemed. Encouraged, Malipiero went on, "I did this that I might lay my poor services at your disposal; for at heart, Highness, I have ever been your most devoted. My only son is in your service."

"You lie, you foul, infernal traitor. You lie!" And Cesare advanced upon him as if to strike him into dust. Gone now was the impassive calm on his face; gone the inscrutable softness of his eyes; their glance enveloped Malipiero as in a flame – a flame that swept about his heart and left it ashes.

"My lord! My lord!" he babbled foolishly.

Cesare halted in his approach, and resumed his quiet manner as abruptly as he had cast it off.

"Look at that dagger at your feet," he said, and Malipiero obeyed him stupidly. "It was broken an hour ago against my breast. Can you guess whose the hand that wielded it? Your son's – this precious only son of yours, who is in my service."

Malipiero recoiled, bearing a hand to his throat as if something choked him.

"You came hither for such scraps of knowledge as that spy might have gleaned. My invitation to Varano was your opportunity. Without it you would still have come, bearing as spontaneous the offer that you brought as answer. The object of your spying you best know – you that never yet kept faith with any man. Oh, there is no doubt, Malipiero, that at heart you have ever been my devoted servants – you and your son."

"O God!" groaned the unhappy wretch.

"Your only son is to be hanged at daybreak tomorrow. It shall be from this window here, in sight of this Varano whom he served, in sight of you who have ever been my most devoted."

Malipiero cast himself upon his knees; he flung out his arms wildly. "My lord, I swear to you that I knew naught of any plot to – to hurt you."

"Why, I believe you for once. There may have been no such plot. But I caught your son in the act of spying, and so he took, perhaps, what seemed to him the only course. It makes no difference. He would have hanged without that."

Malipiero, on his knees, raised a livid face, his brow glistening with the sweat of the agony that racked him.

"Highness," he cried, in a quavering voice, "I have it in my power to make amends for my son's folly. I can rid you of this bankrupt of Camerino. Shall it – shall it be a bargain between us? My son's life for the raising of this siege?"

Cesare smiled. "It was to make me some such proposal, I think, that you desired to speak with me alone. Nothing is altered but the price – for not a doubt but that you intended some other profit from the treachery you had conceived."

Malipiero flung dissimulation to the winds. What, indeed, could it avail him against one who looked so deep and unerringly into motives? The greed of gold which had made him a constant traitor to any whom he served had been his only stimulus in this fresh treachery. But now, the life of his boy was all the recompense he asked. He frankly said as much.

"I will not bargain with you," was Cesare's contemptuous answer.

Tears welled to the eyes of the distraught man and coursed down the furrows of the livid cheeks. Wildly he implored clemency and urged upon the Duke's attention the gain he stood to make.

"There is not in all Italy a knave with whom I would so scorn to deal as you, Malipiero. Man, you have steeped yourself in the filth of treachery until you stink of it. The very sight of you offends me."

"My lord," the wretch clamoured, "I can raise this siege as could no other man. Grant me Gustavo's life, and it shall be done to-morrow. I will draw Varano away – back to Camerino. What are his men without him? You know their worth, Highness – a parcel of hirelings with no heart in the business, who would never stay to oppose a sally if Varano were not at hand to urge them."

Cesare measured the man with a calculating eye. "What means have you to perform so much?"

At that suggestion that the Duke was inclined to treat with him, Malipiero rose. He shuffled a step nearer, licking his lips. "Varano loves his throne of Camerino dearly. But there is one thing he loves still more – his honour. Let it be whispered to him that the lady, his wife – " He leered horribly. "You understand, Magnificent? He would leave his camp out yonder and dash back to Camerino, where she bides, as fast as horse could bear him."

Cesare felt his soul revolt. The thing was vile, the fruit of a vile mind, uttered by a vile mouth; and as he looked at the leering creature before him, a sense of nausea took him. But his face showed no sign of this; his beautiful passionless eyes betrayed none of the loathing with which this arch-traitor inspired him. Presently his lips parted in a smile; but what that smile portended Malipiero could not guess until he spoke.

"Possibly there is in Italy a viler thing than thou; probably there is not. Still, it is for me to use thee, not convert thee. Do this thing, then, since you are assured it may be done."

Malipiero drew a deep breath of relief. Insults were of no account to him. "Grant me my son's life, and I undertake that by tonight Varano shall be in the saddle."

"I'll make no bargains with you," Cesare answered him.

"But if I do this thing you will be clement, you will be merciful, Highness?"

"Rest content. You shall not fail to find me just."

"I am content," said Malipiero. "I count upon that. And yet – and yet... Reassure me, Highness! I am a father. Promise me that, if I serve you in this, Gustavo shall not hang."

Cesare eyed him a moment and shrugged contemptuously. "He shall not hang. I have said that you shall find me just. And now to details." Cesare crossed briskly to the writing-table. "Have you power in Varano's name to grant a safe-conduct?"

"I have, Highness."

"Here is what you will need. Write, then – for twenty men from Imola."

Malipiero snatched a quill, and in a hand that shook, for all his efforts to steady it, he wrote and signed the order Cesare demanded. The Duke took the paper and sat down.

"How shall I have knowledge that Varano has departed?" he inquired.

Malipiero considered a moment. Then, "As soon as he goes tonight I will extinguish the cresset that burns outside his tent. You can see it from here."

Cesare nodded shortly, and blew upon his silver whistle. To the men-at-arms, re-entering in answer to that summons, he consigned the person of the ambassador, bidding them reconduct him to the gates.

When the door had closed again, Cesare turned to Agabito with a smile of grim contempt. "I had best served the world had I violated the sacredness of that ambassador's person, and held a family hanging in the morning. The toad! Madonna! The foul, crapulous toad! But there! Summon Corella, and bid them have young Malipiero at hand."

When, presently, Cesare's Venetian captain, whom so many supposed to be a Spaniard, stalked into the room – a tall, stately man, all steel and leather – the Duke tossed Malipiero's safe-conduct across to him, and gave his orders.

"You will watch tonight the cresset that burns outside Varano's tent. Ten minutes after it has been quenched you will ride out with the twenty men you choose, and make for Camerino." Cesare unrolled a map and beckoned Corella to his side. "But not this way, Michele – not by Faenza and Forli. You shall take to the hills and thus outstrip another party going by the main road. Contrive that

16

you reach Camerino in advance of it by at least six hours, and remember that those others will ride desperately. Agabito will instruct you later in what else you have to do. The manner of it shall be in your own hands."

Michele da Corella gasped. "They will set out before me," he said. "They will take the shorter road, and they will ride desperately. Yet I am to be in Camerino at least six hours ahead of them. In short, I am to work a miracle, and I am just Michele da Corella, a captain of horse."

Cesare looked up quietly. "Chucklehead!" said he. "You will detach the two best-mounted men of your company, and send them after the other party by the Rimini road. Let them pass and precede them, and so contrive with the relays to delay them upon the road sufficiently to enable you to do as I command."

Corella flushed out of shame of wits that must appear so dull.

"Now, go, Michele," the Duke bade him, "and make ready."

As Corella was withdrawing the Duke recalled him. "I said twenty men. I should have said nineteen – counting yourself; the twentieth will be Messer Gustavo Malipiero, who is to ride with you. Bid them bring him in now."

Corella saluted and withdrew. Cesare sat back in his great leathern chair and glanced at Agabito. "Well?" he inquired. "Do you perceive what a web of justice I am weaving?"

"Not yet, my lord," confessed Agabito.

"Not? I sometimes think you are as dull-witted as Michele."

And Agabito kept it to himself that he sometimes thought his master possessed all the guile and craft of Satan.

As Malipiero the older had undertaken, so did he perform; though in the performance he went near to being strangled by the powerful hands of Venanzio Varano.

He repaired at nightfall to Venanzio's tent with his foul invention, and at the first hint of his meaning the passionate lord of Camerino flung into a fury. He caught Malipiero by his scraggy throat, swung him off his feet, and went over with him in a dark corner of the tent.

There he pinned him to the ground under a knee that seemed to be crushing every bone in the old traitor's breast.

"Dog!" he snarled, and Malipiero writhed and squirmed, half-dead from shock and fright, expecting to feel the other's teeth close on his windpipe, so brutal was Varano become in his great rage. "Do you proclaim my wife a trull?" he roared. "Say that you lied! Confound yourself, you rogue, or, by the Host I'll wring your carrion neck."

Then Malipiero, coward though he was at heart, was fired with the courage of despair. "Fool!" he panted, struggling for breath. "Fool, I spoke out of love for you, and I can prove the thing I say."

"Prove it?" roared the infuriated Varano, and he heaved the wretch up to dash him down again. "Prove it? Can lies be proved?"

"No," said Malipiero. "But truth can."

It was a simple and very obvious retort. Yet it produced its effect upon Varano, and Malipiero was able to breathe more freely at last. Varano had released him; he had risen and was bawling for lights. Malipiero sat up, nursing his bruises, making sure that no bones were broken, and breathing a prayer of thanksgiving to Our Lady of Loreto – who had ever been the object of a special devotion on his part – that he had had the wit to forge proofs betimes that should lend countenance to the foul charges he made against a pure lady's honour. He comforted himself, too, with the reflection that those same proofs would avenge the mishandling he had suffered, and that for the bruises Varano had dealt his body he would presently deal such bruises to Varano's soul as should go some way to make them quits.

Lights came, revealing the shrivelled, yellow-faced man sitting there upon the floor, with tumbled hair and rent garments and a very evil glimmer in his rat's eyes, and the other – the great lumbering Varano – standing over him, no less pale and evil to behold.

"Now, dog, the proofs."

This was Malipiero's hour of vengeance. Slowly he loosed the points of his purple doublet; slowly he groped within the breast of it, and slowly he drew forth a package tied with an orange ribbon.

Slowly he was proceeding to unfasten it, when Varano, with an oath of impatience, stooped, snatched the package, and tore away the ribbon. Then he strode to the table, unfolded a letter, and spread it under his great hand.

Malipiero, watching him with fearful, unblinking eyes, saw the great head slowly sink forward on to his breast. But Varano rallied quickly. His faith in his wife was no mere thistledown to be so lightly scattered. He sank to a chair, and turned to Malipiero, who had now risen.

"Tell me," he said, "tell me again, how came these into your hands?" There was now no anger in his voice. He spoke like a man who is struggling between dark unconsciousness and painful consciousness.

"Madonna's chamberlain Fabio brought them an hour ago during your absence. He dared not come while you were here. Love of you made him traitor to your lady. Fear of you kept him from delivering the letters to you himself. And no sooner had he said so much to me than he was gone again, leaving the cursed package in my hands."

"If – if they were false!" cried Varano, wrestling with that fierce natural jealousy of his upon which the cunning Malipiero had built his schemes.

The traitor's face grew long with simulated sorrow. "My lord," he murmured dolefully, "to bid you build on that were not to love you. What ends could Fabio wish to serve? And Fabio loves you. And Fabio, who purloined those letters from madonna's treasure casket, knew of their existence, else he had not sought them."

"Enough!" cried the wretched Varano – a cry of anguish. Then with an oath he opened out another letter. "Oh, vile!" he groaned. "Oh, worse and worse," and he read the signature – "Galeotto" – then knit his brows. "But who is this Galeotto?"

On the livid face of the satyr behind his chair a faint smile was smeared. He had a sense of humour, this Malipiero, and in the fiction of that name, in the equivoque it covered, it had found a sly expression. Aloud he parodied a line of Dante's:

"Galeotto fu il nome, e chi lo scrisse!"

With a snort the lord of Camerino turned to a third letter. His hand clenched and unclenched as he read. Then he raised it, and smashed it down upon the table with a fearful oath. He came to his feet. "Oh, shameless!" he inveighed. "Adulteress! Trull! Oh, and yet – so fond to all seeming, and so foully false! God help me! Is it possible – is it – "

He checked, his blood-injected eyes fastened upon Malipiero, and Malipiero recoiled now in horror of the devil he had raised. He drew hastily aside, out of Varano's way, as the latter, moved by a sudden resolve, strode to the entrance of the tent, beating his hands together and calling.

"Saddle me three horses on the instant," he commanded, "and bid Gianpaolo make ready for a journey." Then, striding back into the tent, "The third horse is for you, Malipiero."

"For me?" clucked the traitor, in a greater fright than any that had yet touched him since embarking on this evil business.

"For thee," said Varano sternly. Then towering above the shivering wretch, "Hast ever known torture, Malipiero?" he inquired. "Hast ever seen the hoist at work, or the rack disjointing bones and stretching sinews till they burst, till the patient screams for the mercy of a speedy death? If God in His great clemency should please that you have lied to me – as I pray He may – you shall make acquaintance with those horrors, Malipiero. Ah, it makes you faint to think on them," he gloated, for he was, as Cesare had said a cruel, bloody man. Then suddenly, sternly, "Go make you ready for this journey," he commanded, and Malipiero went.

Here was a tangle, a complication on which the astute Venetian – for this Malipiero hailed from Venice, the very home and source of craft – had failed to reckon. That Varano should still be suspicious amid all his passion of jealousy, and should wish to make sure of Malipiero against the chance of precisely some such situation as the existing one, was something that had never entered the traitor's calculations.

What was he to do? Mother of God, what was he to do?

As he stood in his own tent a sickness took him, a sickness that was physical as well as spiritual. Then he rallied, played the man a moment, and drew his sword. He ran his thumb along the edge of it to test its keenness; he set the hilt against the ground, and paused. He had but to place himself with his heart over the point – so – and drop forward. A Roman death was here – swift and painless. Surely he had reached the end, and if he took not this easy means of egress there were the horrors Varano had promised him – the rack and the hoist.

Then he bethought him of his son. His son would hang at dawn unless Varano went. And if he killed himself now, Varano must guess the truth, and would remain. That and the reflection that between Imola and Camerino much might betide, restrained him. He took up his sword again, and restored it to its sheath. Steps sounded without; a soldier stood at the entrance, with a summons from Varano. The traitor braced himself to go.

As they reached Varano's tent he bethought him of one thing there was yet to do, and turning to the mercenary who paced behind him, "Quench me that cresset," he commanded shortly.

The fellow caught up a pail of water standing near, and flung the contents on the blaze, extinguishing it.

"Why, what is this?" asked Varano, stepping forth.

"There was too much light," said Malipiero glibly. "They can see us from the castle."

"What then, man?"

"Would you have Cesare Borgia know that you ride forth?" cried Malipiero, with a very obvious sneer for the thing the other overlooked.

"Ah, true! You are a thoughtful knave. Come now. To horse!"

As they mounted, and were ready to set out – Malipiero between Varano and Gianpaolo da Trani, his esquire – Schwarz, the captain of the mercenaries, came up. The rumour of Varano's departure running round the camp had reached the Swiss, and, incredulous, he came for orders.

"Plague me not," growled the Lord Venanzio in answer.

"But, Excellency," the man protested, "shall you be absent long?"

"As long as my business needs."

"Then from whom shall I take orders in the meantime?" cried the condottiero, out of patience.

"From the devil," said Varano, and gave his horse the spur.

All night they rode, and so desperately that by dawn they were in San Arcangelo, and Malipiero bethought him with a pang that here, under this bridge, which gave back a hollow echo of their horses' hoofs, flowed the ancient fateful Rubicon, which he was crossing figuratively as well as literally.

Varano, riding half a horse's length in advance of his companions, pushed on, his face set, his eyes ahead. A mile or so beyond Arcangelo they were overtaken and passed by two riders going at a gallop, who thundered away towards Rimini in a cloud of dust. They were the men despatched by Corella, and they had taken fresh horses at Cesena in the Duke's name, thus outstripping the weary cattle of the men of Camerino.

Varano watched their speed with eyes of furious envy, and cursed the spent condition of his own horse. So they pressed on towards Rimini, their pace slackening now with every mile and in spite of all their flogging. At last the town was reached, and at the "Three Kings" Varano bawled for fresh horses with never a thought for breakfast. But horses, the host regretfully informed them, there were none to be had that morning.

"Perhaps at Cattolica…" he suggested.

Varano never stayed to argue. He drank a cup of wine and ate a crust, then heaved himself back into the saddle and urged his companions on. He was to pay for this unreasoning haste; for it was a haste that did not make for speed in the end. It took them three hours to reach Cattolica – three weary men on three spent horses. And here again they were met by the same tale of no relays. There would be none until the evening.

"Until evening?" roared Varano hoarsely. "Why, 'tis not yet noon!"

Malipiero, utterly worn out, had sunk on to a stone bench in the inn-yard. "Horses or no horses," he groaned, "I can go no farther." His face was grey, his eyes encircled by black lines. Yet Varano observed nothing of this, as he turned upon the fellow in a fury of suspicion. Before he could speak, however, his esquire had come to Malipiero's rescue.

"Nor I, body of God!" he swore. "Before I ride another mile I must eat and sleep. What odds, my lord?" he reasoned with the scowling Varano. "We'll sleep by day, and ride by night. When all is said, it is the speediest travelling."

"Sleep?" growled Varano. "I had not meant to sleep this side Camerino – perhaps, indeed, not then. But since I ride with women... Pshaw!"

Thus matters stood, then. They rested all that day in Cattolica, and what hopes of escaping Malipiero may have fostered were quenched entirely by the lack of means. They resumed their journey again at dusk, upon fresh horses then provided – indifferent beasts, however, and far from such as Varano's hot impatience craved. Again they rode all night, going westward by Urbino, which was in the hands of Cesare's revolted captains, then south to Pergola, where they came soon after daybreak on the morrow.

Thence to Camerino was little more than thirty miles, and Varano would have gone straight on, but that again the lack of fresh horses foiled his purpose. It was in vain he swore, besought or threatened. The country was all topsy-turvy, he was answered, infested with men-at-arms, and horses were scarce. He must wait until his own were rested. Until noon, then, they abode there, and now it was that Malipiero had the inspiration to feign illness, since flight was impossible.

"My head swims," he had whimpered, "and my loins burn. I am an old man, my lord, unfit to ride as you have made me ride."

Varano's eyes, dull, aching and bloodshot from his sleeplessness, measured the other fiercely. "Shalt have a physician in Camerino," said he.

"But, my lord, it is my fear that I may never get so far."

23

"Dismiss the fear," Varano enjoined him. "For you shall be there this evening – living or dead." And he stalked out, leaving Malipiero cold with a great fear that already he was suspected. When the hour to resume the journey came, Malipiero renewed his protestations.

"Mount!" was all the answer Varano returned him, and Malipiero, resigning himself to the awful fate that awaited him, climbed painfully to the saddle. He was ill, indeed; between fear and saddle-weariness he was all but spent. Yet he sat his horse in a sort of desperation, and so came into Camerino at eventide between his companions.

The place was garrisoned by a small company of Borgia soldiers – nor were many needed, for had the Varani attempted to return, the whole state would have taken up arms to beat them off. Under cover of the dusk, Venanzio led his companions to a mean hostelry in the borgo. There he left Malipiero with Gianpaolo – the latter virtually gaoler to the former. Alone, Varano went forth to seek for himself the truth of this vile tale that had been told him.

Meanwhile, Malipiero, wrapped in his cloak, lay stretched on a settle shivering with horrid anticipation of the hoist and the rack. Soon, soon now, Varano would discover the treachery, and then – He groaned aloud, disturbing Gianpaolo, who sat at table eating.

"Do you suffer, sir?" quoth the esquire; not that he greatly cared, for he loved Malipiero little, but that it seemed an inquiry which courtesy demanded. Malipiero groaned again for only answer, and the esquire, moved to pity, brought the unhappy man a cup of wine.

Malipiero gulped it down. It warmed him, he protested, and begged for more. Then having drained a second, and after that a third goblet, he relapsed into his forlorn attitude. But the wine creeping through his veins inspired him with new courage. He had been too fearful of consequences, he now perceived. He should have made a dash for it before this. Even now it might not be too late. There were Borgia troops in the town. He would find refuge at the citadel. He had but to inform the captain or the governor, or whoever might be in command, of Varano's whereabouts in the town, and he would find shelter and gratitude.

Fired by the notion, he flung off the cloak, and got briskly to his feet.

"I need air!" he cried.

"I'll open the window," said the too-obliging Gianpaolo.

"The window? Bah! This place is foul. I will take a turn outside."

Gianpaolo, eyeing him curiously – and with good reason, for the man had lately sworn he could not move without pain – barred his way to the door.

"Best await my lord's return," said he.

"Why, I shall be back before then."

But Gianpaolo had his orders – that Malipiero was not to be allowed out of his sight. Moreover there was this sudden vigour in one who so lately had been prostrate from exhaustion. Gianpaolo could not believe that wine alone had wrought a change so portentous.

"Why, if you will, you will," said he. "But in that case I'll with you," and he reached for his cap.

Malipiero's face fell at that. But his recovery was swift. Let the fool come, by all means, if he insisted. Malipiero would march him into a trap, and quickly. And then, even as he was on the point of consenting, the stairs groaned under a heavy step; the door was flung open so violently that it struck against the wall, and Venanzio Varano, with mad blazing eyes and a brow of thunder, strode into the room.

Malipiero backed away in terror, with an inward curse at his own tardiness in perceiving the obvious way of escape. Now it was too late. Varano had learnt the truth already, and again Malipiero bethought him of the rack; already in imagination he felt his sinews cracking and the rude hands of the executioner upon him.

And then, marvel of marvels, Varano dropped into a chair, and took his great black head in his hands. A while he remained thus, Gianpaolo and Malipiero watching him – the traitor understanding nothing of this bearing, unable to think what could have happened?

Presently Varano sat up, composed himself, and looked sorrowfully at Malipiero.

"Malipiero," said he, "I have prayed God ever since we left Imola that, for some reasons which the rack should tear from you, you had lied to me. But – " A sob cut his utterance. "Oh, there is no more pity in heaven than on earth. This thing is true, it seems – most vilely, hideously true."

True! Malipiero's senses reeled an instant under the shock of it. Then a great warmth thawed his terror-frozen veins; a great exultation sang within his vile soul; a great thankfulness welled up from his heart to heaven for this miraculous escape. His spirit capered and jested within him. He would set up for a diviner, a seer, after this.

Outwardly he remained a pale embodiment of sorrow. He licked his dry lips, his little eyes sought Varano's and fell away before the awful glance that met them. So may the damned look.

He wanted to question Varano, to ask how he had discovered this thing, that he might satisfy himself of the incredible truth of it; and yet he dared not. Nor was there the need; for presently Varano gave him the information that he craved.

"I was recognised in the street as I quitted the inn. A man who saw me come forth followed me, overtook me, and called to me by name. He had been my servant once, he said, and had ever loved me, wherefore he had meant this very night to ride forth in quest of me to tell me of the things that were happening in my absence.

"When I had heard this story I would have gone at once to that accursed palace where by the Borgia clemency that vile adulteress is housed. But he stayed my impatience with his counsel. He bade me wait – wait until dead midnight, and so make certain. He himself – this good soul that loves me – will watch for me, and will be at hand when I arrive."

He rose violently. His grief and shame dropped from him, and were replaced by an anger dreadful to behold. Imprecations rained from his mouth, which was twisted like that of a man in physical suffering. A mirror hanging from a wall of that poor chamber caught his eye. He strode to it and scanned himself, rubbing his brow the while. Then with his clenched fist he shivered the thing to atoms.

"It lied," he roared, and laughed most terribly. "It showed a fair smooth brow – no horns – no horns! I that am antlered like a stag!" And his awful laugh shook the windows in their crazy frames.

At midnight the Lord Venanzio rose from his chair where he had been sitting motionless for upwards of an hour. His face was haggard, his eyes stern and his mouth hard.

"Come," he said quietly, "it is the hour."

Gianpaolo, with a deep sorrow in his heart, and Malipiero, with an unholy glee in his, followed their lord down the narrow stairs, and out into the scented autumn night. They went up the steep street to the palace that crowned the hill. But passing the main doors they struck down a narrow lane and so came to a wicket in a high wall. A man rose up before them, seeming to materialise out of the gloom.

"He is within," he murmured to Varano. "He went the usual way, leaving the gate unlocked."

"That was considerate in him," said Varano heavily, and dropped a purse into the hands of the spy. Then he pushed the wicket till it opened, and beckoned his companions after him into a garden that was thick with shrubs. They came by an alley black as Erebus into a fair clearing under the stars; and here Varano checked, and gripped Malipiero's wrist.

"Yonder," he snarled. "That is her chamber." And with his other hand he pointed to a lighted window – the only window of the palace that still showed a light. "See with what a warmth it burns – a Vestal fire!" he sneered, and laughed softly. Next he sped swiftly forward across the yielding turf, his companions following. Under her balcony he paused.

"See," he whispered back to them. "Is he not considerate, this gallant? Look!" And they saw dangling from the balcony a great ladder of silken rope.

Had Varano still hoped against hope, still set his trust in his wife against the things he had been told, the letters he had seen, then must his last hope have foundered here.

He swarmed the ladder with the ease and speed of an ape. They saw him fling one leg over the stone parapet and then the other; there followed a crash and ring of shivered glass, as with his shoulder the infuriate husband smashed a way into the room.

He found his quarry standing in mid-apartment, startled by this terrific entrance – a fair young man, tall and comely, decked like a bridegroom all in white and gold, his discarded doublet still hanging in his hand.

Varano swooped upon him ere he could utter a word, locked an arm about his neck, wrenched him backwards, and, dropping on one knee, caught him, as he fell, across the other. The wretch, half-strangled in that awful grip, saw a long dagger gleam above him, heard a terrific voice: "Hound of hell, I am Venanzio Varano. Look on me, and die!"

The dagger sank to the hilt; it was raised again, and yet again, to be replunged into the heart of this man who had dishonoured him. Then, by an arm, Varano dragged the warm, twitching body across the room towards the bed, leaving a great crimson smear in its wake along the mosaic floor.

"Shalt lie snug tonight," he sneered, "snug and warm, snug and warm. And this wanton – " He dropped his hold of the dead arm and turned to the bed, his thoughts running now directly upon his wife. Clutching his dagger firmly in one hand he swung aside the heavy curtains with the other.

"Now, harlot…" He checked. The bed was empty, undisturbed.

The door behind him opened suddenly. He swung about, a horrid, blood-spattered sight.

On the threshold stood a tall man with a grave dark countenance and a very martial bearing, a man whose fame was almost as well known to every soldier in Italy as was the Duke his master's.

"Michele da Corella!" quoth Varano, thunderstruck. "You were in Imola. What make you here?" Then, his mind swinging back to the weightier matter that oppressed it. "My wife?" he cried. "Where is Madonna Eulalia?"

Corella advanced into the room. Behind him pressed a posse of javelin-men in the Borgia livery of red and yellow.

"Your wife, my lord, is in Bologna – safe," said he.

Varano, bewildered, stared at Cesare's captain. "Why – why – what treachery is here?" he mumbled thickly, like a drunkard.

"A very foul one, my lord – yet not one that touches you so nearly as that other. The traitor is that knave, that scavenger, Malipiero, a part of whose plot it was most vilely to slander the fair name of the spotless lady of Venanzio Varano."

"Slander?" echoed, Varano, and "Spotless?" fastening upon those words amid all that Corella had spoken. "It is not true, then?" he cried.

"As heaven hears me, it is not true," Corella answered. "The people of Camerino were venting upon Madonna Eulalia their resentment against your house, my lord; and so, a week ago, she sought shelter with her father in Bologna. No doubt her courier would reach your camp almost in the hour in which you left it."

A great sob broke from Varano; tears coursed down his war-worn cheeks. What signified to him that he had been betrayed in other matters? What signified losses and reverses so that his Eulalia was true and spotless?

Corella was speaking. Briefly he gave Varano the details of the treachery by which Malipiero had drawn him away from Imola, so that Cesare might rout the mercenary rabble that would never stand in its leader's absence. He had sought to bargain for the life of his son who was to have hanged for spying and for attempting to murder the Duke. Cesare, loving the treason but loathing the traitor, had refused to make terms, promising Malipiero in return for the betrayal he proposed no more than justice.

"It was by Malipiero's contriving," he pursued, "that I left Imola, and did what else was necessary to accomplish my lord's wishes in this matter, even to housing comfortably in this chamber a person whom his Highness had entrusted to me. My thought was that he would attempt to escape by the ladder provided for the purpose and that you would take him as he came forth. Your impatience, my lord – "

By the Host!" roared Varano, breaking in, "Cesare Borgia shall answer to me for having put upon me the slaying of an innocent man."

Corella looked at him a moment with lifted brows. "You have not understood," he said. He pointed to the corpse. "That carrion was Gustavo Malipiero."

Varano recoiled. "Gustavo Malipiero? His son?" And he jerked a thumb in the direction of the window.

"His son."

"My God," said Varano hoarsely. "Is this the justice of your Duke?"

"Ay, my lord, upon the assassin there and the traitor outside; upon both at one blow – and that by the hand of yourself, whom Malipiero so foully abused, and through the very scheme that he invented. Such is the very perfect justice of my Duke."

Varano looked at Corella. "And incidentally his own purposes are served," he sneered.

Corella shrugged. But already Varano had turned from him. He took up the body in his powerful arms, and staggered with it to the shattered window. He heaved it over the balcony into the garden below.

"There, Malipiero," he cried, "is the price of your services to me. Take it, and begone."

Chapter 2

THE TEST

There was in the army of Cesare Borgia a young Sicilian officer, Ferrante da Isola by name, who through his military genius, his wisdom in council and his cunning in strategy rose rapidly to be one of the Duke's most trusted captains.

This Ferrante was a bastard of the Lord of Isola's; but considering his father's numerous legitimate progeny, he perceived that in his native Sicily little scope could await his considerable ambitions. All his possessions were youth and courage, a long active body and a handsome face, a quick brain and a blithe, mercurial heart. With these he went forth from his father's house in quest of a market where such wares should command their price. He had come to Rome in the autumn of 1500, the year of the Papal Jubilee, the very season in which Cesare Borgia was arming for the second campaign of the Romagna. He had found ready employment; promotion had followed swiftly during the war, in which he had been constantly conspicuous by his valour and address; and, at length, when Tiberti was killed before Faenza by the bursting of a gun, the command that had been Tiberti's was given to Ferrante. Thus within six months of joining Cesare's army he found himself a full-blown captain with a condotta of horse under his control, admitted to the Duke's councils, and enjoying the confidence, and in some measure the friendship, of his master.

To have achieved so much in so little time augured well for the future. Ferrante felt that high destinies awaited him, and in this assurance he permitted himself the luxury of falling in love.

The thing came about in the following summer, as the army emerged from the Bolognese on its homeward march – an army much reduced in numbers by the troops that had been left to garrison the conquered states, and still further to be reduced by the forces to be sent against Piombino. Cesare Borgia lay in the pleasant city of Lojano and rested what time he awaited the solicited sanction of the Signory of Florence to march his troops through Tuscany, and considered at the same time some easy means of reducing the little state of San Ciascano which, despite the fall of Faenza, still held stubbornly against the Duke.

This San Ciascano was something of a thorn in the flesh of Valentinois. To reduce it were, after all, an easy matter were he to move against it in force, and devote two or three weeks to besieging and bombarding it. But other matters claimed his attention. The Pope was urging his return to Rome; the King of France required his support in the Neapolitan campaign, and it was not the time to turn aside and spend perhaps a month in combating the stubbornness of those hillfolk; nor could he spare any portion of his forces for the work, since all that he could spare must go against Piombino.

His only course, therefore, was to send some of the troops left in the Romagna to do this work; and this was a matter that required consideration and careful planning. Guile should best serve his purposes – as it ever did – if the chance but offered to employ it. So he schemed and planned what time he waited in Lojano, and in the meantime our gallant young Ferrante cast eyes of ardent longing upon Cassandra, the only daughter of the noble and High and Mighty House of Genelleschi.

The captain had first beheld her in the Church of the Annunziata, whither he had gone to inspect a much-vaunted fresco by Messer Masaccio – for he was something of a dabbler in the arts himself, and had at one time studied painting, though we have no evidence of the results that followed. It would seem, however, that on this occasion the Madonna of the Annunciation from the brush of Messer Masaccio was entirely obscured in the eyes of our young captain by the Madonna Cassandra of the House of Genelleschi.

Had you questioned him, as he came forth from the church at sunset, he could not have told you so much as the colour of the veil of the Madonna in the picture he had gone to see, whilst he could have described with tedious minuteness every lineament, every detail of colouring, every particular of shape and every item of raiment of the living madonna whom he had seen by chance, and upon whom his eyes had fed for a full hour. And not a doubt but that he would have waxed rhapsodical in the telling, being of a sudden plunged into that mood of amorous ecstasy that will make a poet of the meanest of us.

And yet there would have been no need; for there in front, with an elderly woman in attendance, tripped the lady herself, so that you might behold her and be spared Ferrante's long-winded rhapsodies.

It was her going that had drawn the soldier forth. It was to the end that he might still behold her that he came, with never another thought for Masaccio and the treasures of art, now that so great a treasure of nature was revealed to him.

He had the wit to reach the holy water font ahead of her, and having dipped his fingers turned courteously to offer her the moisture that was clinging to them, which she most graciously accepted, her eyes downcast after one swift upward glance which, Ferrante said afterwards, went near to blinding him. He leaned back as for support against the porphyry font, and never noticed that he was effectively frustrating the attempts to approach it exerted by her elderly companion. Abandoning these, at last, the dame made off in the wake of her charge, flinging back a malevolent glance at the tall young captain who had thwarted her pious intentions.

Ferrante leaned on, a while, entranced, his eyes following the two women as they crossed the little square in the gathering dusk. But he saw them not. What he saw was a little oval face of the colour of old ivory, framed in shining tresses of black hair confined in a golden net; lips that were red with the warm red of pomegranate blossoms, and eyes that were blue as the Adriatic – eyes whose one fleeting glance had burned itself for ever into his memory.

At last he stirred; stirred as she reached the farther side of the square and was on the point of vanishing into the gloom of one of the narrow streets that flowed from it. He came down the wide steps of the church, and moved to follow her. It was not an evening on which such a maid should be abroad with no more protection than that of an old dame. The town was a-swarm with soldiers – great, aggressive Swiss, peppery Gascons, passionate Spaniards and too-gay Italians. Not even the iron discipline of the Duke might save that child from untoward consequences of her innocent daring in venturing forth thus at nightfall. He was chilled at the thought of the indignities that might be offered her as she went, and he quickened his pace. He overtook them swiftly, and not a moment too soon, it seemed.

Four men, two of whom he recognised as of his own condotta, were lurching down the street with arms linked, forming a human chain which now barred the women's progress. The dame, taken with fear, came to a standstill, and clutched her companion's arm. Thereupon jests flew from the men-at-arms – the rude, heavily salted jests of campaigners – and they swooped down suddenly upon the women.

Simultaneously came quick steps and the ring of spurs behind the latter, and so they stood rooted there in a great fear, deeming themselves taken between two fires. Then, suddenly, a brisk voice rang out, stern with command, and at the sound of it the soldiers obediently fell aside, leaving the way clear.

The dame looked up, to find the tall young captain of the font standing at her side. And at sight of him, and in view of the effect of his presence and command, relief overspread her broad face, to be quickly followed by mistrust of the singlemindedness of this intervention.

Ferrante addressed himself – cap in hand, and bowing with the grace of the perfect courtier – to the mistress. "Madonna, you may pursue your way; yet suffer that I pursue it with you. Lojano is unpleasantly full of soldiers, and my escort may not come amiss."

It was the dame who answered – quickly, as if to forestall her mistress – and Ferrante, hungering to hear the lady's voice, was angered.

"Sir," said she, "it is not far. Madonna's brothers shall thank your Excellency."

"I ask no thanks," he answered, a thought surlily; then added, with more characteristic grace: " 'Tis I shall thank madonna for the honour of having used me as her escort."

The lady seemed on the point of answering; but again the dame forestalled her, rendered more mistrustful than ever by the sugariness of the soldier's speech. Ferrante vented his vexation on the four men-at-arms who stood grinning there, holding of their captain's conduct in this matter precisely the same view as did the dame.

"If you would be spared the attentions of the provost-marshal," said he, "you would do well to remember the orders of his Highness, and respect all persons and property."

The men stood silent under the rebuke. But ere he had taken a dozen paces up the street beside his charges, he heard a smothered laugh behind him, and then one of the soldiers, mimicking his accents: "We are to respect persons and property, remember."

"And when," said another, "the person is the property, or the intended property, of the captain, why – by Bacchus! – we are to turn our eyes the other way, like good little brothers of St Francis!"

Ferrante glowered wrathfully, and for a moment was on the point of turning back to chastise this overdaring jester. But chancing to glance aside at the dame, he found her eyeing him with an expression of mingled fear and malevolence that stung him into an even swifter anger.

"Foul-minded knaves," said he, leaning towards her, and jerking his thumb backwards over his shoulder. "Foul-minded as waiting-women."

She bridled, and flushed to a dull purple. Not a doubt but that her anger was no more than just controlled by prudence. She spoke, in an acid, vinegary voice: "I think, sir, we need not trouble you further. We shall be safe alone."

"Say 'safer,' mistress, since 'tis what is in your mind," he snapped; then to the lady, "I trust, madonna," said he, in a different tone, "that you do not share your woman's unworthy fears?"

Still he was not to hear her voice; again it was the dame who answered him.

"I said but, sir, that we should be safe alone. If you construe more than that into my words, you do so out of your knowledge of yourself."

Even as she spoke, two burly Swiss swung into view, turning a corner of the street. They were singing lustily but tunelessly; for they were very drunk. Ferrante looked at them, and from them to the dame, a thought mockingly, for there was fear writ large on her broad face – fear lest he should take her at her word, and leave them.

"Woman," said he, "you are a bargue tossing between Scylla and Charybdis." Then he stooped to add confidentially: "Courtesy, believe me, makes a good pilot." And with that he led them past the noisy Swiss, and on with no more word spoken.

Thus in a silence that in the end grew sullen they came to a very noble palace in the town's main street. Over the door was a great escutcheon of stone supported by two lions couchant; but Ferrante could not discern the blazon in the failing light.

The women had halted, and now surely, he thought, he should hear the lady's voice at last. He peered at the little face that showed so white and ghostly in the dusk. In the distance a boy was singing; down the street two men were passing with heavy tread and clanking spurs, and Ferrante cursed one and the other producer of these noises, lest they should cause him to miss a note of the music with which his ears were about to be rejoiced. But he might have spared himself the pains. For yet again it was the dame who spoke, and in that moment he hated her voice more than any sound that he had ever heard.

She thanked him curtly, and dismissed him. Dismissed him thus, like a groom, on the doorstep, she who had said that madonna's brothers should thank him. True, he had disclaimed the need for thanks, and by that must now abide; but was it courteous to have accepted his disclaimer? Oh, the thing had its bitterness! True, the lady had thrown him a smile, and had curtsied prettily; but what are a smile and a curtsy to one who hungers for words?

He bowed profoundly, and turned away, hurt and angry, as the women vanished within the cavernous portals of the mansion. He gripped by the shoulder a citizen who chanced to pass him at that moment. He had a lean sinewy hand, and the citizen's flesh was pampered and tender, his soul timid. The fellow squealed in this sudden grip.

"Whose arms are those?" quoth Ferrante.

"Eh? Arms?" gasped the citizen. "Oh – ah! Those? The arms of the Genelleschi, Excellency."

Ferrante thanked him, and went his way to his own quarters.

And now of a sudden it seemed that this Ferrante became a man of most fervent piety. Leastways he was to be found in the Church of the Annunziata each morning for early Mass, though the form of devotion that took him thither was not one that had to do with the salvation of his soul. He went that he might daily feast his eyes upon Cassandra de' Genelleschi. He had learnt her name by now.

Thus a week sped, and in that little time a great change was wrought in the captain's nature. Hitherto he had been a soldier to the exclusion of all else, the very pattern of what a condottiero should be, holding his men submissive as the limbs of a body whereof he was the brain. Now he became a dreamer, taking little account of his company, and swiftly losing his grip of the unruly troopers who served under him, so that they fell to committing offences against the Borgia discipline until the matter came to the ears of Cesare, who summoned Ferrante to his presence, and sternly admonished him.

Ferrante excused himself lamely; put forth the lamentable plea of ignorance of what might be toward; wherefore he was reprimanded and bidden to guard against the repetition of such outrages as had lately been perpetrated by his men. He left the Duke's presence in an anger that promised ill for his followers, but which was presently forgotten in a daydream revolving about the white beauty of Cassandra de' Genelleschi.

His love-sickness touched a crisis. He could not so continue. The daily sight of her in church was no nourishment for his starving soul; indeed it was a provocation. His repeated attempts to engage her in speech had been frustrated by the ever-present dame, and so, being driven to despair, he determined that the citadel must be bombarded if he would ever hoist his colours there. To this bombardment he proceeded, and for his missile he employed a letter – a most wonderful perfervid composition reflecting the extent of his distemper.

"*Soavissima Cassandra, madonna diletissima,*" he addressed her, having cut a pen, for good omen, from the feather of an eagle's wing. "You have heard tell," he wrote, "the sad story of Prometheus, and the pangs he suffered of having his liver daily fed upon by the bird of Jupiter. 'Tis a very piteous tale, which must have moved your gentle heart. But how infinitely more piteous am I, how infinitely greater is the anguish I endure, whose very heart is daily rent, torn and devoured by my ardent longings, I who am chained by love's fetters to the dark rock of despair! Compassionate me, then, madonna mia," he pursued, and much more in this hyperbolic strain, which in saner moments must have moved him to derision.

The mad letter he despatched to her by an esquire, who was to see it safely into her own hands, waylaying her for the purpose at the palace door. This did the esquire, as he was bidden. Nevertheless, the letter passed unread into the hands of Leocadia, the waiting-woman. She would have read it, but that she lacked the art; so she bore it to Cassandra's brothers, informing them whom she suspected was the sender, and also how this same Borgia captain had hung about their heels for this week past as though he had been their very shadow.

Tito, the elder, heard and frowned, read the letter and laughed between contempt and anger, then passed it to Girolamo, who swore unpleasant oaths and lastly bade Leocadia call their sister.

"Who is this man Ferrante?" inquired Girolamo, when the woman departed on her errand.

Tito, who was pacing the chamber, stopped short and snorted contemptuously. "A by-blow of the Sicilian Lord of Isola by a peasant woman – a base knave of no fortune, an adventurer, who likely seeks to use our house and an alliance with it as a means to his ends."

"As an end in itself, more likely," answered Girolamo, shifting in his chair. "You are very well informed concerning him."

"As to that – he is of some prominence in the Borgia train, and has command of a condotta," Tito explained. "A handsome dog; and Cassandra, being a woman and a fool – " He spread his hands, sneering. Girolamo scowled.

They were both swarthy, hawk-faced men, these Genelleschi, and much older than their sister, towards whom their attitude was paternal rather than fraternal.

She entered presently, ushered by Leocadia, and she looked at them with a something of fear clouding the effulgence of her eyes.

Girolamo rose, and proffered her a chair; she smiled at him, and took her seat, folding white useless hands in the lap of her blue gown.

It was Tito who addressed her. "So, Cassandra," said he, "it seems you have a lover."

"A – a lover? I?" said she. "Of your choosing, Tito?" She had a rather high-pitched voice that was quite colourless, and – to one skilled in tones – gave index to the extreme feebleness of her mind.

"Of my choosing, ninny?" echoed Tito, mimicking her accents. He never had much patience with her. "Via! Pretend less innocence, my lady. Read me this letter. It was intended for you."

Cassandra took the paper from Tito, and knit her brows. Slowly and with great labour she set herself to decipher the heavy scrawl of her soldier-lover. At length she appealed to Girolamo.

"Will you read it for me?" she begged. "I am but indifferent skilled, and the writing here is – "

"Pah! Give it me," broke in Tito, sneering; and snatching it impatiently away from her, he read it aloud. When he had done he looked at her, and she returned his glance quite blandly.

"Who is Messer Prometheus?" she inquired.

Tito glared savagely, inflamed by the inconsequence of her question. "A fool who overreached himself like this one," he answered, tapping the letter. "It is not of Prometheus that I would hear you talk; but of this Ferrante. What is he to you?"

"To me? Why, naught."

"Hast seen him none the less. Hast ever spoke to him?"

It was Leocadia who answered. "Nay, my lord. I saw to that," said she.

"Ah!" said Tito. "He has addressed you, then?"

"Daily, my lord – on leaving church."

Tito considered her sternly; then turned again to his sister. "This man," he said, "seeks to court you, Cassandra."

Cassandra giggled. There was a tiny mirror in the heart of her fan of white ostrich plumes. In this she now surveyed herself, and the gesture was very eloquent.

"You think it little marvel, eh?" put in Girolamo. Yet, though sardonic, he was more gentle than his brother in addressing her.

She giggled again, looking from her mirror to her brothers. "I am very comely," said she, with conviction. "And the gentleman is not blind."

Tito laughed loud and harshly. He scented danger. Fools such as his sister, whose only sense was a sense of vanity – he had no illusions on the score of her – were all too prone to responsiveness to a man's admiration, and to go to foolish lengths in that responsiveness. Her views regarding Messer Ferrante must be corrected.

"Fool," said he contemptuously, "do you conceive that this adventurer is taken by your white face and baby eyes?"

"With what else, then, pray?" quoth she, her brows arched upwards.

"With the name of Genelleschi and the portion that is yours. What else have you that shall draw a needy adventurer?"

A flush overspread the pretty, foolish face. "Is it so?" she asked, turning to Girolamo. "Is it indeed so?" Her tone quivered a little.

Girolamo flung out his hands and shrugged. "Beyond all doubt," he assured her. "We have sound knowledge."

Her eyes glistened and were magnified by sudden tears. "I thank you for this timely warning," said she – and they saw that she was in a great rage – the rage that springs of vanity scarified. She rose. "Should this fellow again address me, I shall know what answer to return him." She paused a moment. "Shall I send a reply to that insolent letter?" she asked them.

"Best not," said Tito. "Silence will be the best mark of your contempt. Besides," he added, sneering, "your writing being more difficult to read even than his, might leave him in some doubt as to your real intentions."

She stamped a very shapely foot clad in a shoe of cloth-of-gold, turned, and angrily departed with her woman.

Tito looked at Girolamo, and sat down.

"You have been well advised," said Girolamo, "and you have set up an effective barrier."

"Pooh!" said Tito. "A woman's vanity is an instrument upon which the merest fool may play any tune he pleases. But I shall set up a more effective barrier still – the barrier of a tombstone – ere I've done. This insolent upstart shall be punished. To dare – to dare!" he cried.

Girolamo shrugged. "We have done enough," said he. "Be content with that. More might be dangerous to ourselves. This knave of Isola stands well in the esteem of Cesare Borgia. If he should come to any harm, the Duke might exact a heavy price."

"Maybe," said Tito, and there for the moment let the matter lie, chiefly for lack of means to accomplish the thing that he desired.

But when on the morrow he went to pay his court to this Borgia, for whom he had scant love, he heard a matter discussed in the ante-chamber that set him thinking. This matter concerned Ferrante. Men were talking of the change that had come upon the captain; of the want of discipline in his condotta, which had been the most orderly in the entire army, and of the Duke's grave displeasure at this state of things. Messer Tito, gathering a sudden inspiration from all this, went presently to beg private audience of the Duke.

Cesare was at work with his secretary in a pleasant sunny chamber whose balcony overlooked a garden all ablaze with blossom. Gherardi was writing, to the Duke's dictation, a letter to Messer Ramiro de Lorqua, Cesare's Governor of Forli. It was a letter that concerned the reduction of San Ciascano; and Valentinois, as he lightly paced the chamber, smiled as he dictated, for at last he had hit upon a plan to make a sudden end of that troublesome resistance.

Gherardi concluded the despatch, and rose to make way for Cesare, that the latter might append his signature. At that moment a chamberlain entered with Messer de' Genelleschi's request for a private audience.

Cesare paused, holding his ink-laden pen suspended, and his eyes narrowed.

"Genelleschi, eh?" said he, and there was no pleasure in the tone. "Admit him."

He looked at his secretary. "What's here, eh, Agabito? This man's friendship for Bologna is notorious, yet he hangs about my court and now he demands audience of me. It would little surprise me to find him a spy of the Bentivogli, or of those interested in San Ciascano."

Gherardi slowly pursed his lips, and slowly shook his head. "We have had him closely watched – quite fruitlessly, my lord."

"Ah!" said Cesare, plainly unconvinced.

Then the door opened, and the chamberlain ushered in Messer Tito de' Genelleschi. The Duke drew the letter to him, and signed it "Cesare" swiftly and with a great flourish. He passed it to Gherardi, who stood at his elbow, and bade him seal it. Then, at last, he slowly turned his eyes upon the newcomer, who had advanced to the middle of the room, and – great man though he was in Lojano – stood there, like a lackey, awaiting the Duke's pleasure.

Cesare's beautiful eyes turned dreamily upon him, with no hint of the scrutiny they were exerting, and Cesare's voice very gentle and musical, invited him to speak.

"Highness," said Tito, "I have a grievance."

"Against us?" quoth Cesare, in a manner that invited confidence.

"Against certain men-at-arms of your following."

"Ah!" There was undoubtedly a quickened interest in the tone. "Proceed, I beg, sir. This is a matter which it imports that we should know."

And now Tito unfolded the pretty tale he had prepared, which had it that on three occasions his sister and her waiting-woman had suffered rudeness at the hands of certain soldiers in the town – such rudeness that they dared no longer go forth save under an escort of armed lackeys.

Cesare's eyes kindled with anger as he listened. "An example shall be made," said he. "Can you afford me particulars that will help me to lay hands on the offenders?"

"No more than that they were men of Messer Ferrante da Isola's condotta."

The anger grew in the Duke's tone and glance. "Ferrante again!" he exclaimed. "But this exceeds all bounds." Then suddenly, his voice sharp as a knife's edge, "How know you they were Ferrante's?" he asked.

The question took Tito entirely unawares. The fool had not dreamed that a great man like Cesare would stoop to petty details of "how" and "why." It was unworthy, and it was unusual, and so, unfortunately, Messer Tito had no answer ready. This he betrayed by his foolish expression, by the foolish blinking of his eyes under that glance of Cesare's which of a sudden had become cold and searching.

"Why –" he began, drawling that he might have time to think, and laughing to cover his confusion, "in the first place they were horse soldiers, and in the second – why – it was gathered from remarks that they let fall."

"Ah! And these remarks – what were they?"

"You see, Highness," explained the other, "I am but giving you the facts as related to me by my sister and her woman; unfortunately it did not occur to me to examine them so minutely."

Cesare nodded his head. "And you were justified by the manner in which justice has been dispensed in Italy. But my justice is not so. Your oversight shall be repaired at once," he continued briskly. "I'll sift this to the dregs, that there may be no misapprehension. Agabito, let a messenger summon Messer Tito's sister and her woman instantly."

But as Agabito was departing on this errand, the Duke stopped him. Tito's face – the sudden consternation of it – had told Cesare all he sought to learn.

"Wait," he said, and leaned back in his chair, laying tapering fingertips together, and smiling as if in self-contempt. "After all, where is the need? No, no, Agabito; we may confidently take Messer Tito's statement to be correct. For of course these men of Ferrante's would be known to the lady by their device."

"Ah, yes, yes," cried Tito eagerly. " 'Twas that, Highness. It had escaped my memory."

"It might well," said Cesare. "So slight a detail. But now that you recall it, do you by chance remember what the device was?"

Here Tito knit his brows, took his shaven chin in his hands, and appeared to be in a very travail of recollection. "Now let me see," he muttered. "Surely, surely, I remember. I –"

"Would it be blue and white?" quoth Cesare gently.

Tito smacked fist into palm. "Blue and white – blue and white, of course," said he. " 'Twas so – 'twas blue and white indeed. How came I to forget it?"

Agabito stooped low over the papers at the table, to hide the smile he could not repress – for the men of Ferrante's condotta wore no such badge at all.

"The matter shall be dealt with," said Cesare. "Ferrante shall be called to account at once. Note that, Agabito," the Duke commanded. Then he leaned forward, pondering for a brief moment. That Tito had lied to him he was assured beyond all doubt; but it remained for him to discover Tito's full aim and motive. Was it Ferrante he sought to harm? Cesare set himself to find an answer to that question.

"I deplore this matter, Messer Tito," said he, with a very gracious courtesy. "It is not usual in my troops to give occasion for complaint. They are sternly schooled. But this Ferrante latterly – by the Host! – I know not what ails him!"

"Like enough it will be the company he keeps," suggested Tito, and thus advanced another step into his morass of falsehood.

"Why, what company is that?"

But now Tito made a feint of seeking to draw back. "Ah – no, no! I've been indiscreet. I have said more than was my intent. Forget it, Highness."

"Messer Tito," said Valentinois very sternly, "do you trifle with me? Am I a man from whom things are thus to be concealed?"

"But, my lord, I beseech you! If I were to say what it was in my mind to say, it might…it might – " He waved helpless hands.

"Might it?" said Cesare, his brows raised. "Then let it, I beg you – and without more delay, for I have other suitors awaiting audience this morning. Come, sir, speak! What company do you imply is kept by Ferrante da Isola?"

"Imply? Oh, Highness!"

"State, then – I care not. Come, man, come. In what company have you heard of his being seen?"

"Heard? Should I accuse a man on hearsay? Ah, no. I speak of what I have seen, Highness. On more occasions than one have I beheld this man of yours in a tavern of the borgo in the company of some gentlemen of Bologna who are well known to me. It may be innocent. It may be."

Cesare looked at him very coldly now. "You are implying, sir, that Ferrante da Isola consorts with enemies of mine to my hurt."

"Oh, my lord! Acquit me of that, I beseech you. I imply nothing. I but state what I have seen. The rest is but what you, yourself, infer, Highness; not what I imply."

"You could if necessary make oath concerning these same facts?"

"I am quite ready, should you doubt my word," said Tito, with a sudden access of dignity.

"To perjure yourself?" quoth Cesare softly.

"To perjure myself?" cried Tito, his tone of a sudden mighty haughty.

Cesare was silent a moment, his fingers toying at his tawny beard, the faintest shadow of a smile quivering about his lips. Then he shrugged contemptuously, and looked the other straight between the eyes.

"Messer Tito, I do not believe you," he said.

An angry scowl crumpled the smoothness of Genelleschi's brow, and his quickened blood glowed through the tan of his cheeks. That he had lied, and knew it, did not temper his indignation at being given the lie thus coldly and calmly – and before a witness, too. There were men enough in Italy who would there and then have leaped at the Duke's throat for such a speech. But Genelleschi was not of these.

"Highness," he exclaimed, in haughty and indignant protest, "you forget that my name is Genelleschi."

Cesare smiled, displaying teeth of a dazzling whiteness. He rose, slender and graceful in his deep purple surcoat.

" 'Tis you forget that mine is Cesare Borgia." His eyes caught Messer Tito's glance, and held it captive. "As deeply as I abhor a liar, just so deeply do I love an honest, loyal soul; and such an honest, loyal soul is Ferrante da Isola."

"Complete your meaning, Excellency," cried the other, his voice now thick with wrath.

"Is there the need?" smiled Cesare.

Genelleschi all but choked. He felt that, if he remained, the wave of fiery anger that his soul sent forth would whelm all caution; so he bowed low – too low for courtesy pure and unalloyed.

"Your Highness will suffer me to take my leave," he said, and turned to depart.

"I trust that is the most that you shall ever take of me, sir," said the Duke, and dismissed him with a gesture.

But as Genelleschi reached the door Cesare's voice arrested him. "Stay, Messer Tito. You may be conceiving that I have used you harshly." His eyes had narrowed suddenly, but Tito saw naught of this. "You may conceive that you have had an ill return for the service you came here to render me in warning me of this man's treachery; that it would better sort with the ways of justice in which I claim to walk that I should satisfy myself that Ferrante is indeed innocent before convicting you of falsehood."

"I confess, Magnificent," answered Tito, with a mock deference that did not escape the Duke, "that some such thought was in my mind."

"Bethink you, though," returned the Duke, speaking slowly, "that Ferrante's infatuation for your sister is known to me, as is also known that you and your brother account him an upstart of low birth, whose suit is an offence to your lofty station, whose throat you would cut but for the fear that I might take heavy payment for the life of an officer I rate so highly. Consider that I know all this, and ask yourself how can I believe your accusation, unsupported by any proofs, against a man whose loyalty to me has been tried a dozen times."

Messer Tito blinked in sheer surprise at the extent of Cesare's knowledge, and was confounded by it – not realising that much of this same knowledge was inference, and the inspiration of the moment in that most subtle brain.

His recovery was swift from that confusion which showed Cesare how truly aimed had been his shaft. To deny his attitude towards Ferrante, Tito realised, would be futile. But he could still belittle it; still claim that he brought Cesare this warning out of pure loyalty –

must have brought it him though his own brother had been the traitor.

Cesare smiled at that phase of Tito's protestations, and his smile added fuel to the other's flaming wrath.

"You say that my word is unsupported by any proofs, Magnificent. In Lojano the word of Genelleschi is accounted proof enough of anything he says."

"I do not gainsay it. But why should not I prefer to place my trust in Ferrante, whom I have ever found loyal?"

"I have warned you, Magnificent," cried the other. "I have no more to say."

The Duke stood pondering a moment, staring through the window at the red roofs of Lojano. Then he turned again to Messer Tito.

"My disbelief in you shall be justified," he said. "I will put him to the test. If he fail me, I shall do penance to you for my unbelief. But woe betide you if he comes unscathed through the ordeal. Will you accept the wager?"

Genelleschi, knowing the utter falseness of the accusations he had brought, knowing the loyalty of the man he had defamed, quailed at the question. But he stood committed by what he had said.

"I accept," he answered, and went so far as to invest with pretended eagerness his answer. Whatever might follow, he must now appear sincere.

Cesare cogitated him in silence a moment, then crossed back to the table from which he had moved, and took up a package freshly sealed – the letter to Ramiro de Lorqua which Agabito had just prepared.

"At Imola," he said, "lies Ramiro de Lorqua with two thousand men, awaiting my orders for the attack upon San Ciascano. Those orders are in this letter. Ferrante knows that Caserta and the defenders of San Ciascano would pay handsomely to learn the contents. This letter shall go by Ferrante's hand tonight. That shall be the test."

"But, Highness," cried Tito, with cunning concern, "if he should betray you! Have you counted the cost to yourself?"

"I know the cost, sir," was Cesare's answer, his face inscrutable. "Thus do I justify myself for testing him." And with that he gave Genelleschi his dismissal.

Tito Genelleschi went home with very mingled sensations. Things had fallen out in a most amazing manner, and had exceeded by much any intentions of his own when he had sought audience of the Duke. He had the feeling of one who has been swept along by sheer chance, and force of circumstances, into committing himself to far more than he had ever dreamed of at the outset. He was pervaded, too, by a grave misgiving – an uneasiness as to what steps Cesare might take against him when Ferrante emerged triumphant from the test, as Ferrante must; for Messer Tito had no cause to doubt the man's exceeding loyalty to his master. The Duke had threatened him with vague consequences of his accusation should Ferrante's conduct prove it false. There was need for action on his part; he must take his measures; in some way he must contrive that Ferrante's letter should miscarry; it but remained to devise the means, to determine upon a plan. Thus, and again compelled by sheer force of circumstances in very self-defence to carry through this matter to which he had so rashly set his mind, did Tito Genelleschi become an active traitor to Cesare Borgia. Ferrante must fail; Cesare Borgia must pay the price of having said to Tito Genelleschi, "I do not believe you."

Tito sought counsel with his brother. The latter's face became grave when he heard how Tito stood committed, and he criticised the matter freely and harshly. His elder brother lost patience.

"What's done is done," he broke in, very surly. "And what's to do is to do; we should do better to consider that."

"Ah!" said Girolamo. "And what is to do?"

Thus abruptly questioned, Tito as abruptly replied, and in doing so answered not only his brother's words but his own perplexity.

"The contents of that letter," said he, "must be made known to the defenders of San Ciascano, that the plans of Valentinois may be wrecked, and that thus he may be persuaded that Ferrante is a traitor."

Girolamo looked at him, his lips pursed, his eyes scared.

"Yes," he said slowly, "that of course is what you would wish. It is daring to the point of madness. Fortunately it is also impossible."

"Say you so? Ha!" It was a snort of anger. Tito felt that his endurance that morning was being sorely taxed. "Impossible, eh?" And then, on the instant, as he eyed his brother, inspiration came in answer to the urgent call of his rage. His rising anger sank again upon the instant. His eyes dilated with surprise at his own conceit. A superior smile twisted his thin lips.

"Impossible, eh?" he repeated, in such a manner that it became plain to Girolamo that his brother had solved the riddle. But Tito vouchsafed him no enlightenment just yet. He sent for Cassandra.

"What has Cassandra to do with this?" inquired Girolamo.

"Everything," said Tito, with a great assurance.

When she came, Tito set a chair at the table for her, motioned her into it, then placed ink, pens and paper before her.

"You are to write a letter, Cassandra, to your fine lover – to this Ferrante da Isola," said he.

Her great eyes regarded him with astonishment, which for the moment lighted the dullness of her beautiful, vacant face.

"You are to confess yourself moved by this letter – stirred to the very soul of you. Ah – you have a soul, Cassandra?" he inquired, with the sneer that he held ever in readiness. Her stupidity was a constant irritation to him, the keener when he considered her faultless beauty.

"Fra Giorgio has taught me so," she answered, impervious as ever to the subtleties of sarcasm.

"Fra Giorgio is a fool," said he.

"You must not say so, Tito," she admonished him. "Fra Giorgio says that it is sinful to mock at priests."

"By which, conscious of the mockery he must provoke, he means that it is sinful to mock at him. But our business is with Messer Ferrante."

Yes, Tito," said she.

"You shall write, then, that, moved by his burning epistle – and – and the thought of his heart suffering the same fate as the – liver of Messer Prometheus, you desire more knowledge of him."

"Oh, but I do not. He is too tall and lean and ugly; and he is beardless, and I love a beard."

"Tchah!" snapped Tito peevishly. "Attend to me. You are to write him as I bid you; what you may think is another matter, with which we have no concern. You shall say that we – Girolamo and I – are from home, and bid him come to you this evening at sunset. Ah – and by the garden gate; that will have a more furtive, romantic air, which, doubtless, will impress the Sicilian dog, eh, Girolamo?"

Girolamo shrugged. "You forget I do not share your confidence," said his brother.

"But you can guess the rest. He will come, Cassandra, not a doubt of that, and for a while – an hour, say – you may pretend to him and to yourself that he is indeed your lover, and hold him in dalliance with you in the garden, there. Then – But I'll school you in the rest. The letter first. Come, girl; here is what you need."

She took a pen, dipped it, and poised it above a sheet of paper. Her delicate brows were drawn together in perplexity, wondering what all this should portend. At last she asked Girolamo; she preferred always to address her questions to him; he was wont to answer her with less impatience than Tito.

"Why am I to do this?"

"It is Tito's affair," said Girolamo. "But the object is to punish this upstart for the affront he has put upon us in daring to lift his eyes to you."

"How will you punish him?" she asked, smiling interestedly now, athirst for details.

"That you shall learn presently," cut in Tito. "First the letter – the letter. Come, begin."

"How shall I begin?"

Tito flung himself into a chair, and peevishly dictated the epistle, she laboriously penning the words he flung at her with ever-growing impatience. And by eccentricities of spelling, and vagaries of handwriting, she achieved a document at last which should afford Messer Ferrante some considerable mental exercise. So said Tito when he scowlingly surveyed the scrawl. He dispatched it none the less to the captain's quarters by a young maid of the house, and then made known to Girolamo the remainder of his plot, and to Cassandra just so much as it imported her to know, schooling her carefully in what was required of her.

Girolamo acknowledged the plan to be shrewd, deplored certain elements of danger it contained, and finally expressed the opinion that Ferrante, charged with such a mission and in the very hour of setting out upon it, would not come, whatever his feelings for Cassandra. Tito scoffed at his brother's conception of a lover.

"Oh, he will come; he will come, never fear," said Tito, "and in the fact that he will never dare confess that small breach of duty lies our own security from those minor dangers that seem so big to you."

That there were full grounds for Tito's assurance the evening proved. For as the Angelus was ringing from the Duomo adown the street at the back of the Palazzo Genelleschi came the rattle of hoofs, to halt by the green door by the tall brown wall.

The brothers were sitting with Cassandra at the trysting spot by an old lichened fountain that spouted into a little lake in which Girolamo – who was an Epicurean – cultivated frogs and eels.

At the sound of hoofs Tito became attentive; when they halted he rose, caught his brother by the arm and vanished with him into the house.

Alone on the stone seat beside the fountain Cassandra waited, and was faintly taken with a desire to laugh. But her waiting was brief, and presently she saw the tall figure of her lover advancing towards her in the twilight. He was all cased in grey leather, save for the band of claret hose which showed between his thigh-boots and his jerkin, and the steel cap and gorget gleaming like silver on his head and at his neck. His face was pale with emotion under the tan of it, and his eyes, when he came to fall upon one knee beside her, were the eyes of a fanatic at prayer.

"Madonna," he murmured, "you have shown me a mercy beyond all my deserts; given me a happiness such as I dreamt not that life could hold. I scarce dared to hope that you would deign return an answer to my poor scrawl. That you should bid me come to you and give utterance in words to all the fierce longings that are my torture was something that not even my dreams had dared to promise me."

She sat – the demurest maid in all Italy that evening – with folded hands and downcast eyes, listening to this madman's babble. And now that he paused she made him no answer, for the excellent reason that she could think of none.

"You will forgive me that I come before you thus – in this campaigner's raiment. It is not so I had seen myself paying my court and homage at your feet. But I go tonight upon a journey and a mission. Indeed, but for the hunger of my eyes to look once again upon your peerless beauty, but for the hunger of my ears to hear the melodies of your sweet accents – I had by now – were I full dutiful to the Duke, my master – been out of Lojano. Do you, madonna, absolve me for my want of duty and for my condition?"

He knelt there looking up almost timidly – and he the captain of a score of battles – at this fair child, who was to him the incarnation of all that is good and beautiful and noble upon earth.

She viewed him languidly – and he was good to look upon: dark and swarthy; shapely and tall; young and strong, with a fine, male beauty in his shaven face, and a rare fire in his full, black eyes. But she had been too well schooled by Messer Tito to lapse now from her lesson, and fall into admiration of him. Besides, was he not a low-born knave, when all was said, and was not this devotion he professed for her an insult? She had her brothers' word for it, and this beautiful, soulless fool had no judgment that was not her brothers'.

"I find that you are very well," she said, and he flushed with pleasure. "And as for your want of duty – why, what is an hour?"

His face clouded for a moment. She did not understand that an hour filched from such a duty as was his might be a serious matter were it known of.

"What is an hour?" he echoed slowly, and then, his passion rising he gave it tongue. "Ah, what is not an hour? What may it not be? The sweetness of heaven, the bitterness of hell may all be crowded into an hour. Were this hour all of my life that I should spend thus in your beloved presence, then my life were but an hour – the rest but prologue and epilogue to this one hour of living."

"Oh, sir," she said, her lids drooping, and the long fringe of them lying upon her perfect cheek; and again, "Oh, sir!"

A fool you had vowed her, surely, had you witnessed her then and heard the vacuous simper of her tones. But the captain – so blinding was his distemper – was translated into ecstasy.

"I am called Ferrante," he murmured. "Will you – will you not speak my name, Cassandra?"

She flashed him a glance, then drooped her lids again. "Ferrante!" she murmured, and turned his brain to fire, for never had he dreamed that his name contained such melodies. He put forth a trembling, faltering hand to take one of her own, that was surrendered to him and lay passive in his grasp.

"Wilt give me this, sweet angel?" he implored her.

"Give you what?" quoth she.

"This hand – this little hand."

"Why – to what purpose? Have you not two great able hands of your own?"

"Delicious wit," cried the enraptured wight. "Be merciful, dear maid!"

She laughed, that foolish treble laugh of hers, which rang in his infatuated ears like a peal of silver bells, what time he feasted his eyes upon the matchless beauty of her face. His breathing was shortened by the excess of emotion that possessed him; a languor slowly crept along his veins. And then she bade him sit beside her, and he obeyed her, eagerly yet timidly – very foolishly, thought she.

As he sat thus in the tepid eventide, in that fair-scented garden, he came to think that heaven and the world had used him very well. He was at peace with all men; he loved all men. And presently he spoke of that, spoke of the change that loving her had wrought in his whole life; how it altered the drift and current of it; how from harsh and overbearing that he had been accounted, he would henceforth strive to be meek and gentle, that he might be worthier of her gentle self – in all of which he employed the very choice and flowery eloquence that comes to some men in the season of their inamoration, but which she found wearisome and very foolish.

This, however, she dissembled. She listened demurely, as becomes a maid, and occasionally gave such answers as she had been tutored in, false words suggesting her reciprocation of his passion.

Thus the hour that he had said might hold his lifetime sped swiftly for him in his delicious intoxication, slowly for her to whom each minute brought an increasing weariness. The shadows deepened about them; the purple afterglow was fading from the sky; the trees and shrubs became dark blurs against a gloomy background; the windows of the house behind him sprang into light, and from the lake came the harsh croaking of a frog.

He rose, alarmed, mindful of his mission, and sought to shake his sweet entrancement from him.

"You are not leaving me?" she sighed.

"Alas, madonna, that must I, though grieving!"

"It is but a moment since you came," she protested, and ravished him by the innocence that could utter such words of open wooing. He had won a pearl among maidens for his own.

He took her hand, and stayed to speak again of love; then spoke again of going. But her little fingers had coiled themselves about his own. In the gloom he saw the pale shimmer of her upturned face; her voice came up to him on the scented summer air. He bent over her as he answered: "Listen, beloved. Tonight I ride to Imola with messages of state. But on my return I shall seek your brothers, to beg of them this treasure in their keeping."

She sighed. "When will you return?" she asked.

"In three days' time, if all goes well. An age, sweet lady. But oh, the reward that my patience shall receive!"

She broke in quickly: "You shall not go without a stirrup-cup; you shall not leave until you have pledged me. Come!" And she drew him, no longer resisting, to the house.

Through glass doors opening from the terrace she led him into a spacious, handsome chamber, and there in the light shed from the golden candle-branch he stood and his eyes devoured the glorious beauty of her.

She beat her hands together and a page appeared, whom she bade bring wine.

And what time they waited they stood before each other, and a something of pity took her in that moment. She was a woman after all, and the call of his splendid manhood could not go unheeded. It may well be that had he left her to herself she had now lacked the courage for her treacherous task. But in that moment his passion, so long held in check, welled up in a great tide that swept him to his ruin.

He caught her slight, frail body in his arms. Crushing her to him, he fiercely sought her lips. She battled to resist him, and for a second he had sight of her white face; and what he saw there checked him. It was a look of fear and loathing blent. He let her go, and fell back, foolish, awkward and ashamed. And then – for Ferrante was shrewder than most men – it came to him that this aversion to his clasp was odd in an innocent who had so lately offered him such liberal encouragement.

Even as the thought disturbed him the page entered, bearing on a golden salver a jug of beaten gold and two opalescent, thin-stemmed goblets of Venetian make. She moved to meet the page, with a fluttering laugh. She poured the wine.

He watched her closely out of gloomy eyes, and noted the deathly pallor of her face, the trembling of her hand. Was it still the effect of his embrace, he wondered.

She came to him prettily now, a goblet in each hand. He took the one she offered him, and bowed as she pledged him, smiling, though still pale.

"God speed you on your journey," said she.

"God hasten my return to you," he answered, and drank the half of the contents of his cup.

It was a potent wine, hot in the throat and quickening to the blood.

Its effect upon him was very swift. Scarce had he drunk but that there appeared to him less need for urgency in his departure. He considered that his horse was safely tethered to the ring outside the gate. A few moments more would matter little; he would make them good upon the road; and the present was very sweet. A mood of happy optimism enwrapped him as a cloak. He sank languidly to a chair. Indeed, with each breath he took his languor grew. It was the summer air, he thought; the day had been excessively hot.

"You are faint," she cried, and there was a gentle concern in her tone very sweet to hear, seeming to assure him that he was forgiven his momentary amorous violence.

He laughed foolishly, inebriately almost. "Why...yes..." he gasped.

"Drink," she bade him. "The wine will revive you."

Mechanically he obeyed her, emptying his cup at a draught. Again that sense of heat in the throat, that sense of fire in all his veins. He strove to rise, suddenly, subconsciously alarmed. His knees failed him and he sank back gasping. The room swam; a red mist was rolling and billowing before his eyes; and then, through that mist, shining as shines the moon, clear and distinct, he beheld the face of Cassandra de' Genelleschi – no longer the sweet, innocent, childish face he loved, but a face that looked at once foolish and wicked, a face detestable. It was as if in that moment of physical obfuscation the eyes of his soul were opened. Alarmed, he strove to concentrate all his powers to cast off the torpor that possessed him. For just one moment he succeeded, and in that moment he understood. He rose heavily from his chair, his eyes blazing, his livid, glistening face terrific to behold.

"Traitress!" he cried, and had God given him strength a moment longer he would have killed her with his hands, such was the awful revulsion that possessed him, making her beauty the most loathsome thing in all the world.

But ere he could move another step his knees were loosened again and he sank back into the chair from which he had risen. The priceless Venetian goblet slipped from his fingers and was shivered on the tesselated floor. Black night descended upon his brain; his senses left him, and his head fell forward on his breast.

Cassandra stood staring down at him a moment, in horror and in fear. He looked as he were dead. Then she turned, and as she did so the door opened and her brothers entered. She would have stayed – inquisitive as a child – to see them at their work. But her part in that black business was concluded, and they drove her to bed ere they set about what more there was to do.

Tito drew the heavy curtains across the windows, whilst Girolamo made swift search in the sleeper's clothes. He drew forth a package sealed with the Borgia steer. It was the letter Tito had seen that day. With a dagger heated in a flame he raised the seal unbroken, and together by the candle-branch – Tito peering over Girolamo's shoulder – they made themselves masters of the contents. Then Girolamo fetched ink and quill – he was the swifter penman of the two – and sat down to make a copy of that document.

This letter bade Ramiro de Lorqua march with his two thousand men upon Tigliano on the morrow, reduce and occupy it before attempting the attack upon San Ciascano itself. For that he was to await Cesare's further orders, meanwhile setting up a blockade.

"This," said Tito, showing his fine teeth, "will be in the hands of the men of San Ciascano long before Messer Ferrante shall have reached de Lorqua at Imola. How Caserta will welcome the information! You must carry it yourself, Girolamo."

Girolamo was cunningly replacing the seal. "Caserta should pay us a fine price for it."

They laughed together. "A great night's work!" said Tito. "We have destroyed that upstart fool there, and we shall deal the Duke of Valentinois a blow that will stagger him."

Girolamo thrust the package back into the breast of Ferrante's doublet.

"What of this carrion?" quoth he.

"Leave me to deal with it," said Tito. "I'll carry it to a wine-shop in the borgo. When he wakes his adventure at the Palazzo Genelleschi will seem a dream to him. Besides, he'll be in haste to redeem the time he has lost, and he'll ride like the wind for Imola. He may be stirring again before dawn."

"Start enough for me," said Girolamo, and took the letter. "There will be a surprise in store for Messer Ramiro de Lorqua when he marches upon Tigliano. If Caserta knows anything of the art of war he should annihilate the Borgia captain."

On that they parted, Girolamo to ride to San Ciascano and Tito to dispose of Ferrante against his waking.

By the following evening Girolamo was back again, stiff from riding, haggard and covered with dust. But he was in high spirits. The affair had sped well. Caserta's gratitude for the warning had been profound; he had set about taking his measures; the credit of the Genelleschi with Bologna should be enhanced, and their zeal rewarded. As he was returning, and after he had crossed the River Po, Girolamo had met Ferrante, riding as if the devil were behind him, on his way to Imola. From a screen of trees by the roadside he had watched the belated messenger's furious passage.

And now the Genelleschi, well content, sat down and waited for news of the rout of the Borgia forces under de Lorqua – the news that should prove Ferrante da Isola a traitor who had sold his duke, and vindicate Tito de' Genelleschi's character. Cesare Borgia should bitterly repent him for having given that gentleman the lie.

It was on the morrow that news began to penetrate to Lojano of a bloody battle in the territory of San Ciascano; and with it came a summons to Tito de' Genelleschi to wait upon the Duke of Valentinois. He went with a grave countenance and a mocking heart.

"You will have heard the news?" was Cesare's questioning greeting. The Duke had been writing busily when Tito was ushered into his presence.

"I have heard a rumour of a battle, Highness," said Tito, and he found it in his heart to admire the Duke as he had never yet admired him. His calm was indeed magnificent. Part of his army routed, his most trusted follower proved a traitor, yet there he sat, his countenance smooth and inscrutable, his tone level and impassive as ever.

"That letter that Ferrante bore," said Cesare, "bade de Lorqua march upon Tigliano and invest it. But it seems that the folk of San Ciascano had news of its contents, for Caserta lay in ambush at Tigliano awaiting the attack."

Tito's heart leapt within him. With difficulty did he keep the joy he experienced from showing in his countenance. "You would not be advised, Highness!" he cried. "You would have faith in this rogue Ferrante in spite of my warnings."

Cesare smiled quietly into the other's face. "Was I not well advised?" he asked.

"Well…well advised? Well advised ! But – "

"Ay – well advised. Had it fallen out otherwise than this, Ferrante had indeed been proved a traitor."

"Otherwise?" faltered Messer Tito, who understood nothing now.

"It seems you have not heard the end of the story," said Cesare. "Whilst Caserta and his forces waited at Tigliano for de Lorqua, the latter crossed the river some miles to westward, and marching upon soldierless and undefended San Ciascano, made himself master of it with scarcely a blow struck. Caserta, seeing his rear threatened, and the state lost to him, is, I am informed, in full flight."

With eyes that laughed in mingled scorn and amusement, the Duke considered white-faced, uncomprehending Genelleschi for some moments.

"You see, sir," he explained at last, "Ferrante bore two letters; the contents of the one were intended for Caserta to lure him thus to his ruin with false information; the contents of the other – which

Ferrante bore in his boot, where you did not think of looking – were for de Lorqua alone. As I bade him, so did he act, and proved his loyalty. I did not choose that you should know the full extent of the test to which I submitted him, and in which you helped him to succeed. For when, in obedience with my orders, Ferrante went to offer to sell the false dispatch to San Ciascano, he was driven out as an impostor by Caserta, who had already bought their contents from your brother." Cesare laughed grimly. "But for the circumstance that Caserta is fled, I think I should send you to him that he might recompense you fittingly for the false information you conveyed to him."

A great terror took Genelleschi then, and with it – odd assortment – a fierce anger. He had been an unwitting tool – he and his – in the Borgia's cunning hands. But terror beat his anger down, and very soon he came to his knees before the pitiless Duke – the Duke whose justice was so swift, and terrible; the Duke who never erred on mercy's side.

"Mercy!" he begged, in broken accents.

But Cesare laughed again and waved his hand contemptuously. "I am well content," said he. "I may break camp at once and resume my march, thanks to you, who have helped me solve the riddle that delayed me. I will consider also and set against your evil intentions that you have rendered a good service to my friend Ferrante da Isola, in curing him of his lovesickness. A man so afflicted makes an indifferent soldier."

Still paralysed with terror – a terror that increased under the utterances of that mocking voice, under the contempt of those beautiful eyes – Tito still kept his knees, with hands upheld. The sight began to weary Cesare; then disgusted him. He rose abruptly. His glance hardened; his tone changed, and, from softly mocking, it grew of a sudden harsh.

"Out of my sight, toad," he bade that proud gentleman of Lojano. "Get you gone, and never show your face – your own, your brother's or your sister's – in my dominions again. Go!"

And Genelleschi went, and counted himself fortunate.

Chapter 3

FERRANTE'S JEST

The career of Ferrante da Isola – or, to be particular, the sudden cessation of all record of it – is a matter that must have intrigued many a student of history. In a blaze of military glory he comes into its pages; flashes across them like a meteor, leaving a trail of fiery deeds in his wake; and is gone into an extinction as utter as it is abrupt.

The tale of that passing, and of the jest that led to it, is the tale I have set myself to tell. It was early foretold this Ferrante that his jesting would undo him, for he was overfond of the practice, and for all that he loved the merry tales of Messer Giovanni Boccacci he seems to have taken their lessons little to heart, else he might have heeded the admonition of Pampinea, to guard against making jest of others. And it happened, too, that this humour of his was of a warped and bitter kind, so that his own laughter, as often as not, was purchased by the grief and tribulation of others.

It had been so from the commencement of men's recollection of him, but since he had himself suffered so sorely at the hands of Cassandra de Genelleschi that cruel quality of his humour had undergone increase.

Now Ferrante's condotta formed part of that division of the army of Cesare Borgia that descended the Valley of Cecina to go against Piombino. But he was not destined to take part in that siege, for the Duke, it seemed, had other work for his very capable hands. At Castelnuovo – on the night the army encamped there – Cesare Borgia summoned him to his tent. He found the Duke in a furred gown, seated upon his campbed, studying a map; and before he had completed his bow, Cesare had abruptly come to the business upon which he had summoned him.

"You are acquainted with the country hereabouts?" he asked sharply.

Ferrante had some knowledge of it, and being a Sicilian, and not one to belittle his attainments, he answered promptly: "As with the palm of my own hand, Magnificent."

The Magnificent slightly raised his brows, and slightly smiled. "Nevertheless, you may find this helpful," said he, and held out the map, which Ferrante obediently took. Then came the Duke's next question: "What force do you judge would suffice for the taking of Reggio di Monte?"

Now Ferrante had enjoyed for some time the confidence of the Duke, and had been a member of his councils; but never yet had he been honoured to the extent of having his opinion thus privately sought by Cesare. His pride in himself awoke; he grew suddenly in importance in his own eyes, as he drew himself up, knit his brows, and thoughtfully stroked his shaven chin, considering.

"It would largely depend upon the time at that force's disposal," he replied, to avoid committing himself.

Cesare made an impatient gesture. "Do I not know that?" he said. "Let us assume that there is haste, and that an army cannot be spared for a siege. What force could master the place?"

The problem was a tough one; and Ferrante waxed uneasy, lest, by failing satisfactorily to solve it, his opinions should lose the vast esteem in which it would seem that they were held by the Duke.

"Why, as to that, now," said he reflectively, "Reggio di Monte is no such easy place to capture. It is pitched on a hill-top, like an eagle's nest, and boasts of its impregnability to assault." He paused a moment. "Force will not crack that nut as soon as strategy."

Cesare Borgia nodded. "That," said he, "is why I sent for you."

Ferrante was flattered; yet not unduly. It was as a strategist that he had won distinction; his military imagination was far above the common even of great soldiers; his talent for scheming and devising, and his audacity in executing, had been duly recognised and were widely admired – though by none more ardently than by himself.

"I propose," said Cesare, "to give you charge of the affair when I know what men you will require."

Ferrante's heart was quickened in its beating. To conduct a campaign; to lead not a mere condotta, but an army – here, indeed, was a great stride in his promotion. In imagination he beheld himself already a lieutenant-governor. But he broke into no thanks or protestation of devotion as another might have done; he bowed soberly, as one acknowledging a charge, taking the matter calmly as his due.

"I shall require – " (he paused, considering) "two thousand men."

"You shall have a thousand," said Cesare quietly. "That is all the force that I can spare. Will you undertake it with that?

"Since you can spare no more, that must suffice," said Ferrante, with a fine show of confidence in his own powers to achieve the impossible.

"Very well," said the Duke. "You will take your own condotta of horse; Ramires shall lead it for you; della Volpe shall command your foot, and Fabio Orsini shall act as your lieutenant. Are you content with these officers?"

Content with them! Two – Diego Ramires and Taddeo della Volpe – were among the most famous condottieri in Cesare's train. And they were to serve under him! His fortunes soared on giant pinions. Had he imagined himself a lieutenant-governor? He had been too modest; he perceived this now, and saw himself already Governor-General of the Romagna. Yet he contained his satisfaction, contenting himself with bowing soberly.

"I shall require some artillery," said he.

"I have none for you – not indeed enough for my own needs against Piombino," was the answer.

Ferrante was disappointed. What was an army without artillery? He posed some such question to the Duke. "If you could spare me were it no more than four guns," he sighed in conclusion.

"Four guns? Why, what shall you do with four guns?" quoth Cesare. "To grant you them would be to weaken myself without strengthening you."

"They might serve me well for display," said Ferrante, giving the first reason he could think of – a reason that was to recur to him later, and afford him the very kernel of the scheme he was to develop. At the moment, however, all that he thought of it was that the explanation was a paltry and unworthy one.

Not so, it seemed, thought Cesare, for his glance quickened as it rested upon Ferrante, as though the condottiero's words had awakened in the Duke's mind some notion of the means by which the task he was imposing might be carried through.

"Be it so, then," he said. "You shall have the guns. All will be ready for you by sunrise. You will set out then."

Ferrante bowed and departed, well content. But outside, under the stars of that summer night, his satisfaction and self-complacency met a check. How – how was the thing to be accomplished? It had been easy to speak confidently of doing it with a thousand men, and to look confident; it would have been the same had the Duke suggested that he should do it with a hundred – and just as easy, he grimly reflected now. Here was a great chance of distinction, true; but there was a still greater chance of disaster. He felt now that the task of capturing Reggio di Monte with a thousand men was one he would like to allot to his worst enemy – and on that he went to bed, hoping for the counsel that sleep is said to bring.

He awoke despondent; but his spirits rose when he came forth from his tent to find his army all drawn up awaiting him. It was in his eyes a very noble sight, and never did lover look with greater ardour upon his mistress than did Ferrante upon those men-at-arms.

There was his own condotta – a phalanx of steel-clad horsemen – rearing skywards a forest of four hundred lances, and here the close-packed ranks of sturdy Romagnuoli foot; yonder the baggage-carts and the ordinance mounted upon carriages drawn by bullocks; and above was the morning sun shining upon all and striking fire from morion, corselet and lance-head.

Through the bustle of the camp from which they were departing came Ferrante's officers to greet their leader; first the Spaniard Ramires, tall and handsome, leading his charger, bridle over arm; after him rolled the sturdy Taddeo della Volpe – that valiant one-eyed veteran, who had left his other eye at Forli and had boasted that he was glad of it since it enabled him to see but the half of danger; lastly came the youthful Fabio Orsini, a very pretty fellow in variegated hose, who dissembled his valour under a cloak of foppishness. If they entertained any jealousy of Ferrante's promotion, they dissembled it, and very friendly were they as they stood there to receive his orders.

These he issued briskly; and presently the horse, with Ramires at its head, began to move. After it, della Volpe defiled his foot; and lastly came the guns and baggage-carts. Ferrante rode some little way in the rear, accompanied by Orsini and followed by two mounted esquires.

In this order they went back by the road that but yesterday they had travelled, and climbed the first hill of that rugged country. From the crest of it, Ferrante looked back upon the main body of the army which was on the point of resuming its westward march. Then he rode down the incline, and turned his thoughts once more to the business to which he stood committed.

Anon, letting the reins lie on the neck of his ambling charger, he drew forth the map that Cesare had given him, and pored over it as if to gather inspiration from its tracings. One matter this study did determine – how Reggio di Monte should be approached. Not by the highway running up the valley along the river, whence their coming might be witnessed and their strength – or, rather, their weakness – observed by the men of Reggio on the heights. Rather must they approach it under cover, and to this end Ferrante ordered the troops – after the noontide rest – to strike away to the south and the hills. As a consequence they rested at nightfall on the slopes of Monte Quarto, with that stout hill as a screen between themselves and the eyes of Reggio.

There they pitched the tents of the officers, and there the men bivouacked under the summer sky. Ferrante ascended the hill alone that night, and from the summit he looked across the narrow gap of valley at the lights of Reggio on the hill-top opposite, a bowshot away. That was his first view of the town. He had come and he had seen; but to the conquering he perceived no way just yet. Would a way be opened to him? He sat down to think, and so near did the lights of Reggio seem that he entertained the perfectly idle reflection that a bridge thrown across the gap would afford an easy solution of the riddle.

Now this papal fief of Reggio di Monte, you are to know, had been unlawfully sold by the late Pope, Innocent VIII, to Count Prospero Guancia, and upon the latter's death had been inherited by his brother Girolamo, Cardinal-Deacon of Santa Apollonia, who now held it, in open rebellion against the authority of the Holy See. For whilst the Cardinal-Count as cleric must, and did, acknowledge the sovereignty of Pope Alexander VI, as tyrant he refused – so far as Reggio di Monte was concerned – to recognise in the latter his temporal overlord. He was by no means blind to the danger of this insubordination; but he was a crafty and far-seeing opportunist, employing well-paid spies at Rome to keep him informed of his danger's precise degree.

Hitherto, Cesare Borgia had been fully engaged beyond the Apennines, in the conquest of the Romagna, with no time to turn aside to gather so comparatively insignificant a fruit as Reggio di Monte. The Cardinal-Count well knew that in the course of things his own turn should come, and that he might be forced to yield his fief. But it was also possible that chance might serve him; and he deemed it as well to wait in his out-of-the-way corner of Tuscany until the enemy was at his gates. He had known a spasm of fear when word was brought him that the Pope's son was in Tuscany, marching upon Piombino, and he wondered uneasily whether Cesare would turn aside to dislodge him from his stronghold. But he did not consider the peril imminent, knowing as he did that Cesare was in haste, that he was awaited in Rome, and that he was to join the French in the Neapolitan campaign. That Neapolitan campaign was a sweet subject of reflection to the Cardinal-Count. Much might happen in the course of it, and a French defeat would mean such loss of power to the Pope that it was unlikely Reggio or any other Northern tyranny would be further disturbed by Borgia ambition. So overwhelmingly clear was this to the Cardinal-Count, so firmly did he found his hopes upon it, that he was resolved to withstand any but an overwhelming attack that might be made upon him in the meantime. To this end he had made due preparation. He was well victualled to resist a siege, and, if poorly garrisoned, he could rely upon the natural strength of Reggio, the stoutness of its walls and its almost inaccessible position on its craggy heights.

The game he was disposed to play was a very plain and obvious one, and it was obvious to Messer Ferrante, who was considering it as he sat there on the hill-top and looked across the valley at his prey. Not to such a detachment as Ferrante commanded would the Lord of Reggio surrender, and Ferrante could imagine the laugh of scorn with which his lordship would greet the appearance of the full force that had been sent against him. Therefore, it followed logically in Ferrante's mind that, if the Cardinal-Count was to see the force at all, he must be kept in ignorance of its weakness, be led to suppose it greater than it was – that a prompt surrender might be inspired.

So far – and strictly in theory – all was easy. In practice even this easy beginning seemed none too possible; and, if it were, what was to follow after? He sat there far into the night, devising impracticable stratagems, and weaving romantically impossible plans.

"If my men had wings now, or every horse of my condotta were a Pegasus," he said aloud, and checked there, realising that this sort of speculation was unprofitable and could lead him nowhere. Yet it was a very perfect type of such plans as flitted through his mind.

In the end he became angry. It was immensely flattering of the Duke to show such confidence in him by sending him with so entirely inadequate a force; but he now found it in his heart to wish that he had been given less confidence and more men.

He sat on, resolved to await the coming of day, that he might take a survey of the ground before he went to rest. And presently the early summer dawn crept over the silent land, pale and colourless as a moonstone at first, then quickening to the iridescence of the opal, and lastly flaming into a glory of gold and purple in the east, behind the stark black mass of mountains that were Italy's backbone.

Ferrante surveyed the valley in the clear morning light. Below him was a farmstead with pasture-land and arable, beyond it a vineyard, and below this again an olive grove that ran down to the sparkling river winding at the bottom. From the water wisps of mist were rising, like steam from an overheated beast. Beyond it, to the south, a wedge of woodland spread some little way along its course. Before him, on a level with him, stood the red-brown mass of the city of Reggio, the Maschio Tower of the citadel standing square and clear above the rusty roofs. With the eye of the soldier he considered the stout walls and their roofed battlements, saw how these sprang from grey rock that was no whit less sheer, and observed how the rock in turn rose out of meadow-land that became ever gentler in slope and richer in hue as it descended to the emerald green of the valley by the river. He remarked the grey road, wound spirally about it, like a rope, and commanded by the city at every point of it, and he determined that that way lay no hope of effecting an entrance by surprise.

Undoubtedly the Duke had set him a choice task. He stood leaning against a boulder, chin in hand, and very thoughtful. The sun's hot face looked over the Apeninnes, and dispelled the last shadow from the narrow valley at his feet. He watched the river tumbling and sparkling in the morning light, watched the thin mist, rising more swiftly now. The sight of that mist brought him an inspiration; at least, it showed him what might be done if it were a fog, and indulging his dream he conceived a very subtle, crafty plan, for which, however, a fog was wholly essential. He came back to realities with an oath. There was no fog, and, since it was not in the power of man to make fogs, what purpose could it serve to waste time considering what he might do with one.

He turned away in a mighty ill-humour, and went down the hill to his camp, more out of conceit with himself than ever he had been in his twenty-five years of life – which in Messer Ferrante, after all, was not so bad as it might have been in another.

To the sentry standing by his tent he gave an order. "There is a farmstead over the hill. Let six men go there at once, secure every member of the household and bring all prisoners to the camp here."

It was a precautionary measure against word of their presence being prematurely conveyed to Reggio. He entered his tent, flung off his cloak, all sodden with dew, pulled off his long boots, and flung himself on his couch, tired from his long vigil. Presently the flap was lifted and Fabio Orsini came in.

"Well returned," the lieutenant greeted Ferrante. "Where have you spent the night?"

"On Pisgah," answered Ferrante sleepily, "surveying the promised land."

"At what hour do we march?"

" 'Tis what I most desire to know. By your leave, I'll seek counsel in sleep."

Orsini made shift to depart. At the entrance he looked back. "Have you commands for me?" he asked.

Ferrante's answer seemed an odd one. "Can you make fogs?" quoth he.

"Fogs?" echoed Orsini.

"Ay, fogs – dense fogs, white fogs, fat fogs."

"Why, no," laughed Orsini.

"Then," said Ferrante, "I have no commands for you." And he turned over to go to sleep.

When he awakened he found his three officers assembled in his tent.

"It is noon, Sir Captain," said Ramires.

"Did I make it so?" grumbled Ferrante peevishly. "What now?"

"We have come for your orders."

"Then I'll order breakfast," said Ferrante, and sat up rubbing the sleep from his eyes.

"We refer to marching orders," della Volpe explained, rolling his one eye fiercely.

Ferrante drove his fingers through his rumpled hair and flung his jaws wide in a yawn. "Whither do you march?" he inquired, when he had recovered.

"Whither?" they cried in chorus, and looked at one another. Ferrante began to find them entertaining; also his opinion of them as soldiers sank considerably. They were mere fighters, stout fighters, but no more. "Let us take counsel," he said. He rose, went to the entrance, and bawled for one of his esquires, calling for meat and drink.

"I spent the night up yonder," he informed them, "considering the matter of our attack, and surveying the land. I discovered one important thing, sirs." He paused.

"Yes, yes?" they cried.

"That this is no easy business," he informed them easily.

"Thus much we knew," roared della Volpe.

"Ah, you knew? Good! That is where your intelligence surpasses mine."

The single eye of the grizzled captain of foot fixed itself sternly upon Ferrante.

"The question is," said Ramires slowly, "when are you going to attack?"

"I crave your pardon," said Ferrante, "but that is not the question at all. The question is – how are we going to attack?"

His esquires entered, bearing bread and meat, fruit, and eggs beaten in wine. Ferrante took the things, spread them beside him on the camp bed, and began to eat.

"What do you counsel?" he inquired, his mouth full.

71

The question seemed to perturb them, suggesting considerations hitherto ignored.

"Why," said Ramires, "here's a deal of bother about seizing a thieves' nest."

"There is likely to be a deal more before it's seized," said Ferrante, and quaffed his mess of eggs and wine with relish. Yet their stupidity, their failure to see his difficulties even when he suggested them, began to put him out of patience.

"I am all for the direct attack," said della Volpe, with the fighter's scorn of the schemer.

"It should be dear to you," said Ferrante. "It has cost you an eye already."

The remaining eye glowered fiercely out of that scarred face. "My eye was my own to lose."

"As is your temper – though you were wiser to retain it, Ser Taddeo."

"And I thank God I lost my eye," went on the condottiero, "since, had I two, I might see as much danger as do you."

"I think," said Ferrante, "that you have made that jest before."

"Sirs, sirs!" cried Ramires, intervening. "We are concerned at present with the attack on Reggio."

"For myself, and to be frank," said Ferrante, "I am more concerned with breakfast. But let that be. I can listen as I eat. Expound me your plans." And he sank his teeth into the succulent fibres of a peach.

Ramires braced himself to the task, and with the occasional interpolations from della Volpe he propounded strategies that were old in the days of Cyrus, but none of which would have led that same Cyrus into Babylon, nor was likely to lead them into Reggio. Orsini stood listening, but venturing no opinion. Ferrante ate, drank, and heard them as soberly as he might.

"You assure me of one thing," said he, when they had done. "That you have never seen this city of Reggio. Go up, and look at it, I beg."

"What will take one place will take another," said della Volpe.

"Always granting that that other is not Reggio," put in Ferrante. "Go up; go up, and survey the town; and, ere you go, put off your armour, lest it glitter. When you have seen, perhaps you will have help to offer me."

As they were departing, by no means in the best of moods, he stayed them.

"Can you make fogs, Messer Taddeo?" he asked.

"Fogs?" quoth Taddeo, bewildered.

"It is plain you cannot. Can you, Ramires?"

"Is it a jest?" quoth the Spaniard, with a great dignity.

"It is plain you cannot either. I have a plan for bringing the arrogant Messer Guancia to his knees. But my plan requires a fog. Since you cannot make me a fog, perhaps you'll go pray for me; and whilst you're gone, I'll try to think of something better."

They went out accounting him mad, and the Duke no better for having given him charge of this expedition. They comforted one another by vilifying him as they climbed the hill to get a view of Reggio.

After sunset Ferrante's tent was once more invaded by his officers. Taddeo had a plan, he claimed – a most original plan. Ferrante looked up hopefully.

"A night attack!" Taddeo announced, with pride.

Ferrante sneered. Taddeo argued; let them set out in an hour; there would be no moon; they could reach Reggio undetected and surprise its gates.

Ferrante's sneer grew broader. "An excellent plan, Messer Taddeo, but for one thing which you have overlooked."

"And what may that be?" challenged the truculent veteran.

"That they are not all stone-deaf in Reggio, and therefore that a thousand men winding about a hard mountain road would be heard before they were half-way up. Then, Messer Taddeo, we shall have as pretty a shower of rocks and boiling pitch to greet us as ever rained on a parcel of fools."

Taddeo was angry, and he had the support of Ramires, whilst Orsini – as became his youth – stood neutral. It was all very well for Ferrante to sneer at their suggestions; but what better could he offer?

None, he admitted. "If only we had a fog, now – " he began; and at the very mention of the word they flung out in a passion and left him.

But despite the ease he affected in their presence his mind was tortured by perplexity. He slept but ill that night, and he awoke at peep of day. He rose, dressed, and went out into the clear, steely light of dawn. Very slowly, and his wits very busy about this appalling riddle that had been set him, he ascended the hill. He fostered a faint hope that the renewed contemplation of Reggio might inspire him.

The light grew rapidly as he went up, and by the time he had gained the summit it was broad day. Arrived there he uttered a soft ejaculation, and it was not across at Reggio, standing dark and sharply outlined against the pale southern sky that he stared, but down into the narrow valley at his feet. He stared and stared, misdoubting his senses, fearing that he must be asleep in his tent and dreaming – dreaming of the thing that so obsessed his mind. For half the valley was blotted from his sight in the thick billows of a mist that hung there above the now hidden river. It was the fog of his dreams. Then he roused himself. Here was no time to be lost. Every moment was of value, for none might say how soon that mist would rise.

He turned and flung down the hill again like a madman. Like a madman he burst upon the awakening camp, bawling for trumpets, and kicking sleepers out of their dreams.

"To horse! To horse!" he bellowed, and presently to his own were added the brazen voices of half-a-dozen trumpets.

His officers, half-dressed and unkempt, came hurrying for his orders. He issued them sharp and briefly; the officers dashed off again to see them executed. Soon all was a confusion of scurrying men and stamping horses. Soon out of that confusion order began to resolve itself. The foot was ready first and, as it formed up, Ferrante waited for no more. He flung himself on to the charger one of his esquires had fetched him, summoned trumpeters to his side, caught up the great red and gold standard bearing the device of the bull, and shouted to the foot to follow him.

"Ramires, marshal the horse; but do not stir until my trumpets summon you. Fabio, see to the guns. Taddeo, follow me. On, on!"

At a run he led them up to the crest of Monte Quarto, his mounted trumpeters busy all the while, rousing the countryside with their brazen din, and bringing all Reggio to the walls in quick alarm. Over the hill's crest he led those six hundred men, marching four abreast, for the way was narrow; down he led them until himself and the foremost ranks were plunged into the mist, and hidden.

"Now run," he bade them – for their descent of the hill had been sedate so far; and he led them – not down, but away to the right, and round the flank of the hill until they rejoined the rear of the column near the summit once more. There he stood aside, bidding them on; and Taddeo, who grasped his meaning, went on with them, and over the crest and down and round again in an unbroken chain. At last, when the whole column had five times repeated the manoeuvre, and five times been round and over the shoulder of Monte Quarto, Ferrante bade Taddeo halt and marshal them there as they returned. Then he sent forward Orsini with the guns and baggage-carts – the latter empty, for there had been no time to break camp – and after these he followed again, with Ramires now and the horse, his trumpeters more vociferous than ever.

The manoeuvre of the foot was repeated with the horse, and after these came again more foot, more guns and baggage-carts, and lastly more horse. For upwards of an hour did the fearsome pageant which Ferrante's cunning had devised to terrorise the defenders of Reggio continue to parade before the scared eyes of the watchers on the walls. For an hour and upwards did the Cardinal-Count himself observe those vast forces pouring over the summit of Monte Quarto in a never-ending torrent of steel-cased men and splendid horses, flashing and glittering in the morning sun that shone upon the heights. Into the mist below they passed – to ford the river, and cross the valley, thought the Cardinal-Count – to be led round and back, in fact, over the shoulder of the hill again, and down and round in never-ending legions.

By the time the thinning mist warned Ferrante that he should make an end, the Cardinal-Count computed that ten thousand men at least composed the army that was come against him, and drew from this the only possible conclusion – that the very thing he had deemed unlikely had come to pass, and that Cesare Borgia had turned aside and come with his entire army to compel Reggio to surrender.

It was a sour draught for the Cardinal-Count; a force of a thousand, of two thousand or even of five thousand, he would defiantly have withstood, setting his faith in time. But with such an army as this marching against his gates, the Tyrant of Reggio realised in bitterness that the time was come for other measures. He must consider, and to consider he withdrew, calling his council to attend him.

His council was panic-stricken. With one voice its members urged him to surrender – to make betimes a becoming show of humility, and save the city from the fire and sword that must wait upon the defiance of such a host as lay encamped below. For Ferrante had encamped, meanwhile, in the valley; and in this matter he was effectively assisted by the forest to pursue the comedy of his pageant.

When the curtain of mist was rolled aside, Reggio had beheld on the wood's edge no more than a matter of a thousand men. But there was such constant coming and going, into and out of the forest, that it was clear the Duke had bivouacked his countless legions under the shelter of the trees, and that this matter of a thousand men or so was but an overflow – a supposition confirmed by the fact that there were no horses to be seen.

The Cardinal-Count sat listening to the appeal of his counsellors – a long, lean, majestic man, whose haughty countenance was livid now. He gnawed his heavy lip awhile, considering; and presently there came an usher to announce a herald from the Lord Cesare Borgia, Duke of Romagna and Valentinois.

The herald was admitted to the council-chamber – a very pretty fellow in a surcoat of scarlet and gold with the pontifical arms embroidered upon his breast, with stockings that were one red and the other yellow.

He bowed profoundly to the assembled company, unnecessarily proclaimed his office, and still more unnecessarily the many titles of the Duke of Valentinois, in whose name he spoke. Thereafter he did his errand very courteously, and it was a more courteous errand than the Cardinal-Count had looked for. It summoned him to surrender. Just that, and no more. It was backed by no threat of hideous alternatives, and in that lay the most deadly threat of all. Cesare Borgia was so sure of Reggio that he did not even deign to threaten.

It was over. Nothing remained them but surrender. The Duke held them in the hollow of his hand. He gave Messer Guancia until sunset to determine. The Cardinal bowed his head.

"Upon what conditions does his Highness bid me yield?" he asked, in a dull voice.

"He offers you safe-conduct for yourself and your garrison," said the herald.

A bitter smile crossed the lips of the rebellious prelate.

"I thank his Highness for so much forbearance," said he. "I will take counsel, and determine. My ambassadors shall wait upon him later."

The herald bowed and took his leave.

The Cardinal-Count sat on, in a brooding silence that none dared disturb. He suffered horribly from the wound his pride had taken, and he cast about him for a salve that should assuage the pain of it. And then, suddenly, his counsellors, sitting mutely expectant, observed his dark eyes to harden and glitter evilly.

"Be it as you wish," he said, in a level voice. "Surrender shall be made today. You have leave to go, sirs." And he motioned them away.

Alone he sat there, clutching the arms of his chair, and smiling softly and cruelly to himself. Reggio must fall. But Cesare Borgia and his captains should not outlive their victory.

He rose, and went to strike a gong; then bade a servant summon his secretary, his seneschal and the captain of his garrison.

In the plain below, by the wood's edge, some tents had been pitched, Ferrante's amongst others, and in this sat Ferrante and his officers that afternoon to receive the ambassadors of the Cardinal-Count. The condottiero had gone far towards redeeming his character in the eyes of his lieutenants by the morning's manoeuvres; yet Ramires, whilst lavishing praise of its astuteness, still wanted to know what Ferrante would have done had there been no fog, and Taddeo, whilst admitting and similarly praising that shrewd piece of humbug, was sceptical of its having the full effect that Ferrante looked for, and he wanted to know what was to happen if Messer Guancia still resisted.

Ferrante's good humour, however, was nothing damped. Things had sped so miraculously well for him that he could not but believe that his luck was flowing strongly; that he was right was proved presently when the ambassadors arrived.

They were three: Messer Annibale Guancia – generally reputed to be the Cardinal-Count's nephew, though scandalmongers alleged the kinship to be a nearer one – the captain of the garrison and the president of the council.

A crowd of men had surrounded them on their approach, and so hemmed them about that they had feared for their very lives and had been in no case to look round and take notice of the real extent of the Borgia forces. Thus they were hustled into Ferrante's presence.

Messer Annibale, the spokesman, looked from one to the other of the occupants of the tent, and blinked. Ferrante was seated, with Taddeo standing on one hand and Ramires on the other, both the lieutenants being armed at all points. At a small table to one side and rather behind them sat Fabio Orsini, quill in hand, a sheet of parchment unrolled before him.

"My errand," Annibale announced, "is to the Duke of Valentinois' Excellency."

"I am his Excellency's lieutenant, deputed by him to receive your errand," answered Ferrante, very haughty. "His Excellency was expecting the Cardinal-Count in person, and would have conferred with him had he come. But to meet a deputy he sends a deputy. So say on, sir."

Annibale hesitated a moment; but the point raised by Ferrante was a just one, and being moreover impressed by the calm assurance of these officers, he formally made offer of surrender in the lord of Reggio's name, subject to safe-conduct being granted to Reggio's defenders, one and all.

"That is to say, you accept the offer made you by the Duke's Highness. It is well." He turned to Orsini. "Set it down," he commanded. Then to the ambassadors: "Is there aught else?" he asked.

"A prayer, sir," said Annibale.

"Prefer it."

"My lord implores the Duke's Magnificence to spare the city occupation by so vast an army, or indeed by more than just such troops as it may be his good purpose to place in garrison. My lord having the well-being of this poor city at heart, and fearing for its inhabitants dire consequences of such an occupation…"

"Enough!" broke in Ferrante. "So much I have power to grant. Set it down, Fabio, that saving two hundred men of Messer della Volpe's foot, who are to garrison the city, Reggio di Monte's hospitality shall not be taxed by his Highness' troops." Then to the envoy, "That, sir, I think, is all. It but remains to sign the articles of capitulation, and for his Highness or his deputy to receive the oath of fealty of the council."

"The one and the other may be done in Reggio this night, and to that end my lord dares hope that the Duke's Excellency and the officers in his train will sup with him at the palace, when all may be amicably concluded."

Ferrante's eyebrows went up in some astonishment at the request, and the envoy made haste to explain.

"It is my lord's most earnest wish to make his peace with the Holy Father and with the Duke; and he trusts that this his ready submission will weigh with them, and that, in earnest of forgiveness for his past resistance, his Magnificence will deign to accept my lord's hospitality."

Ferrante considered a moment. "The Duke's Highness desires to show no harshness where he is not constrained to it," he answered deliberately. "And, provided the citadel is in our hands by then, I can accept in his name the invitation of the Cardinal-Count."

The envoy bowed. "You may proceed to occupy the citadel at once," said he. "The captain of the garrison is here to tell you so."

On that and some valedictory compliments the interview came to an end, and the ambassadors of Reggio were reconducted. An hour later Taddeo della Volpe marched two hundred of his foot into Reggio, and took possession of the citadel, whence he sent word to Ferrante that all had run a smooth course and that the Cardinal-Count's garrison – and it was a scant one – had disarmed.

Towards sunset Ferrante, accompanied by Ramires and Orsini, and escorted by a guard of honour of a hundred men-at-arms, rode into Reggio to sign the articles, receive the oath of fealty, and sup with the Cardinal-Count.

Under the deep archway of the gate he was met by Taddeo, the veteran's scarred face agrin now with satisfaction. He felt that he had his share in this amazingly easy victory, and that he would have his place in the brave tale that was to be told to Cesare Borgia. He came attended by a score of pikemen, and with these he now joined Ferrante's party. Together they proceeded towards the palace through streets that were lined with silent, timid, anxious townsfolk.

On the steps of the cloistered staircase that ascended from the vast courtyard of the old palace they found the majestic scarlet figure of the Cardinal-Count awaiting them. The fierce eagerness in his eyes was changed to disappointment when he learned that Cesare Borgia was not with them. It was Ferrante who explained his master's absence.

Now Ferrante loved a jest so well that he was ever loth to keep one to himself. Indeed he found that the revelation of it to the person who had been the unconscious victim added an epilogue almost as humorous as the jest itself. The element of cruelty that was inherent in the man took pleasure in gloating over discomfiture and the humiliation of the arrogant, and he desired to see it savoured to the bitter full.

So now he must stand there, very debonair and smiling, and inform the Cardinal-Count, with the pleasantest manner in the world, not only that the Duke was absent, not only that he had never been present, but, further, the precise manner in which, by the help of the morning's mist, he had befooled the Cardinal-Count into surrendering an impregnable city to a mere detachment of a thousand men.

And he related it all with the gay and easy manner of one who expects his listener to laugh with him.

But no responsive laughter was there from the Cardinal-Count. Whiter and yet whiter grew his face as he realised the trick by which he had been cozened into opening his gates. Sterner and sterner grew his glance as he appraised that tall, graceful figure in pearl-grey silk with here and there a touch of violet to match the sweeping plumes in his grey hat, and in a voice harsh and quivering with rage he desired to be informed what gentlemen he was to have the honour of welcoming to his table.

"I am Ferrante da Isola," said the condottiero, with conscious pride, and on that he presented one by one his three companions.

Messer Guancia smiled now; but his smile was not nice to see. "It remains for me," he said, "to pay with the best grace I can command."

"Why here," cried Ferrante gaily, "is the spirit in which I love to see a jest accepted."

But his officers felt chilled under the lord of Reggio's glance as he bade them welcome.

So great was the rage within the prelate, so overmastering his desire to be avenged upon these men who put this trick upon him, and upon this glib fellow who laughed of it to his face, that he forgot his disappointment at the absence of the Duke. He turned, with Ferrante at his side, and led the way up that grey staircase of carved stone and into the palace.

He had said that it remained for him to pay with the best grace he could command, and Ferrante had cried gaily that here was such a spirit as he loved. Well, well! He should love that spirit less when he knew more of it – when he discovered precisely what payment was intended. So ran the prelate's thoughts. They steadied him, and comforted him for the loss he had sustained.

With great deference and ceremony were Ferrante and his lieutenants led to table, and to keep them company and do them fitting honour there were a score or so of gentlemen and officers of Messer Guancia's following. Ferrante looked about him, and smiled. He knew no fear. Under his court finery he wore a mesh of steel, as did his comrades, and in the yard below his hundred men and Taddeo's twenty were under arms and within call.

They got to the superbly appointed table. At its head sat the Cardinal-Count, enthroned in a great gilded chair that was slightly raised above the level of the others. The rest disposed themselves with a careless disregard of precedence that Ferrante looked upon as odd. He found himself midway down the board – instead of on the Cardinal's right hand as was his due as the honoured guest, the representative of the Duke of Valentinois. Their host, he saw, was hemmed about by men of his own household, and none of the Borgia officers was within six men of him. Again he observed that he and his comrades had been effectively separated, so that on either hand of each were at least two of the gentlemen of Reggio. On his own left hand he had Messer Annibale – that nephew of the Cardinal-Count who had earlier come to him as an ambassador; on his right was a gentleman of lesser eminence.

Suspicion awoke then in the bosom of Messer Ferrante. Here all was not as it should be. What if he had walked into a trap? What if the prelate proposed to murder them, and then ring the bells and lead forth what force he could muster against a little army without officers? He and his fellows wore their swords, it was true, whilst the vanquished came ostentatiously without weapons. But in their robes they might have daggers hidden, and they were twenty men opposed to four. It had ever been a maxim of Ferrante's that who despises an enemy reinforces him; and he wondered, with an angry misgiving, could he have been guilty here of that dangerous error. He wondered, too, upon what pretext he might bring in a party of his guards. That pretext he had soon enough – of his own making. It was not for nothing that he was accounted the very prince of strategists.

He had been engaging his left-hand neighbour, Messer Annibale, in a trivial conversation, when a lackey approached to serve him, bearing a great silver platter of brodetto of fish. In turning – as if by chance – Ferrante drove his elbow sharply into the fellow's side. Over went the platter of brodetto, and full half its contents were strewn upon the condottiero's delicate pearl-grey silk. Ferrante came to his feet in a magnificently simulated passion, and caught the lackey a blow that sent him hurtling against the tapestried wall of the apartment.

"By the Passion!" he roared. "Are you no better served than this in Reggio?"

From the head of the table came the prelate's voice, apologetic and conciliatory; Messer Annibale, too, had risen, and was seeking to pacify the infuriated captain. His own companions – Taddeo, Ramires and Orsini – sought also to calm him and to recall him to some sense of good behaviour. But Ferrante waved all wrathfully aside, pushed back his chair, and strode doorwards, a mess of fish and savoury ingredients dripping from his ruined finery as he went. He tore aside the door-curtain with an angry hand, and in an angry voice he shouted for the men of Taddeo's foot.

The entire company had risen now, the Cardinal-Count among the rest, dismay and vexation overspreading his white face. "What would you do, my lord?" he asked. "This man has done no more than – "

"I have no concern with him." Ferrante broke in rudely, facing the table again, and towering there, the very incarnation of wrath. "But if I am to sup with your Magnificence I'll not be served by swineherds and bathed in fish-stews. I'll have my soldiers to wait upon me and teach your lackeys their trade."

A dull flush was tinting the Cardinal-Count's cheekbones. "It shall be as you will, Most Excellent," said he.

"I mean it so to be," said Ferrante, snorting, and he turned to his men – a score of them – who thronged the threshold. "Lay aside your pikes," he commanded, "and attend us here at table. So, my lord of Reggio, you shall see what service means." And he came back to his place at the board.

His comrades began to understand, and so, too, did the Cardinal-Count – gathering understanding from the number Ferrante had bidden to attend them. He smiled a trifle scornfully. "You gentlemen of Rome have much to teach us," said he, by way of restoring good humour in their ranks, and Ferrante laughed, and this object being achieved, made haste to remove the constraint which his burst of anger had left upon the company. He had partly succeeded when the wine was brought. From the hands of the seneschal one of his men received a great jug of beaten gold on which was choicely figured the story of Bacchus and the Nymphs of Nysa.

With a clumsiness that made a mock of Ferrante's boast, the half-armoured man-at-arms clattered to the Cardinal-Count with his great jug. He was about to pour, when the prelate stayed him, covering his goblet with his hand.

"First to my guests," said he, with a courtly smile; and good-humouredly he twitted Ferrante on the manners of his Ganymede. Ferrante took it in excellent part. Indeed, it was his design, now that he had gained his ends, to promote good feeling, or, at least, the outward seeming of it.

His own glass was filled and those of his three lieutenants, and upon that the seneschal snatched the jug from the soldier to replenish it – for all that there was not the need. Nor did he return it to him, for already a man-at-arms with a similar vessel, directed by the seneschal, was serving now the gentlemen of Reggio. No doubt the thing would have been less noticeably accomplished had the servants of the Cardinal-Count had the performing of it, as had been intended. Yet clumsily as it was done, and although half-consciously noticed by Ferrante at the time, he saw nothing unnatural in it, certainly nothing to arouse suspicion.

He reached for his goblet, and had it half-way to his lips, when over the rim of it his eyes met those of his host. It was no more than a transitory glance, for Ferrante, of intent, let his eyes sweep on, idly and unconcerned. But in that flash he had seen something that now gave him pause. It was not much; but men of a high order of intelligence, as was Ferrante, are of a singularly swift receptivity to impressions. The Cardinal-Count, he had observed, was watching him furtively from under lowered brows, a something cruel and cunning in his glance. Then it was that, as in a flash of recollection, he remembered his subconscious observation that the wine for his followers and himself had not been poured from the same jug as that which had supplied the gentlemen of Reggio. And that trifle, which he had scarcely noticed at the time, assumed now gigantic proportions in his mind. The wine before him and his three officers was poisoned! He knew it as much by intuition as by the slight evidences he had.

In some fraction of a second did all this flash through Ferrante's mind, and before that second was complete he had determined how to act.

Another in his place, and presuming upon the presence of his men-at-arms, would have risen there and then, and flung his accusation. Not so Ferrante. He would not have the laugh against him if, after all, he should be wrong; would not have it said that timidity had misled him. Besides, it pleased him to deal more subtly, more humorously, with Messer Guancia.

So he stayed himself in the very act of raising his goblet, and in the most natural manner – as one who has just bethought him of something that is of moment – he leaned across the board, and called to Orsini, who was seated some way below him on the opposite side. Orsini looked up.

"Your tablets," said Ferrante. "I have remembered that I have a note to make." And whilst Orsini fumbled for his tablets and Ferrante waited, leaning across the board, he took the opportunity to mutter two words quickly in Spanish to Ramires who sat immediately facing him.

"*No bibas!*" said he, under cover of the murmur of conversation about him, and trusting to the fact that, in Reggio, Spanish – particularly when it was slurred and muttered – would not be understood. By the quick lift of the Spaniard's eyebrows he saw that he had caught the words.

Ferrante sat back, and lest Messer Guancia should suspect his motives he leisurely lifted his goblet, and appeared to sip the wine. In reality he did no more than hold it a moment against his tightened lips, which he was careful to wipe when he set down the cup again.

The eyes of the Cardinal-Count became alight with satisfaction. But Ferrante was blind to this. His neighbour handed him Orsini's tablets. He opened them, and wrote the imperative command, "Drink not! Warn Taddeo." He closed them and passed them back.

"Read what I have written, Fabio," he said. "I wish you to bear it in your mind."

Orsini obeyed him, and Ferrante admired the manner in which the youngster kept his countenance, and played his part. Fabio looked up smiling and nodded; then turned the tablets about in his hands as one who hesitates. At last, leaning over to della Volpe.

"I think this matter concerns you as much as it does me, Taddeo," he said. "Does it not?" he added, and passed the tablets across to the veteran.

And he was no more than in time. He stayed Taddeo in the very act of lifting his cup. Taddeo read, was baffled for a moment, then understood, and nodded to Ferrante.

"I will see it done," said he, and pocketed the tablets.

Ferrante heaved a sigh of infinite relief, and considered the second move in this queer game to which he had set his hand. In that instant the Cardinal-Count rose to his feet, and called upon his friends to quaff the health of their noble guests.

There was a premonitory scraping of chairs as the company prepared to rise. But Ferrante, swifter than the rest, leaped to his feet before them, snatching up his goblet as he did so.

"One moment ere you drink," he cried, and with outspread left hand he stayed the company in the very act of rising. "Let me beg your Magnificence to resume your seat," said he. "I have some words to say in my master's name touching the surrender of Reggio – a message for you, which I make no doubt will lead you the more gladly to pledge us, and him with us."

His eyes sparkled, there was a delicate flush on his still youthful cheek. But neither of these signs was the herald of an eager eloquence, as those others deemed them. They were the outward manifestation of the delight that Ferrante took in this game of strategy he had set himself to play; this pitting of quick wits against the clumsy murderous plan of the Cardinal-Count. In anticipation, he was already relishing the deadly jest he had prepared.

"My message to you," he began – and carelessly, abstractedly, as he spoke, he passed the goblet into his left hand, "is a message of good will. Had bloodshed been necessary ere Reggio di Monte had raised her gates to us – "

He broke off abruptly, staring at the Cardinal-Count.

"What ails your Excellency?" he cried, alarm ringing loud in his question.

Instantly all eyes were turned upon the lord of Reggio, all necks were craned that men might obtain a better view of the prelate, who sat back, blinking in surprise. In that moment Ferrante's left hand set down his cup beside Messer Annibale's. His eyes never left the Cardinal's face.

"Why nothing ails me," said the prelate, nonplussed. "I am well."

Ferrante's fingers closed now over the stem of Annibale's goblet. His own body thrust forward screened the act from those below him on his side. Annibale's body, similarly placed allowed the lord of Reggio to see nothing of it. For the rest all eyes were too intent upon the Cardinal-Count to observe that swift exchange, and ere any glances returned to Ferrante he was holding his goblet at the height of his breast, as they had last beheld him.

"A trick of the lights, perhaps," laughed Ferrante. "It seemed to me that your Excellency had turned pale, and that you sank back exhausted."

"No, no," said the prelate, with a reassuring smile. "I am well. I may have sat back. No more than that. Continue, pray, Messer Ferrante."

Ferrante continued – a rambling speech full of words of great sound but little meaning, out of which it transpired that the people of Reggio might rest assured that in the Lord Cesare Borgia they would find an overlord to care for them as for his very children. It was hardly what he had seemed to promise at the outset, and it provoked the secret scorn of most of the Lord Guancia's friends. When he had done he raised his goblet on high.

"I drink," he said, "to the peace and prosperity of Reggio di Monte, and to the success and victory of our Duke's arms."

And slowly, with head well back, he drained his cup.

Whoever pledged Cesare Borgia, as he had called upon them to do, he was sure that the Cardinal-Count would not; and he observed that the prelate did no more than make a pretence of sipping at his cup, what time he watched Ferrante with evil, exulting eyes.

Ferrante's officers watched him, too, their eyes dilating with alarm, whilst in obedience to his message of warning they did no more than pretend to touch their wine.

But one or two there were who drank, and among these was Messer Annibale, the Cardinal's nephew. No doubt the luscious fare of his uncle's table had quickened his thirst, for he drained his cup to the dregs ere he set it down.

And then, as Ferrante was resuming his seat, the Cardinal still watching him – Messer Annibale uttered a scream, clutched at his girdle as if to loosen it, and went over backwards, taking his chair with him. Chair and man crashed to the ground. Out of it rolled the nephew of the Cardinal-Count, and some little way along the floor; then he lay prone, his legs drawn under him, his contracted hands clawing at the tesselated floor, whilst his drawn mouth emitted scream after scream of anguish.

That and other horrid sounds rang upon the panic-stricken silence. The gelid hand of terror closed about the hearts of that noble company. Stricken sat all, with white faces and staring eyes, no face more white, no eyes more wide, than the lord of Reggio's own. Soldiers and servants stood aghast, and most aghast of all the seneschal who had handed out the poisoned wine and feared now – as feared his master – that there had been an error in the jugs.

Ferrante covertly watched the ghastly face of Messer Guancia during the time of his nephew's cruelly long-drawn agony; he watched, and waited until the figure on the ground lay mercifully still. Then he rose once more, the only one at ease in that assembly. Mockery smouldered in his eyes and curled his strong lips as he broke the awful silence.

"It seems, my lord of Reggio," said he, "that here is some mistake. Your seneschal has lacked the care that is so necessary when it is proposed to serve the guests with poisoned wine. It seems that you have been caught in your own toils."

An effeminate youth across the board, who had no doubt drunk freely, uttered a piercing scream, and fell forward in a swoon. Ferrante smiled inwardly to see his plans thus furthered by the terror of a fool.

"Ramires," said he quietly, "send up a score of men. Then close the gates, and make yourself master of the palace."

Ramires went out. The dozen men that had come to fill the place of lackeys sprang to their pikes at a word from Ferrante.

"Sirs," said he amiably to the company, "you will assemble at that end of the chamber – all save my lord, the Cardinal-Count." And seeing a hand or two steal furtively to the breast of a doublet: "The man who bares a weapon," he told them fiercely, "shall be strangled out of hand in the yard below. Be warned, sirs! I do not lack the means to constrain the unwilling."

And they went, a flock of frightened sheep, all but three – the lord of Reggio, the one who was dead and the one who had fainted.

Taddeo's pikemen, reinforced now by a score of others that Ramires had brought in, stood guard over them, a line of bristling steel through which none was mad enough to attempt to break.

Ferrante turned once more to the Cardinal-Count. Messer Guancia sat gripping the arms of his chair, but showing no other sign of life. The condottiero said but one word to him, said it pointing to the goblet that stood, almost untasted, before the prelate.

"Drink!"

The wits of the Cardinal-Count were in a mist; but at that sharp word of command they sought to struggle through. He stirred, shrank farther back into his chair at first. Then he reared his head and sought to summon courage to his glance and bearing that he might mask the terror inspired him by that cup which he believed to contain poison, but which Ferrante knew did not.

"I will not drink," he answered.

Ferrante shrugged his shoulders. "We shall see," he said, and called a soldier to him. "I make you Messer Guancia's gaoler," said he. "You will lock him in his chamber with a soldier to guard him constantly, and you shall give him neither meat nor drink until in the guard's presence he shall have consumed that cup of wine." He turned to his officers. "Come, sirs. Here is no more to do."

His men-at-arms drove the gentlemen of Reggio out of the chamber and out of the palace, of which Ferrante remained in full possession. And ere they sought their beds he explained to his mystified lieutenants how he had juggled the affair, how fooled the Cardinal-Count for the second time that day.

"And now he sits there," he ended, smiling, "with a cup of wine before him that is as wholesome and innocent as the milk he suckled in his infancy, yet believing it poisoned he dares not touch it; sooner will he suffer agonies of hunger and of thirst; possibly he may even die sooner than set lips to it. Is it not humorous?"

"It is horrible," said Orsini, shuddering.

"It is just," said Taddeo; and Ramires nodded.

"It is merciful," Ferrante protested. "Another would have had him strangled. When he can endure no more, let him drink, and I'll punish him no further."

Next morning they went betimes to pay the prisoner a visit. They found him huddled in his great gilded chair, his scarlet robes drawn close about him. Before him on the table stood the tall gold goblet still untouched. As they entered he looked up at them with wild, blood-injected eyes. His face was ashen to the lips.

They considered him a while in silence. Then Ferrante spoke. "You are very obstinate, my lord," said he. "You have but to drink to obtain release."

It was intentionally an ambiguous speech, and the Cardinal-Count's only reply was a shudder. Ferrante changed the guard and departed with his officers.

They returned at evening and found the scene unchanged – the old man huddled in his chair; the tall goblet standing on the board before him. But early next morning word was brought Ferrante that he had died in the night, and Ferrante called his officers and repaired with them at once to the great chamber.

There they found the long scarlet figure lying prone, already stiff and cold.

"How is this?" Ferrante asked the sentry.

"He drank some of the wine at midnight," replied the soldier, "and he died upon the instant almost."

Ferrante's brows went up; his officers muttered their astonishment. He crossed to the table, and peered into the goblet. It was more than half full. He smiled thoughtfully. It was not the end he had expected, but it was very curious; it was most quaintly humorous in its way. The man had been fulminated by his terror; destroyed by his imagination.

As he stood there, considering the dead prelate, Ferrante gave utterance to his thoughts.

"Most strange," said he, "how deadly a man's terrors may become. Beware of fear, my friends; it is man's worst enemy. It has laid this one low. He thought that he drank poison – and there he lies, poisoned; poisoned by his own imagination, for he drank no other." And he stirred the body thoughtfully with his foot.

"Impossible!" cried Taddeo.

"There is some mistake in this," added Ramires.

Ferrante looked at them and sneered. "It is the way of you; you can see no more than what is placed before you – not always that. This wine," he said, taking up the goblet, "is as free from poison as when it was first crushed. Behold the proof of it." And bearing it to his lips he drained the cup.

Then he hurled it from him with a force that sent it crashing against the wall. He reeled a moment, his hands to his face; stood another instant fighting for breath and rocking on his feet; then his knees gave way and he fell supine, with arms outstretched – dead.

In the Cardinal-Count's right hand they found anon the explanation. It clutched a phial that gave off an acrid scent as of bitter almonds. The rest was easily imagined. The lord of Reggio, deeming himself doomed beyond all hope, and assured that sooner or later he must die by this cup of wine which he believed was poisoned, or else perish slowly of hunger and of thirst, had determined to drink, and so have done. But remembering the long-drawn agony of his nephew, which he had witnessed, and seeking at least to avoid the like, he had determined to increase the poison in the wine, and had emptied into it the phial which, it so chanced, he still had with him.

And that is the story of the passing of Messer Ferrante da Isola, and of the jest that killed him.

Chapter 4

GISMONDI'S WAGE

Benvenuto Gismondi, thief and scoundrel, rode slowly northward along the old Aemilian Way, upon a stolen horse. The country all about him was a white glare of sun-drenched snow. Before him stretched the long straight road, of a less virgin whiteness, and in the distance – some four miles away – loomed hazily the spires of Forlimpopoli.

Benvenuto ambled on, cursing the cold and the emptiness of his stomach, and thrusting the numbed fingers first of one hand then of the other into his capacious mouth for warmth. His garments, that once had been fine, were patched and shabby; his boots were ragged, and in places a livid gleam from his sword peeped through the threadbare velvet scabbard. On his head he wore an old morion, much dinted and rusted, by which he thought to give himself a military air; from under this appeared long wisps of his unkempt black hair, to flutter like rags about his yellow neck. His white pockmarked face, half-hidden in a black fur of beard, was the most villainous in Italy.

He was in sad case. There was too much respect for the property of others demanded in the Romagna these days, since the Lord Cesare Borgia had come to rule there, and such men as Benvenuto

Gismondi were finding it difficult to make a living. For there was nothing heroic about Benvenuto's villainy. He was no reckless masnadiero, to demand fat purses at point of sword in the open country. There were risks in that profession which he had no desire to face. He was essentially a town thief – of the kind that lurks in doorways on dark nights awaiting the chance to put a knife into the back of some wayfarer and, thereafter, plundering the corpse at leisure. And of that class the Lord Cesare Borgia had all but made an end in the cities where he ruled.

Therefore was Messer Benvenuto on his travels. He was for the north – for Bologna, perhaps or even Milan – anywhere where an honest God-fearing thief might ply his trade undisturbed by the excessive zeal of a meddling podestà. But he went with no good grace; he had matter for grievance in this enforced departure out of the Romagna; for he was a Romagnuolo to the core of him, and he loved his native land, accounting all others barbarous. Besides, in Cesena there was a certain sloe-eyed Giannozza, deep-bosomed and hipped like an amphora – the Hebe of the "Half-Moon" Inn – who had stirred our hero very violently to love, as he understood the emotion. The thought of her and of the warm luxuriance of her charms was torture to him as he rode there on the snow-spread Aemilian Way, whipped by the keen north wind; and it caused him to curse more bitterly than ever that Pope's bastard whom he blamed for his misfortunes.

In the distance, a mere speck as yet on the eternity of a road, a horseman was approaching. But Benvenuto had no concern with him. His concern was entirely with his own distress, and particularly with the gnawings of his stomach. Beyond Forlimpopoli he could not go fasting. There were limits to a man's endurance. Yet how was he to find a meal? He might sell his horse. But without a horse, how should he reach Bologna, or still more distant Milan? Besides, what should such as he be doing with such a horse for sale? There would be questions, not a doubt of that – there were always questions now in this distraught country – and if his answers failed to satisfy the questioners, as like as not they'd hang him. They were a deal too free with their hangings nowadays.

He ambled on, disconsolate; almost desperate enough for valour. Nearer drew the other horseman, and Benvenuto began to take an interest in him. He began to wonder whether a bold, browbeating manner and a harsh voice might produce a purse, and he began to wonder whether, if he set his mind to it, he could not sustain the one and the other. He shivered, and his yellow teeth chattered. Before resolving he would wait and see what manner of man was this who came alone and at so brisk a speed. Meanwhile he unsheathed his heavy sword and held it naked in his left hand, ready for work but concealed in the folds of his ragged cloak. Thus he rode amain to meet this wayfarer.

As the other drew nearer, Benvenuto observed that he was well mounted and very richly dressed, wearing a quilted brigandine – a garment that is dagger-proof – and over that a cloak of wine-coloured velvet heavily trimmed with lynx fur. At still closer quarters Benvenuto observed that he was young and of a very noble air, and he remarked the heavy gold chain that lay upon his breast, the jewelled brooch that held the black plume in his velvet cap. He concluded that here was a nut worth cracking.

He watched the fellow furtively as they drew together, and edged his horse towards the middle of the road so that they must pass each other at close quarters. The young man scarce glanced at him; he rode absorbed in his own thoughts. Benvenuto fell to trembling violently and his courage went near to deserting him completely. But he braced himself at the last moment, and as the stranger passed abreast of him he stood up suddenly in his stirrups, flashed up his sword, and aimed with all his strength a blow at that young head.

Too late the stranger saw the movement and the weapon. His hands tightened on his reins even as the murderous stroke descended. He swayed a second, being smitten, and then plunged downwards from the saddle. His frightened horse broke away at the gallop. The young man's spur hung in the stirrup, nor was released until he had been dragged a dozen paces through the snow. He lay there, and the horse, unhampered now and unchecked, sped on like a mad thing.

Benvenuto wheeled and rode up to the fallen man. For some minutes he sat breathing hard and grinning, as he considered that figure supine there in the snow, grinning too, but breathing not at all. Free of the confining cap, which had fallen off and lay some way behind, the youth's fair hair was flung back from the head and embrued from the wound that had been dealt him. Blood, too, lay in small patches along the trail made by his body as it was dragged.

Benvenuto looked back along the road towards Forlimpopoli, and forward towards Cesena. No living thing was in sight. So, well content, he got down from his horse to reap the harvest of his bloody work. But the rich raiment that had tempted him with its promise into daring so much now seemed to mock him. He rose from an almost fruitless search, cursing the poverty of the dead man's pockets, and weighing in his palm the gold chain he had taken from his victim's neck and a silken purse containing but three gold ducats. His prize, it seemed, was gilt, not solid gold.

To have risked so much for so little, angered him. To have been put to the necessity of killing a man to earn three gold pieces and a trumpery chain was an irony practised upon him by an unfriendly fate. He reflected that to commit murder was a grave matter. It was to imperil the salvation of his immortal soul – and Messer Benvenuto accounted himself a truly devout and pious fellow, a dutiful son of Mother Church. He had a special devotion for the black Madonna of Loreto, and was a member of the Confraternity of St Anna, whose scapular he wore day and night upon his dirty skin.

It was by no means the first time he had killed a man; but never had he been so poorly compensated for the mortal sin and the risk of hell which the deed entailed.

He glanced down at the blue-white face of his victim, and it seemed to him that the dead eyes were leering with evil conscious mockery. A panic seized him. He turned, snatched his horse's bridle, flung himself shuddering into the saddle and rode off. Twenty paces away he reined in again. He was behaving like a fool. The man's cloak with its heavy lynx fur was worth at least five ducats; and there was a jewel in his cap.

He went back, and in going he pondered. What should he do with a rich cloak? To sell it would be no easier than to sell his horse. Out of that train of thought came inspiration. The dead man could give him all he lacked, and never feel the loss of it, being dead.

He dismounted again, tethered his horse by the roadside, and set about his horrid task. But first he closed those hideously mocking eyes. To propitiate the departed spirit he even went so far as to kneel there, in the slush and snow, and patter a prayer for its repose. Then he set to work. He took the body under the armpits, and dragged it from the road. Down into the broad ditch and up again into the field beyond he dragged it. There, with chattering teeth and fingers that shook so that his work was retarded despite his frenzy of haste, he stripped the dead youth of his dagger-proof brigandine of quilted velvet, his undervest of silk, his great boots of grey leather, and his trunk-hose. Next he stripped away his own greasy rags, shuddering all the while and making queer whimpering noises – partly because the cold was punishing him acutely, partly because of other things.

There in the bright January sun he arrayed himself piece by piece in the gay plumage of the cockerel he had plucked. Thus he should travel in ease and dignity to Milan; thus command respect and courteous treatment – matters with which his acquaintance hitherto had been subjective. Thus should many a door be opened to him and many an opportunity discovered.

The dead man was much of his own proportions; even the boots, one of which he had already donned, should comfortably encase his feet. As he took up the second boot he discovered a certain stiffness on the inside of the leg. He fingered it, bending the leather in his hand; the matter intrigued him. He ran his fingers over the other boot; there was no corresponding stiffness there. Again he returned to the one he had not yet donned; and now a foxy gleam shone from his close-set eyes; thoughtfully he rubbed his long lean nose. That something was hidden in that boot was very clear; and it was a common enough hiding-place. Now a thing that is worth one man's while to hide is, reflected Messer Benvenuto, worth another man's while to find. It looked as if this enterprise of his were not to be so fruitless as he at first supposed.

To rip the outer leather from the lining was a moment's work. Then from the gap he drew a package of papers wrapped in a blank sheet on the edge of which was the broken half of a green seal. It was held together by some threads of silk. To snap these threads and to fling off the wrapper took Messer Benvenuto no longer than it takes to blink an eye. He spread one of the three contained sheets, and ran his glance over the large angular hand that sprawled across it.

It was a letter couched in Latin, and from that letter our rascal gathered, first and foremost, that his victim's name was Crespi, and that Faenza was his native place. He learned what more there was to learn; for Ser Benvenuto was no illiterate clod. A fond mother had vowed him to the Church, and so he had perforce done his humanities, and for all that years were sped since then, he had not yet forgotten that Latin tongue which so painfully he had acquired. His eyes gleamed as they followed and spelled out the sprawling characters. Here indeed was matter that might be worth a hundred times its weight in gold. But not here in the open would he stand to investigate the full value of his prize. Someone might chance to come that way, and find him there with the incriminating body. He looked about.

In the far distance, towards Forlimpopoli, specks were moving along the road. A cavalcade approaching; though no sound reached him yet. In haste he thrust the papers into his bosom, and his foot into the boot – never heeding that his stocking was all wet from standing in the snow. Then he took Messer Crespi's sword, and buckled it about his loins; lastly he snatched up the cloak, shook the snow from it, and flung it jauntily upon his own shoulders. Of his own discarded rags he made a bundle, and with this he sprang back to the road. There yet remained Messer Crespi's cap, which still lay where it had fallen. He took it up. It was slashed across the crown; but, being very ample of folds, this was easily dissembled, and there was no blood on the outside and little on the inside of it. But there was something else inside it – a black mask, a complete vizor for t̶ face, such as gentlemen sometimes wore when they went abroad.

Benvenuto replaced it in the crown of the cap, and set the latter a-top his lank, ill-kempt black hair. In his finery his countenance – half-wolf, half-fox – looked more villainous than ever.

He glanced over his shoulder at the little cavalcade, still very distant; then he got to horse and set off. But he no longer rode northward; he was returning in his tracks; returning to Cesena, urged to this course by the papers he had discovered. For at Cesena lay Cesare Borgia himself, in winter quarters, and Benvenuto's business now was with Cesare Borgia, whom these papers so very closely touched. The Duke's open-handedness was a byword. Benvenuto pondered that liberality of the Duke's, and relished the reflection that he bore him matter to cause him to open his hands wide indeed.

Having ridden a mile or so, Benvenuto flung his bundle of rags into the ditch. He saw it sink through the half-frozen crust of snow, and pushed on unburdened.

Presently he drew forth the papers again, that he might complete their perusal. This warmed him to the very core. He had done a glorious, a patriotic thing, it seemed, in disposing of this Messer Crespi – whoever he might be. And he was clearly clean of sin; since who kills a murderer is no worse than who robs a thief. That Messer Crespi was a murderer – a very desperate murderer – these letters fully showed, for they revealed a barbarous plot against the life of no less a person than the High and Mighty Lord Cesare Borgia, Duke of Valentinois and Romagna. They showed Messer Crespi to have been one of a band of patriots from various states of the Romagna – the letters did not disclose how many – who had leagued themselves to do this work. They moved in secret, he gathered, and were not known one to another, to lessen the dangers of betrayal. This was plain, since Messer Crespi was bidden to come masked to the assembly that was to be held that very night in the Palazzo Magli, in Cesena. But the leader, the inspirer, the soul and brain of the conspiracy, was evidently known to all; for he signed the letter, and his name was Hermes Bentivogli – the name of as bloody and treacherous a tyrant as lived in Italy, the murderer of the Marescotti, the son of Giovanni Bentivogli, Lord of Bologna.

Benvenuto was, himself – as you have gathered – no lover of Cesare Borgia, and, far from deploring his assassination, he would have hailed his slayer as a hero among heroes. But a man of his peculiar temperament is not to be expected to sink self-interest in political considerations, and to forgo the chance of doing Cesare Borgia a service for which Cesare Borgia should reward him with a pretty, twinkling heap of golden ducats.

Benvenuto had those ducats very clear in his imagination. He saw them piled before him on the dirty table of the "Half-Moon" Inn; saw the yellow, rippling gleam of them; heard the rustle and chink of the heap as it was stirred. He saw the black eyes of his luscious Giannozza grow big at the sight of so much gold; he felt her soft, warm body yielding generously at last to his embraces.

Oh, most brightly shone the star of Messer Benvenuto Gismondi, thief and scoundrel. His fortune rose in a neap tide. And in the pleasant consideration of this heartening fact he rode across the bridge over the Savio, and so entered the strong city of Cesena.

First to the Half-Moon to leave his horse in charge of the gaping, cross-eyed landlord – Giannozza's puny and most unworthy sire; then to a barber's to have his hair and beard trimmed combed and perfumed, that that part of him should be in harmony with the whole; then back to the Half-Moon to dine in an inner chamber which he had bespoken, with Giannozza to bring his meat and pour his wine.

In the common-room men stared at him, as he swept through; and he, perceiving this, broke upon Giannozza in the inner chamber with the exclamation: "Behold me – a jewel set in brass."

Giannozza, hand on hip, measured him with some wonder and more mistrust in her bold, black eyes. She was a handsome baggage, full conscious of it, gracefully sluggish, and very insolent.

"You are soon returned," said she, and added uncompromisingly the question – "What villany have you been working?"

"Villany?" quoth he. "Nay, now – villany!"

"Whence, else, your fine feathers? What gull have you been plucking?"

He took her in his arms, and pulled her to him, leering; she permitting it with a cool indifference. "I have taken service, sweet," he announced.

"Service, thou? With Satan?"

"With the Lord Cesare Borgia," said he – for, being a thief, it naturally follows that he was a facile liar. Though as a liar you do not here see him at his best; for, after all, what he now stated might be construed into intelligent anticipation.

"Has he hired you for his murderer?" she inquired, with the cool insolence that was a part of her.

"I am his saviour," he announced, and fell into big but obscure talk of services rendered and to be rendered and more of the rich guerdons that were to fall to him of the Duke's bounty; she listening, her red lips curling into a lazy smile of insolent unbelief in him. In the end that smile so angered him that he flung her off rudely, and sat down.

"I am to confer with his Magnificence today," he announced. "He awaits me at the castle. You'll believe me when I spread his ducats before your big, fool's eyes. Oho! Ser Benvenuto will be *ben venuto* then!"

She thrust out her heavy lip at him.

"Dost sneer at me, thou trull?" he bellowed, furious. Then with a superior air, "Bestir!" he bade her. "Bring meat and wine. The Lord Duke of Valentinois awaits me. Bestir, I say!"

She looked him over from under half-closed lids, and sneered audibly.

"You knock-kneed, pock-marked foulness," said she. "What airs be these?"

He choked with fury – the more hurt because the straightness of his legs was the pride of one who could lay claim to few physical advantages. He set aside his anger, to argue the matter. But she cut him short.

"Such airs as yours cost money," she informed him. "Where is your purse?"

He produced a ducat, and banged it resonantly upon the dirty table. At the unexpected sight of that yellow disc her eyes widened in surprise and greed, and her manner underwent an instant change. She bustled now in preparation for his meal; fetched a bottle from the cellar, and from the kitchen a steaming shoulder of roast kid, exuding a rich savoury smell of garlic. She placed white bread before him – a rare luxury that – and flung logs upon the fire.

He, being very hungry, forgot what remained of his recent anger, and fell to with a relish; so that for a while the dingy chamber re-echoed with the prodigious sounds of his eating and drinking. Anon, his vigour abating, he bestowed some attention upon the girl as she moved about the chamber with the indolent, feline grace that was natural to her. The food heartened him; and what with the wine and the great fire that roared now in the chimney and threw fantastic light and shadow through the gloomy room, Messer Benvenuto was pervaded by a pleasant torpor.

"Sit here beside me, Giannozza," he besought her, pulling gently at her plump arm.

"And his Magnificence of Valentinois? Does he no longer await you?" quoth she, with her lazy sneer.

He scowled. "A plague on his Magnificence," he grumbled, and fell thoughtful. It was very snug and pleasant here, and outside it was chill and bleak, and there was snow on the ground. And yet – surely it was worth the trouble of walking up to the castle to have his cap filled with ducats!

He rose and strode to the window. He looked out upon a slushy stableyard and a patch of turquoise sky. The afternoon was waning, and the thing must be done that afternoon or not at all.

"Ay, I must go, sweet. But I'll be away no longer than I must." He took up his cloak, and swathed it about him, planted the plump cap upon his ugly head, kissed her noisily – she suffering it with that same detestable apathy – and swaggered out.

Benvenuto took his way to the main street, and then up the hill towards the citadel, the huge Rocca built by the great Sigismondo Malatesta.

Unchallenged he gained the bridge, whence the snow had been swept into the moat below. He crossed it, going with a certain nervousness now, and certain tremblings of spirit which increased with the thud of each step of his upon the timbers.

His imagination set an august and fearful majesty about this duke whom he had never seen, but whose name was known to all men and feared by most. He felt as one about to enter the presence of things supernatural, and he went with such an awe as in his early infancy had attended his first visits to a church.

He had crossed the bridge and stood in the shadow of the great archway, under the portcullis. Strange that no one should be there to ask his business. Strange that the place harbouring that godlike being should be so easy of approach.

There was a sudden clank, and a halbert flashed before him and was poised on a level with his breast. Benvenuto jumped for very fright. A man-at-arms in marion, corselet and cuissarts had stepped out from behind a buttress where he was sheltering from the wind and had levelled his pike to bar our hero's passage.

"*Alto là*? Whither do you go?"

Benvenuto stammered a moment, flung out of countenance by this sudden apparition of a natural foe – a representative, however humble, of law and power. Then he recovered.

"I seek the Lord Duke of Valentinois," he announced.

The pike was lowered, recovered and ground with a thud. "Pass on," said the sentry, and drew back once more behind the sheltering buttress.

Benvenuto went forward, his uneasiness increasing with his surprise at the readiness of his admission. This was not well, he reasoned. Out of a place so easy to enter, it might be difficult to depart again. His conscience and his nerves played tricks upon him. He wished that he had remained in the snug parlour of the "*Mezza Luna*" with the delectable Giannozza, and never ventured thus into the shrine of this awful divinity. For he stood by now shivering in the courtyard of the fortress, and not even the prospect of the ducats to be earned served to encourage him. He wished them at the devil. Presently he braced himself; inwardly mocked his own fears; reassured himself in part; and looked about him.

The court was deserted, save for two sentries – one pacing at the foot of a stone staircase that led up to a gallery on the first floor; the other guarding a deep archway that led to an inner court. Thence came a murmur of voices, and as Benvenuto peered in that direction he saw that it was thronged with people.

The sentries paid no heed to him; but he considered them attentively. The man guarding the staircase was a sturdy, swarthy fellow of forbidding countenance; the other, a tall, fair-bearded knave, looked benign and friendly. Benvenuto's choice was made. He advanced with simulated resoluteness towards the archway and the yellow-bearded guard.

"I seek the Lord Duke of Valentinois," he announced, dissembling as best he might his tremors. "Where shall I find him?"

The guard looked at him. If the livid, pock-marked face was villainous, the clothes were noble; and whilst to a courtier Messer Benvenuto must have looked a lackey, to a lackey he looked a courtier. So without hesitation the guard stood aside before him, and pointed with his pike into the inner courtyard.

"His Highness is in there."

Benvenuto passed on, and, as he went, the sounds from the inner court he was approaching died suddenly away. The crowd had fallen into silence. It greatly intrigued him to know what might be taking place. On the far side of the archway he tapped the arm of a sentry, who stood on a horse block, gazing over the heads of the people assembled there – a motley gathering of perhaps a hundred men of all conditions, in which, however, the soldier and the courtier predominated. The man-at-arms looked down impatiently, and Benvenuto repeated that he sought the Lord Duke of Valentinois.

"He is yonder," said the guard, pointing into the heart of the throng.

Benvenuto was intrigued. What was taking place? He stood on tip-toe; but being short of stature he gained nothing by it. Suddenly the crowd broke into cheers and hand-clappings. Again Benvenuto plucked the sentry's sleeve.

"My business with his Highness presses," he urged. "It is of the first importance. I must see him instantly."

The guard considered him. "I doubt you'll have to wait," said he. He pointed to a page in scarlet and yellow, who, astride a cannon by the wall, was shouting and clapping his hands. "Best tell him," said the soldier. "He'll take your message for you as soon as may be."

Benvenuto thanked him and went on, pressing unceremoniously past one or two who blocked his way. He spoke to the page politely; he shouted to him; finally he shook him by the leg, and thus gained at last his attention.

"I seek the Lord Duke of Valentinois," he said for the fourth time since his arrival in that fortress. "It is a very pressing matter – a matter of life and death."

The page looked him over superciliously, and grinned. "You'll have to wait," he answered. "His Highness is busy over there."

"Over there?" echoed Benvenuto. But the page took no further heed of him. Whereupon, determined to see what might be taking place, Benvenuto climbed on to the gun, behind the boy. Thence he could see over the heads of the throng, and what he saw surprised him.

These spectators formed a ring, from which all snow had been swept. In the centre of this two men faced each other, alert, and with hands held slightly forward. Both were naked to the waist, and they contrasted oddly. One was tall, big-limbed and heavy – a very giant – swarthy, black-bearded, and hairy as a goat about the trunk and limbs; the other, tall also, yet not quite so tall, was of a slenderness that looked delicate by comparison; his long hair and crisp beard were of an auburn fairness, and his naked torso was smooth, and of a gleaming, alabaster whiteness. They were wrestlers about to come to grips, and Benvenuto pitied the comely, white-fleshed fellow, with a contemptuous pity, and looked forward with interest to the mauling he must receive in the embrace of that great bear of a man to whom he was opposed.

Then Benvenuto scanned the foremost ranks of the spectators, looking for one whose regal presence must proclaim the Duke. He beheld several very noble-looking gentlemen; but he was left in doubt as to which of them might be Cesare Borgia, and meanwhile the wrestlers were locked in combat, swaying this way and that, as first one heaved and then the other. The only sound in the courtyard was the sharp hiss of their breath, the quick patter of their shifting feet, and the smack of their hands upon each other's body.

Benvenuto watched, amazed at the fair man's ability to resist so long. He had his fingers locked now about the giant's neck, and was exerting his might and weight to pull the fellow forward and throw him off his balance. And as he put forth his strength, Benvenuto was surprised by the sudden ripple of muscle and sinew upon the smooth, alabaster back. Protuberances as large as apples appeared suddenly under the wrestler's shoulder-blades, whilst from either side of his spine leaped tight ropes of unsuspected power. Clearly the fellow was none so soft as he might seem at a first glance. Yet here his efforts were all vain. As well might he have sought to move a bull. The giant stood with legs wide and feet firmly planted, resisting the exertions of the other.

Then in a flash he moved; wrenched his neck free; seized his opponent about the waist, and swung him from the ground. And then, before he could use his unquestionable advantage, his opponent's two hands had caught him by the chin, and were forcing his head back with such harsh violence that he was compelled to abandon his hold.

They fell apart, breathing hard, very wary of each other.

The page turned a white excited face to Benvenuto. "Madonna!" swore the stripling. "He all but had him then!"

"Who is the fellow?" asked Benvenuto.

"A blacksmith from Cattolica," answered the boy. "They say he has not his match for strength in the Romagna."

"Ay; but the other – the white-fleshed cockerel?"

The lad stared at him. "Why – whence are you? From the Indies or the new world of Messer Colombo? That is his Highness the Duke of Valentinois."

Benvenuto stared back at the page, and frowned. "Look you, young sir," said he, "do you seek to make a fool of me?"

"Diavolo!" said the pert boy. "Who am I to improve upon God's work?"

And then a shout from the crowd drew the attention of both back to the ring.

The fair wrestler had stooped, evaded the blacksmith's long arms, and seizing him by the legs had hoisted him from the ground. But the smith's great hands had closed about the other's neck, and so neutralised the hold, making a throw impossible – for by their rules a throw was no throw in which the thrower went down with the thrown. The shout had been raised while the matter was in doubt, and when it seemed that the blacksmith must suffer defeat, and the word that Benvenuto caught from a hundred throats was "Duca! Duca!"

It informed him that the page had spoken truth; but the surprise of it almost stunned him. Was that, indeed the Duke? That Cesare Borgia? That the demigod whose presence he had approached with such overwhelming awe?

Why, he was no better than another. A duke who wrestled with blacksmiths in the courtyard of his own castle! Faugh! Was that a duke to be feared?

Now that he had seen this pope's bastard, Benvenuto felt himself every inch his equal. What false attributes – he reflected – are bestowed by man's imaginings upon the great! Cesare Borgia was a man like any other – and he wrestled with blacksmiths! He should pay Benvenuto handsomely for the information Benvenuto brought him. No longer would Benvenuto be afraid to demand full value for his wares.

Meanwhile the combat assumed a greater interest in his eyes, and he watched it, marvelling at the folly of this duke. To be a duke and to permit himself to be rudely handled in this fashion! Like enough there would be broken bones under that white skin of his before all was done. It was not thus that Benvenuto understood the trade of dukes; not thus that he had conceived them. Rich wines, a well-spread table, a soft couch, abundance of minstrels to soothe him with their music, and the brightness of female eyes to gladden him. These, Benvenuto had ever conceived to be the natural attributes of dukeship. This rough-and-tumble with blacksmiths in a courtyard on a winter day held no place in his conception.

The page was giving him information. "His Highness has promised fifty ducats to any man who can throw him."

Lackaday! Fifty ducats for such a service! Oh, the Duke was a queer fellow – but most ducally open-handed, as people said; and Benvenuto smiled to think of the tax he should presently levy upon that open-handedness.

Meanwhile, the wrestlers were at grips again, more vigorously than ever; and, as he watched them, Benvenuto was lost in wonder of the Duke's amazing agility. He seemed compact of springs of steel, so lithe and swift were all his movements, so pantherine his step, his crouch, his leap. The end seemed now to Benvenuto less a foregone conclusion than at first. For the brute might of the Colossus appeared to spend itself against the supple strength of the young Duke.

The end came suddenly. Before men realised it, all was done. The blacksmith made a sudden rush to grapple his opponent. The Duke, to avoid him, swung aside from the hips, leaving his feet firmly planted; as the giant missed his grip and hurtled forward, suddenly off his balance, Cesare's arms coiled themselves sideways about his waist. His hands locked and his grip tightened so that the smith could not turn in that embrace to face his antagonist.

Again Benvenuto saw that ripple and rise of muscle under the fair white skin of the Duke's back. Men held their breaths. Here was a well-seized grip. Could the Duke hold it – hold that gigantic mass of writhing muscle?

Hold it he did. He crouched a little, gathered his right leg under him, and thrust out his left hip. It was like the stretching of an archer's bow. And then it was as if the quarrel had been loosed, and the quarrel was the blacksmith. There had been a sudden heave; the protruded hip came straight again, and the blacksmith, swung an instant to the horizontal, crashed down upon his shoulder, and lay there, groaning. But his groans were lost in the deafening cheer that went up from the ring of spectators in the yard and others who had watched the contest from the windows of the quadrangle.

"Duca! Duca!" was the shout. Caps flew aloft; men clapped, and laughed, and bellowed at each other the niceties of the throw.

The Duke meanwhile had gone down upon one knee beside the prostrate wrestler, and was holding up his hand for silence. The man had been hurt. His shoulder was dislocated or his collar-bone broken from the force of the impact with which he fell.

Men-at-arms came forward to help him, half-stunned and suffering, to his feet.

"Let Torella see to his shoulder," said the Duke, adding to the man himself. "You are the stoutest rogue I was ever matched against, and you made me tremble for my reputation." He had his hand on the man's sound shoulder, very friendly as he spoke.

Hearing and seeing so much, Benvenuto's contempt for his Highness steadily increased. He caught the look of dog-like gratitude in the smith's eye, and sneered at both of them.

"You shall have twenty ducats to comfort you," were the Duke's last words to the man. At least, thought Benvenuto, there was no doubt that he was free with his ducats; and that was the main thing now.

An attendant fetched the Duke a silken vest and a fur-lined surcoat, and he donned the garments with the quick grace peculiar to all his actions.

Benvenuto begged the page to announce him to his Highness, urging the importance of the matter upon which he came, which already had been too long delayed. The page obligingly departed on that errand. Benvenuto saw him hover a moment about the Duke, then make a profound obeisance and deliver his message.

Cesare was settling the surcoat upon his shoulders. He inclined his head to listen to the boy; then he looked up, and his eyes fell upon Benvenuto, standing there full now of arrogance and assurance. And that same arrogance went out of Benvenuto when Cesare's eyes fell upon him, as a candle goes out in a gust of wind.

What there might be in the glance of those matchless eyes he could not have attempted to tell you. But something sped upon it to his brain, and partly numbed it. It was as if his body were of glass, and those eyes were looking through it into the dirty little soul within.

Then, abruptly, the Duke beckoned him. He got down from his eminence, and went forward without swagger, his breathing quickened, his skin cold. Soldiers, courtiers and others fell away before him, opening a lane, through which he passed into the immediate presence of that auburn-haired young man.

"You have something to tell me," said the Duke, his voice gentle enough, and yet the coldest that Benvenuto had ever known; his eyes so level and penetrating that Benvenuto could not support their glance.

"Something – something of great moment, Magnificent," faltered the thief.

Cesare was silent an instant, still considering him; and in that instant the wretched Benvenuto felt that he had no secrets from the Duke; that all that there was to know of him was known to this man whose equal he had so lately accounted himself.

"Come with me, then," said the Duke in his gentle voice – a voice rich in melody – and turned away.

Preceded by the page he crossed the courtyard, and mounted six steps to an oaken door studded with great iron nails, which a man-at-arms flung open for him at his approach. Benvenuto followed meekly, uncomfortable under the many eyes that conned him and detected – he was convinced – his true station and quality under his brave stolen raiment.

From the bright, clear sunshine of the courtyard he passed into a large and somewhat gloomy hall, cheered by the ruddy play of light on the floor and walls and ceiling from a great fire that burned in the vast cowled fireplace. The floor was strewn with fresh rushes;

there were tapestries on two of the walls, and a staircase ascended to a gallery on the right. Near the fire stood a large arm-chair in red velvet with an escutcheon in gold which glowed and faded as the firelight caught it. By this was a massive table, elaborately carved, and yonder a buffet upon which stood goblets and a tall golden beaker. From this latter a faint steam was rising, and Benvenuto's nostrils caught and were set a-quiver by the sweet perfume of spiced wine.

Cesare flung himself into the chair by the fire. The page fetched the beaker and a goblet – a single goblet, Benvenuto noted – and poured wine for his master, thereafter setting the beaker on the table.

The Duke waved the stripling away into the background, and turned at last to Benvenuto, who stood there in mid-apartment, foolish and ill at ease.

"Now, sir," said he, "your errand?"

The question fell abruptly. It was by no means the question Benvenuto had expected to begin with. But he must answer it.

"I am in possession, my lord," he said, "of particulars of a plot which aims at your life."

He had counted upon making a profound impression. But this was a day of surprises for him, of incredible revelations into the ways and habits of dukes. Not a muscle moved in Cesare's calm face; unblinking those haunting eyes continued to regard him. There fell a pause, terminated at last by the Duke, whose slender fingers impatiently tapped the table.

"Well, sir, well?" he cried sharply. "What else?"

"What else?" stammered Benvenuto. "Why – that is all."

"All?" the Duke frowned. "But these particulars?"

"I – I have them here. They are contained in these letters, of which I became possessed today, and – and I have ridden at all speed to bring them to you." He was fumbling in his doublet.

"You have ridden? Whence?"

"Eh – from Forli."

He produced the letters. He had, as you know, entertained bold thoughts of the price he would ask, the bargain he would drive before surrendering them. But all notion of that had gone from him with his courage. He had beheld an instance of the Duke's proverbial liberality in the case of the wrestler. He had no doubt the Duke would be no less liberal with him. He would depend upon that. He advanced timidly to the table, and set the letters before the Duke.

Cesare scanned them rapidly. Midway through the first his brows became knit. He gave a sharp order to the page.

"Beppo, summon me Messer Gherardi."

The page went up the stairs, along the gallery, and through a doorway at the end. Cesare resumed his reading. Benvenuto waited, wondering.

At last the Duke set down the letters on the table. Benvenuto had expected outbursts, transports of rage, ferocious satisfaction, then protestations of gratitude to him – the Duke's saviour – and, lastly, a golden recompense. From the beginning nothing fell out as he expected. There was no outburst, no trace of anger even. The Duke's handsome lofty face remained as calm as though such matters were of daily occurrence in his life; his words, when he spoke, did not seem even remotely to bear upon the matter of this conspiracy.

"What is your name, sir?"

Under the play of those awful, beautiful eyes Benvenuto answered truthfully, feeling that he dared not lie – that to lie were idle: "I am Benvenuto Gismondi, your Highness' servant."

"Of Forli?"

"Of Forli, Magnificent."

"And your trade?"

Benvenuto's uneasiness welled up. "I – I am a poor man, Highness. I – I live as I can."

He saw Cesare's eyes pondering his garments – the gold chain on his breast, the jewel in the cap he held – with the faintest yet most sinister of smiles. Too late he perceived how he had blundered; too late he cursed himself for not having come with a tale prepared. But how should he have expected such questions? What manner of man was this who could turn aside from such a matter as Benvenuto had set before him, to make inquiries so alien to the subject.

"I see," said Cesare, and the tone was such that it turned the scoundrel's soul to water, froze the marrow in his spine, filling him as it did with horrid premonitions. "I see. And this Messer Crespi of Faenza, to whom these letters were addressed – he is dead?" It was but the slightly rising inflection of the voice that made a question of that statement.

Livid, shaking now in every limb, and will-less before this man who seemed to draw the very soul out of him, Benvenuto answered: "He is dead, Magnificent."

"Ah! You were well advised in that," the Duke agreed. He smiled, and his smile was the deadliest Gismondi had ever seen. "He was, I take it," the Duke pursued, "a man of much your own height and build."

"It is so, Magnificent."

"That, too, is fortunate, as it is fortunate you should have had the happy thought to array yourself in his apparel. No doubt the condition of your own would be a sufficient justification."

"My lord, my lord!" cried the abject scoundrel, and would have flung himself upon his knees to implore mercy but that Cesare's next words stayed him.

"Why – what now? It is all most fortunate, I say. I would not have it other."

Benvenuto stared into that smiling face, sorely mistrustful. He detected something sinister in that fair speech.

Steps sounded on the gallery. Down the stairs came the page, returning, followed by a well-nourished gentleman in black, whose face was round and white, whose nose was sharp, and whose crafty eyes took, in passing, the measure of Messer Benvenuto.

"Ah, Agabito!" the Duke hailed him, and held out the letters. "These pretend to be from Hermes Bentivogli. Do you recognise the hand?"

The secretary took the papers, and crossed to the window to examine them in the light. Suddenly he cried out: "What is this, my lord?"

"Did I bid you read, Agabito?" quoth the Duke, with the faintest show of impatience. "Is the hand that of Hermes Bentivogli?"

"Assuredly," answered Agabito readily. He was well acquainted with the writing of the Bolognese.

The Duke sighed, and rose. "Then the thing is true, and he is here in Cesena. He has vowed to kill me, more than once. At last, it seems, he has the courage to take the thing in hand."

"He must be seized, my lord."

Cesare stood with bowed head, lost in thought. Benvenuto, seemingly forgotten for the moment, watched furtively, and waited.

"There may be a score of others in the plot," said Cesare slowly.

"But he is the brain – the brain," cried Agabito, slapping the papers in his excitement.

"God help the body that is ruled by such a brain," sneered the Duke. "Ay, he should be crushed. He should be made to feel the full weight, the full terror of my justice."

Benvenuto shuddered to the very soul of him at the words and the tone.

"But –" The Duke shrugged wearily, and turned to face the fire. "He is of Bologna, and behind Bologna there is France, and if I strangle this cut-throat, God alone knows what complications may confront me."

"But with such evidence as this –" began Agabito.

"It is no matter of right or wrong," Cesare snapped at him. "Before I move –" He stopped short, and turned again. His glance, hard and bright, fastened once more upon Benvenuto, whilst he extended his hand to Gherardi for the papers. The secretary promptly resigned them.

"Here," said the Duke, and he now held out the letters to Benvenuto. "Take you these papers, of which in the way of your scoundrel's trade you have become possessed. Learn their contents by heart. Then go at midnight – as the letter directs – to the Palazzo

Magli. Play the part of Messer Crespi, and bring me word tomorrow of what these conspirators intend and who their associates elsewhere."

Gismondi fell back a pace, his eyes dilating. "My lord," he cried. "My lord, I dare not."

"Oh, as you please," said the Duke most sweetly. "But there are enough cut-throats in Italy – too many vermin of your kind – that we should hesitate to dispose of one. Beppo, call the guard."

"My lord," cried Benvenuto again, starting forward, shaken by fresh terror; and the sudden hoarseness of his voice surprised him. "A moment, Magnificent – of your pity! If I do this thing...?" he began; then stopped, appalled by the very contemplation of it.

"If you do this thing," said Cesare, answering the uncompleted question, "we will not inquire into the death of Messer Crespi. Our forgetfulness shall be your wage. I confess," he continued, his tone most amiable, "that I shall do this reluctantly, for I have vowed to exterminate your kind. Nevertheless, out of consideration for the service you are to render, I will hold my hand this time. Fail me, or refuse the task, and there is the rope – first to extract confession from you on the hoist, and afterwards to hang you. The choice is yours."

Gismondi stared and stared into that beautiful young face, so mockingly impassive. His terror gave way to a dull rage, and but for the exhibition of strength he had so lately witnessed in the courtyard, he might not have curbed his impulse to attempt to anticipate upon the Duke the work of Messer Crespi's friends. He cursed his folly in setting his trust in the gratitude of princes; he mocked his own credulity in thinking that his tale would be received with joy and purchased at more gold than he could carry.

In the end he staggered out of the chamber, and out of the citadel, pledged to betake himself at midnight to the Magli Palace, at the imminent risk of his sweet life, assured that he would be watched by Cesare Borgia's spies and that, did he fail to perform the task he had undertaken, the risk to his life would be more imminent still.

Back to the Half-Moon he went, to closet himself in that inner chamber of the inn. He called for candles – for dusk had meanwhile fallen – and set himself to con the papers that should have been his fortune but were become his ruin. To the charms of Giannozza he was for once as unresponsive as to the sneer of her cross-eyed father which had greeted his return and his crestfallen air.

Giannozza being a woman and inquisitive was intrigued by this change in his demeanour, this gloomy abstraction; but powerless to elicit explanation. The seductions with which she sought to loose his tongue all left him cold. At length she fetched him a jug of spiced wine, deeming it the likeliest philtre to charm his soul to confidences. But still he disappointed her. He viewed the jug with apathy; the accustomed gleam was absent from his eyes, and she listened in vain for the usual resounding anticipatory smack of his great coarse lips. Listlessly he took up the vessel. He moved it slowly in his hand, causing the steaming wine to swirl, and made lachrymose philosophy.

"Man," said he, "is no better than a fluid in the jug of circumstance. It is circumstance that moulds and shapes him at her will, as this wine is moulded in this jug; and his end is much as this." And he emptied the jug sorrowfully.

"Touching this service of the Duke's…?" began Giannozza.

He waved her away. "Go. Leave me. I need to be alone a while."

She called him by offensive names, which he scarce heeded, and left him.

Spiritless and dejected sat he there, staring at the fire, which was burning low by now. Thoughts of escape returned to him, to be dismissed again. He was doomed if he essayed it. There were two strangers even now in the common-room, drinking and making friends with Giannozza's unutterable father. That they were emissaries of Cesare Borgia, detailed to watch him, and to seize him should he attempt to leave the town, he had no single doubt. His only chance was the narrow one the Duke had set him – through the gathering of the conspirators that night.

So he returned to the letters and set himself to learn by heart their contents – as the Duke had urged him – that he might carry through this dread affair and play that night his fearful rôle.

Thus it befell that midnight found him at the wicket in the great doors of the Magli Palace. Crespi's purple cloak hung loosely from his shoulders in such a manner as to mask his figure; Crespi's black silk vizor was upon his face, for the letters told him – and in that lay his one chance – that the conspirators were to come masked and remain unknown one to another.

The Palazzo Magli, be it known, was at this time untenanted, wherefore it had been chosen for this secret meeting.

Gismondi found the wicket yield to his pressure. He pushed it wide, and stepped over the sill formed by the actual door, into a blackness as of the very pit. Instantly the wicket closed behind him, and he stood in a darkness so thick that it seemed a thing material and palpable. All was still; no faintest sound disturbed the stillness.

"A cold night," he said aloud, this being the appointed watchword.

Instantly a hand gripped his arm, and Gismondi was troubled by a thrill of fear. Nevertheless he spoke again as was appointed.

"And it will be colder anon."

"Colder for whom?" quoth a voice.

"For one who is warm enough tonight."

His arm was released, and instantly the gloom was dispelled. A cloak was lifted from a lanthorn standing on the ground, and from this a circle of light gleamed feebly along the tiled floor, rose faintly thence to a man's height, but pierced no farther into the upper darkness.

A black figure, indistinct in the misty light, his face masked, signed to Benvenuto to follow; took up the lanthorn and crossed the hall, his footsteps sounding eerily in that empty place. Another similar figure remained – Benvenuto observed – standing immovable by the wicket, ready to admit the next corner.

Across the hall, Benvenuto's guide opened a door, and conducted him into a spacious courtyard within the quadrangular precincts of the palace. A thick soft carpet of snow lay on the ground, and from the lanthorn swinging in the hand of his guide a yellow wheel of light fell on the whiteness, and Benvenuto observed the tracks of many steps that had preceded him that way. They reached another door, passed through another hall, chill and gloomy as a vault, and so on to yet a third door in which a wicket opened to give them passage into a garden.

Here the guide paused. "Follow those tracks," he said, "to the garden's end. There you will find a ladder against the wall. Surmount it and follow the tracks in the next garden. They will lead you to a door, which will be opened to your knock." He turned abruptly, stepped back into the hall, and slammed the wicket, leaving Benvenuto alone and very frightened.

For a moment he paused with fresh and very wild ideas of flight thrusting themselves upon his notice. But he cast them aside. Already he had gone too far for retreat. If only it were daylight. But this gloom, faintly relieved out here by the ghostly luminousness of the all-covering snow, was sharpening his nerves. He looked up at the black sky all flecked with stars that twinkled frostily, then at the track, faintly discernible. He went forward until he found the ladder and the wall. He went over and into another garden; found the track there, and pursued it to the house.

He readily perceived the object of so much travelling. The meeting was not at the Palazzo Magli at all. It had been so announced as a safeguard. By this journey across two gardens, the plotters were introduced into another palace some distance away. Should danger threaten the Palazzo Magli, should it be beset or invaded, the enemy would find an empty nest, and the men who had been left on guard there would know how to convey a warning to the real meeting-place, whence the conspirators might disperse unchallenged.

Benvenuto went up some steps to a stout door and knocked. It was opened instantly, and as instantly closed when he had passed in. He stood once more in Stygian darkness, his pulses beating wildly.

Out of the gloom came an unexpected question – a question for which the letters had not specifically prepared him.

"Whence are you?"

An instant did he hesitate, mastering his sudden terror, and answered as Crespi must have answered: "From Faenza."

"Enter," the voice bade him. And now a door was suddenly flung wide, and a flood of light issuing from it smote and almost blinded him, after the long spell of darkness that had been his.

Peering and blinking he went forward with a bold step and a quaking heart, thanking his patron saint and Our Lady of Loreto for the mask that covered the livid fear writ large upon his countenance.

He entered a spacious chamber, lighted by a dozen great candle-branches suspended from ceiling and from panelled walls. Down the middle of this room ran a long quadrangular table, at which sat seven other plotters masked and muffled as was he – and all in silence, like so many *beccamorti*.

The door closed softly behind him, and the sound chilled him, suggesting to his fevered mind the closing of a trap. He heartened himself with the reflection that he had learned his lesson well; he persuaded himself that he had nothing to fear; and he went forward to find himself a chair at the table. He sat down and waited, glad enough that the secrecy of the proceedings precluded inter-communion. And presently others came, as he had come, and like himself each sat aloof from his fellow-plotters.

At last the door opened again to admit one who differed from the rest in that he wore no mask. He was a tall man with a big-nosed, shaven face, swarthy and bold-eyed. He was a man in the full vigour of youth, and he was dressed from head to foot in black. A long sword swung from his girdle, and a heavy dagger rested on his right hip. This, Benvenuto guessed, must be Bentivogli.

He was followed by two masked figures in black – who had the air of being in attendance – and upon his entrance the entire company – now numbering a round dozen – rose to its feet.

119

Gismondi knew enough of this affair, into which an odd irony had thrust him, to understand why this man, who was the head and leader of the *congiura*, should come unmasked; for, whilst the identity of the plotters was kept secret one from another, their leader was known, at least by name, to each and all, as were all known, by name at least, to him.

Bentivogli stepped to the head of the long table. One of his attendants set a chair for him; but he did not sit. He stood there, his heavy underlip thrust forward, his great brow puckered in a frown, his dark eyes playing over the assembled company. At length he spoke.

"We are all assembled, my friends," said he, "and to me it is strange that this should be so." A chill went through Benvenuto like a sword-thrust in the vitals. But he gave no sign. He stood immovable among the others.

"Be seated, all," Bentivogli bade them, and all sat; but he, their leader, remained standing.

"I have reason to believe," he said, in a cold, hard voice, "that here amongst us sits a spy."

There was a rustle as of wind through trees as the muffled company stirred at that fell announcement. Men turned to scan one another with eyes that flashed fiercely through the eyeholes of their vizors, as though their glances would have burned a way through the silk that screened their neighbours' countenances. It seemed to Gismondi in that moment of choking panic that the entire company was staring at him; then he knew this for a trick of his imaginings; and, betide what might, he set himself to do as others did, and to glare fiercely in his turn at this and that one. Some three or four were upon their feet.

"His name!" they cried. "His name, Magnificent!"

But the Magnificent shook his head and motioned them to resume their seats. "I know it not," said he, "nor in whose place he is here." Whereat Gismondi breathed more freely. "All that I know is this. As I rode hither today, we came, some two miles from Cesena, upon the body of a man, who had been murdered, robbed and stripped almost naked. The body was scarce cold when we discovered it, and in the distance, towards Cesena, rode one who may well have been the murderer. Now it chanced that by the body we found a sheet of paper, which I have here. It bears, as you see, the half of a green seal – a seal bearing the imprint of arms not to be identified with those of any house in Italy today, yet arms familiar to all of you who have received communications from me in the matter upon which we are assembled here tonight."

Bentivogli paused a moment, then continued: "Undoubtedly that paper was a wrapper that had enclosed communications from me concerned with our present business. Whether such a letter had been addressed to the dead man I do not know, nor do I know who he was nor whence he came. But someone here should be able to throw light upon this matter – unless the dead man was indeed one of us, and his murderer has replaced him at this meeting. Can any of you give me the explanation which I seek?"

He sat down and waited, looking from one to another. But no answer came from any.

Gismondi felt his breath failing him. If he had wished to speak at that moment – if he had prepared a likely tale to meet the emergency, he could not have given utterance to it then.

A slow, cruel smile overspread Bentivogli's heavy features as the deathly silence was maintained.

"So," he said at length. "It is as I supposed." Then in an altered and brisker tone: "Had I known where each of you was lodged, I had found means to warn you against coming here tonight. As it is, I can only hope that we are not yet betrayed. But this I know: that the man who became possessed of the secret of our plot sits here amongst us now – no doubt that he may learn its scope more fully before he goes to sell his story to him you know of."

Again there was that rustling stir, and several voices were raised, harsh and hot with threats of what should be the fate of this rash spy. Gismondi gnawed his lip in silence, waiting and wondering, the strength all oozing from him.

"Twelve of us were to have foregathered here tonight," said Bentivogli impressively. "One of us, it seems, lies dead; yet twelve are here. You see, my friends," he added, a sardonic note vibrating in his voice, "that there is one too many. That one," he concluded, and from sardonic his voice turned grim, "that one we must weed out."

He rose as he spoke, a splendid figure, tall and stately.

"I will ask you, one by one, to confer with me apart a moment," he announced. "Each of you will come when summoned. I shall call you, not by name but by the city from which you come."

He turned from the table, and moved down into the shadows under a gallery at the far end of the long room, and with him went the two who had attended him on his arrival.

Gismondi watched them, fascinated. The two attendants, he supposed, would do the uprooting when the weed was discovered; for that reason did they accompany Bentivogli, and for that purpose did they withdraw into the shadow, as more fitting than the light for the deed of darkness that would presently be done. An icy sweat broke on his skin.

"Ancona!" called Bentivogli in a loud voice, and the name boomed mournfully on the chill air.

A masker rose upon the instant, thrusting back his chair, and marched resolutely down the room to confer with the master-plotter.

Gismondi wondered how many moments of life might yet remain him. There was a mist before his eyes, and his heart thudded horridly at the base of his throat with a violence that seemed to shake him in his chair at each pulsation, and he marvelled that the boom of it did not draw the attention of his neighbours.

"Arezzo!" came the voice, and another figure rose and went apart, passing the returning "Ancona" on the way.

Bagnolo followed Arezzo, and Gismondi began to realise that the president was taking them alphabetically. He wondered how many more there might be before Faenza – the call to which he must respond, since Crespi was of Faenza, as he knew. He wondered too what questions would be asked him. From the knowledge he had gathered from the letters he found himself able to surmise them, and he knew what answers he should make. His terror abated, but it did not leave him; some other questions there might be – something for which those papers did not make provision; there must be.

"Cattolica!" came the summons, and a fourth conspirator rose.

And then, of a sudden, the whole company was on its feet, and Gismondi had risen too, mechanically, from very force of imitation, and the heart-beats in his throat were quickened now with sudden hope. In the distance there had been a sound of voices, and this was followed on the instant by a heavy tread in the corridor without – a tread accompanied by the clank of armour.

"We are betrayed" cried a voice – after which, in awful silence, the masked company stood and waited.

A heavy blow smote the door and it fell open. Across the threshold, the candlelight reflected from his corselet as from a mirror, came a mighty figure armed *cap-à-pied*; behind him three men-at-arms, sword on thigh and pike in hand, pressed closely.

Three paces within the room the great armoured figure halted, and surveyed the company with eyes that smiled grimly from a bearded face.

"Sirs," he warned them, "resistance will be idle. I have fifty men at hand."

Bentivogli advanced with a firm step. "What is your will with us?" he challenged, a fine arrogance in his voice.

"The will of his Highness, the Duke of Valentinois," was the man's answer, "to whom your plot is known in its every detail."

"You are come to arrest us?"

"One by one," said the captain, with an odd significance and a slight inclination of the head. "My grooms await you in the courtyard."

For an instant there was silence, as well might be at that pronouncement, and Gismondi understood – as all understood – that here, in the courtyard of this palace, those gentlemen caught red-handed were to expiate their treason at the strangler's hands.

"Infamy!" cried one, who stood beside Gismondi. "Are we, then, to have no trial?"

"In the courtyard," replied the captain grimly.

"Not I, for one!" exclaimed another, and his voice was fresh and youthful. "I am of patrician blood, and I'll not be strangled in a corner like a capon. If die I must, I claim by right of birth the axe."

"By right of birth?" the captain mused, and smiled. "In truth your very birthright, so it seems. Come, sirs…"

But others stormed, and one there was who called upon his fellows to draw what steel they carried, and die with weapons in their hands like men.

Gismondi, apart, with folded arms, watched them, and grinned behind his vizor. It was with him the hour of exultation, of revulsion from his recent terrors. He wondered to what lengths of folly these rash men would go. He thought he might witness a pretty fight; but Bentivogli disappointed him of such expectations. He came forward to the table-head, and his voice was raised to dominate and quell the others.

"Sirs," said he, "the game is played and lost. Let us pay forfeit and have done."

What choice had they? What chance – all without body armour and few with better weapons than a dagger – against fifty men-at-arms in steel?

Again for a moment there was silence. Then one of the masked company, with a sudden, strident, reckless laugh, stepped forward.

"I'll lead the way, O my brothers," he said, and bowed to the captain. "I am at your orders, sir."

The captain made a sign to his men. Two of them laid aside their pikes and came forward to seize that volunteer. Swiftly, and without word spoken, they hurried him from the chamber.

Gismondi smiled. This entertainment amused his cruel nature more than had done that other of a little while ago.

Again and again the men-at-arms returned; and victim after victim was hurried out to the waiting grooms in the courtyard. One set up a resistance as wild as it was futile; another screamed when he was seized. But in the main they bore themselves with a calm dignity. The soldiers went swifty about their work, and after a brief ten minutes there remained but four of the conspirators. One of these was Bentivogli, who as the leader reserved himself the honour of going last; two others were the men who had been attendant upon him; the fourth was Messer Benvenuto, who watched and waited, chuckling to think how the name of Cesare Borgia would stink in Italy for this night's work.

The men-at-arms had re-entered and stood waiting for the next victim. Bentivogli made a sign to Gismondi that was plain of meaning. Gismondi shrugged, smiled to himself under cover of his mask, and stepped forward with a swagger. But when the soldiers seized him, he shook them impatiently aside.

"A word with you, sir," said he to the captain, mighty haughty.

The captain flashed him a keen glance. "Ah!" said he. "You will be he whom I was told to look for. Tell me your name that I may know you."

"I am Benvenuto Gismondi."

The captain nodded thoughtfully. "I must permit myself no error here. You are Benvenuto Gismondi, and – " He paused inquiringly.

"And," Gismondi completed impatiently, "I am here on behalf of the Duke Cesare Borgia."

A quiet, wicked laugh broke from the captain's bearded lips. One of his heavy gauntleted hands fell upon Gismondi's shoulder; the other tore the vizor roughly from his face. Startled, understanding nothing, he was swung round so that he faced Bentivogli.

"Does your Excellency know the villain?" asked the captain.

"I do not," answered Bentivogli, and added: "God be thanked!"

He clapped his hands vigorously; and now it was that Benvenuto realised into what manner of trap he was fallen, and what manner of ruse the master-plotter had adopted to weed out, as he had promised, the one who usurped the place of him that had been slain upon the Aemilian Way. That clapping of hands was a summons, in answer to which there came trooping back into the chamber the entire company of muffled plotters. No farther than the corridor had they been taken;

and on arrival there to each one who had sustained with honour this ordeal had been explained the test that was afoot.

Betimes next morning Ramiro de Lorqua, Cesare's Governor of Cesena, waited upon his master with a dagger and a blood-smeared scrap of paper.

He had to report that the body of a man had been discovered at daybreak on the far bank of the castle moat, by the drawbridge. The dagger that had slain the fellow had been employed to attach to him the label which Ramiro presented to the Duke. On this was scrawled: "The property of Cesare Borgia."

Accompanied by his governor, Cesare descended to the courtyard to view the body. It lay there, covered by the purple, fur-trimmed cloak which Benvenuto had worn yesterday. Ramiro turned this down to disclose the ashen face. The Duke looked, and nodded.

"It is as I thought," said he. "It is very well."

"Your Highness knows him?"

"A poor rogue whom I employed on a desperate venture."

Ramiro – a thick-set, black-visaged, choleric man – swore roundly, as he did upon the slightest provocation. He would see to it that the culprits were tracked and found. Cesare shook his head, and smiled.

"You will search in vain, Ramiro," he said. "Yet I can name to you the leader of the party that is answerable for this murder; I can tell you even that he rode out of Cesena at daybreak today, and what road he took. But to what end? He is a fool who has performed my justice for me, and knows it not. I fear him no more than I fear this poor carrion."

"My lord, I do not understand!" said Ramiro.

"Is it necessary that you should?" smiled the Duke. My will has been done. Understand so much, and bury me this dead – and with him the entire affair."

He turned away, to come face to face with Agabito Gherardi, who was approaching hurriedly.

"Ah, you have heard the news," Cesare' greeted him. "Now behold the face," and he pointed to the dead.

Agabito looked and shrugged. "You would have it so," he said. "But you could have taken them all."

"And had all Italy calling me butcher for my pains – Venice, the envious, Milan, the spiteful, Florence, the evil-tongue – all of them lifting their horrid voices to the dear task of defamation. And to what end?" He linked an arm through Agabito's, and drew the secretary away. "That was an effective scarecrow I set up amongst them last night." He smiled grimly. "They could not dream that the whole thing was chance – that Benvenuto Gismondi was but a thief who had murdered this Messer Crespi for the sake of plunder. They conceive Crespi to have been killed, stripped and replaced in their council, all by my design. They conclude that I have as many eyes as Argus, and the conspiracy is as frost-bitten as your nose, Agabito. They are paralysed with fear of me and the ubiquity of my spies. No man of those plotters counts himself safe, and they have scattered to their several homes, all plans abandoned since they fear the worst.

"Could I improve upon the matter by hunting them down? I think not, Agabito. Benvenuto Gismondi has served my purpose as fully as I intended, and, incidentally, he has had justice and a fitting wage."

Chapter 5

THE SNARE

Messer Baldassare Scipione stepped out into the lane, and closed the green gate by which he had issued from his lady's garden.

He stood a moment in the dusk of eventide, a fond smile upon his honest rugged face; then he flung his ample scarlet cloak about him, and departed with a jingle of spurs, erect and very martial in his bearing, as became the captain of the Borgia forces in Urbino.

At the corner, where the lane debouched into the Via del Cane, he came suddenly upon a very splendid gentleman who was lounging there. This gentleman's eyes narrowed at sight of the valiant captain. He was Messer Francesco degli Omodei, cousin-german to Baldassare's lady.

The captain's bearing stiffened slightly. Yet his bow was gracious as he swept off his plumed cap in response to the other's uncovering. With that he would have passed on had not Messer Francesco deliberately barred his way.

"Taking the air, Sir Captain?" he questioned, sneering faintly.

"By your gracious pleasure – and God's," answered Baldassare, smiling ironically into the other's unfriendly face – a swarthy young face of a beauty almost classical, yet very sinister of eye and very cruel of mouth.

Flung out of countenance by that ironic counter, Francesco had no answer ready, whereupon: "You are detaining me, I think," said the captain airily, and made shift to pass on.

"I will go with you, by your leave," said Francesco, and fell into step beside the scarlet figure.

"The honour notwithstanding, I should prefer to go alone," said Baldassare.

"I desire to speak to you."

"So I had gathered. But I do not desire to listen. Will that weigh with you, Messer degli Omodei?"

"Not a hair's weight," laughed the other impudently.

Baldassare shrugged, and stalked on, his left hand resting naturally upon the hilt of his sword, so that the scabbard thrust up his scarlet cloak behind.

"Messer Baldassare," said Francesco presently, "you come this way too often."

"Too often for what – for whom?" quoth the captain stiffly, yet without truculence.

"Too often to please me."

"Possibly. But not often enough to please myself, which, frankly now, is my entire concern."

"I do not like it," said Francesco, very surly.

Baldassare smiled. "Which of us can command what he likes? Now I, Messer Francesco – I dislike you exceedingly. Yet here I am suffering you to walk beside me."

"It is not necessary that you should."

"It would not be, had you the grace to perceive that your company is unwelcome."

"There are ways of remedying such things," said the other, very sinister now, and striking his hilt with his open palm.

"For you," said Baldassare. "Not – alas! – for me. I am the commander of the Urbino troops. It is not for me to embark upon private quarrels. His Highness of Valentinois is impatient of disobedience to his laws. Messer Ramires – his podestà here in Urbino – is careful to enforce them for his own sake. I have no wish to hurt myself for the sake of hurting you. And you, Messer Francesco, being as craven as you are sly, presume upon this state of things to put upon me affronts which I may not resent."

He delivered the last sentence through his teeth – a very whiplash. Under his outward calm a storm was raging in the bosom of this haughty, fiery-tempered soldier. For this was that same Baldassare Scipione who some years later was boldly to impugn the honour of the crown of Spain, and throw down a gage of battle which not a Spaniard in Christendom had the daring to take up. From that may you infer how he relished the impertinences of this Urbinate fop.

Francesco had checked suddenly, his face aflame. "You insult me!" he said thickly.

"I hope so," answered Baldassare, outwardly imperturbable.

"Your insolence shall be punished."

"I am glad that you see the necessity," said Baldassare, facing the other with a smile.

Francesco's frown showed how little he understood the captain. Baldassare proceeded to explain. "If you were to draw upon me now, here in the street, I should be constrained to defend myself. I could not then be blamed for what might happen; there are enough people abroad to bear witness to the true manner of the event. So proceed, I implore you, to visit with your punishment this insolence of mine."

Francesco's face had gradually lost its colour. His breathing was quickened. A smile twisted his mouth oddly.

"I see," he said. "Oh, I see. But if I should kill you, I should have to reckon with the podestà."

"Let not the consideration of my death deter you," said Baldassare, still smiling, "for I shall see to it that it does not happen."

Francesco stood a moment, scowling at the captain. Then, with a shrug and a curse, he turned on his heel and strode away, Baldassare's soft, mocking ripple of laughter following him.

He went down the street in the deepening dusk, a fine figure of a man, heedless of the many greetings bestowed upon him as he passed – for well known in Urbino was Messer Francesco degli

Omodei. Thus he came to the house of his friend Amerigo Vitelli, and entered in quest of him.

He found Amerigo at table, but disdained the invitation to join in the repast.

"I could not eat," he growled. "I am fed to a surfeit with Scipione's insolence. Fed to a surfeit! I choke with it." And he flung himself into a chair, at the table, opposite his host.

Amerigo's small, pale eyes surveyed him uneasily. A young man was this Amerigo Vitelli, of the Vitelli of Castello, and cousin to that Vitellozzo who served with Cesare Borgia. His age would be about Francesco's own, but nothing else had he in common with his friend. He was of middle height – or slightly under it – of a full habit of body, a flabbiness of flesh and a puffiness of face that told of his habitual excesses. He was dressed in blue velvet, richly jewelled and heavily perfumed, and he was being ministered by two comely striplings clad in silk of his colours – blue and gold.

The room in which he sat was lofty and sumptuous, and the splendour and character of its equipment reflected the voluptuary it enshrined. From a ceiling, on which was delicately frescoed the indelicate story of Bacchus and Ariadne, depended a massive candle-branch of silver-gilt charged with a dozen candles of scented wax, which shed a soft golden light through the apartment. The walls were hung with Flemish arras, on which were figured the erotic metamorphoses of Jupiter: his avian courtship of Leda, his taurine wooing of Europa, his pluvial descent upon Danaë. The table was spread with snowy linen, and bore no dish of fruits or comfits, no cup or beaker that was not a precious work of art.

Behind Vitelli the windows stood open to the summer evening and the perfumes of the garden. The roofs of Urbino formed a dark shadow-mass in the deepening dusk, the tower of the Zoccolanti springing square and rigid, a black silhouette against the deep turquoise and fading saffron of the sky.

One of the silk-clad pages rustled to Francesco, and set a crystal cup before him. From a vessel of beaten gold whose handles were two hermaphrodites carved in ivory, the boy poured an old Falernian wine that was of the hue of bronze. Francesco gulped the half of it so carelessly that Amerigo scowled his displeasure. Such wine was priceless – to be inhaled with awe, and savoured sip by sip; not swilled like so much tavern slop.

Francesco, entirely unconscious that he was offending, set down his cup, and sank back into his chair, his face black with the displeasure that absorbed him.

"What has happened to you?" quoth Amerigo presently.

Francesco briefly related the tale of all this heat of his. Amerigo listened, what time he sliced a peach into a beaker of wine and hydromel.

"You are very clumsy," he said at length. The insult to his Falernian did not conduce to make him sympathetic.

"Clumsy?" roared Francesco, sitting forward in his chair. This was the very last drop wanting to make his cup flow over.

Vitelli smiled quietly, and signed to the pages to withdraw. He waited until they had departed and the door was closed.

"Look, Francesco," said he then – he had a gentle voice and a curiously weary sluggishness of speech that was seldom known to quicken, even in the heat of wine. "This man Scipione stands in our way. Your foolish dotard of an uncle, blind to worldly matters, gives his daughter too much freedom, which she abuses with this upstart." He paused, passed a plump, very white and jewelled hand over his sensual mouth, and his pale eyes fixed themselves upon the bold, handsome countenance of his guest. "There is, so far as I can see, but one course open to you. You must – remove him."

"*I* must!" sneered Francesco. "A fine lover thou, by the Host! to set it upon me to remove the rival who struts an obstacle in your path."

Amerigo smiled, entirely unruffled. "I thought," said he, "that that was a settled matter." He took up a silver skewer, and stirred the peach slices in the wine. "The price was agreed – the half of her dowry shall be yours to patch a fortune that much dicing has rent to tatters. Did I, by chance, misunderstand you?" He did not look up as he spoke. His attention was upon his peach slices. He lifted a fragrant morsel on the skewer and bore it to his lips.

Francesco surveyed his friend in silence a moment, his brow black as a thundercloud. "Were I a lover," he said presently, "I think the duello should serve my ends."

Amerigo shrugged contemptuously. "Madonna!" he exclaimed. "The duello! Oh, I can be as hot as any man to resent an affront. But the duello! God save us! A fool's practice! Because a man is noxious to me, is that a reason why I should afford him the means to kill me? How should that help me?"

"None the less," grumbled Francesco, as if to spur the other, "did this upstart stand between me and my desires, my rival – my successful rival – in a woman's love, I should not let his swordsmanship deter me."

"Then do not," countered Amerigo quietly. "Since the practice finds favour with you, out with your cartel, or set a glove across his smug face, or otherwise contrive that he may have an opportunity of driving a hole through your belly. Out, and to it, I say, since that's your humour."

"It is not my humour," said Francesco, cooling as the other became heated. "For I am not a lover."

"Nay, you are wrong. You *are* a lover – a lover of gold, my Checco," said the host, lapsing again into his more habitual languor. "And what a man, being penniless, will not do for the love of ducats, he will not do for the love of woman. Moreover, there is your own hatred to be served – for not a doubt but that this man has known how to excite it."

"What am I to do?" quoth Francesco angrily.

"Why, the thing that you advised to me." And Vitelli, having consumed the last peach slice, drank off the blend of wine and hydromel with relish.

Francesco considered him. "You love Beatrice?" he inquired.

"As I love peaches in wine; nay, even more. I love her so well that to win her I will not risk a life which it is my aim to devote to serving her." He smiled his supreme mockery of his friend and bondslave in this business.

Francesco rose. "If I were to die by this man's hand where would be the advantage?"

"There would be a certain advantage to you in that you would have peace from your creditors. To me, of course, there would be no advantage – unless they hanged this Scipione for the deed – a matter which I greatly doubt."

"You see, then, that the duello were sheer folly?"

"Your wits are wandering, Franceschino. That is what I, myself, have been urging upon your notice."

"And that we must devise some other way?"

"Rather that you must devise some other way. I confide the thing to you on your own terms."

Francesco smacked fist into palm. He was angry and desperate.

"Ay, but what – what?" he cried.

"I depend upon the notoriously wicked fertility of your imagination, Checco."

"Oh! do not mock. Bend your mind to the solution of this riddle."

"Why plague myself, when it shall profit you to solve it for me? Sainted Virgin!" he added impatiently, "am I to pay you to do this thing and yet do it myself?"

Francesco leaned across the table, his face within a foot of his companion's. "And if I fail you, Amerigo? What then?"

"I shall consider that when you have failed me."

Unreasonably exasperated, Francesco was filled by sudden hatred of his friend, and a temptation to abandon the enterprise. But at the timely thought of the clamouring Hebrews whose prey he was, he wisely repressed his feelings.

"You set me a very heavy task," he complained.

"But I offer you a very heavy payment," the other reminded him.

"The slaying of Scipione was no part of our original bargain."

"Our bargain was that you wed me to your cousin. If Scipione's death is expedient to that end, you must contrive it."

"You know that there is scarce a cut-throat to be found in Urbino these days," Omodei protested. "The pestilent government of this

Borgia podestà has changed the face of things here, as Cesare Borgia – may he rot in hell! – is changing the face of Italy. By the Passion! We were promised liberty by this Duke of Valentinois. What has he given us? A slavery the like of which, I'll swear, the world has never seen." He moved away from the table, and paced the apartment as he talked, rendered restless by the passion that possessed him. "He has made children of us, here as elsewhere. No longer are we free to conduct our lives and adjust our differences as seems best to us. We must order ourselves at his good pleasure, and here is a podestà, who is no better than a nurse to see that we do not break our toys. Yet Italy endures him!"

He flung arms to the ceiling, apostrophising the heaven which he believed to lie somewhere beyond it.

"A man such as this Scipione – an earthworm, a reptile – is noxious to us. Yet, hire me a cut-throat to deal with him, and there is the podestà and the law and a preposterous garboil, ending as like as not in the rope – and not for the cut-throat only." Francesco's voice rose, and he hammered out the words, beating fist into palm to emphasise them: "Not for the cut-throat only, but for the man who hired him to the work, be he never so high. And this – this – is liberty! This – this – is wise government!"

With an oath and a final shrug, he dropped into his chair again, wearily, as if exhausted by his rage.

Amerigo smiled calmly ever. "All this I knew. But I know not how it shall serve you to rail and rant against this state of things. It exists, and must be reckoned with. I depend upon your help."

"I see no way in which to help you."

"But you will, Checco. You will. Give it thought. You are wise and far-seeing. I build confidently upon my faith in you. And remember that when the thing is done and I am wed to Beatrice, your reward awaits you."

Francesco perceived at last that no help was to be expected from Amerigo. Either the man had no invention, or – and more likely – of set purpose he refrained from exerting it, that he should not be incriminated in anything that followed. All he desired was Francesco's help to marry Beatrice degli Omodei. The rest, and whatever it might entail, was matter for Francesco; and Amerigo did not see that he should buy the service with the half of his future wife's dowry, and yet take such risks as might be incurred by so much as a suggestion of his own.

So Francesco realised with what manner of mean-hearted knave he had to deal, and that in this matter he must help himself from first to last.

Vainly was it that he cast about him for some way that should entail no risk to his precious skin. The hired assassin, as he had said, was no longer to be trusted in these days of Borgia dominion and Borgia justice. Two weeks ago a gentleman of Urbino, a friend of Francesco's, had employed a cut-throat to rid him of his enemy. The assassin had been tracked, seized and tortured into betraying the hand that hired him; with the result that Francesco's friend, though of one of the noblest houses of Urbino, had been strangled by the common hangman. Francesco was of no mind to suffer a like fate, however desperate his Hebrew creditors might render him.

He hit at last upon the notion of disposing of Scipione – so far as Beatrice was concerned – without recourse to bloodshed. If he could but stir up his uncle, old Count Omodei, into a proper sense of parental responsibility, all might yet be well.

He repaired to him on the morrow, and found him in his library amid the treasures of learning that to him were more than daughter, family, honour or any other worldly affair; and the white-haired old count gave Francesco a cold welcome. He was deep in a manuscript copy of the "*De Rerum Natura*" of Lucretius, fire-new from the printing-press – that uncanny invention – which had been set up at Fano under the patronage of Cesare Borgia. Naturally he resented this interruption; besides which he had but little kindness for this splendid, profligate nephew who burst upon him now to school him in the art of safeguarding daughters.

"I have come to speak to you concerning Bice," Francesco had announced, his tone bold to the point of truculence.

The Count thrust his horn-rimmed spectacles up on to his

forehead, closed the tome upon his forefinger, and looked up.

"Concerning Bice?" quoth he. "And how may Bice concern you?"

"As your nephew, as an Omodei – on the score of the family honour – "

The Count's brows came together. "And who made you custodian of the family honour, sir?" quoth he with a fine sarcasm.

"Nature, sir," was the hot answer, "when I was born an Omodei."

"Ah, Nature!" murmured the student. "I thought it might have been your creditors."

Taken aback, Francesco flushed. This uncle of his, it seemed, did not live so utterly out of the world as he supposed.

"But you were about to say?" the Count inquired.

"That Bice abuses the excessive liberty you allow her. She lacks the discretion we look for in our maids. Her name – her fair name – is in peril. There is a soldier of Cesare Borgia's – "

"You will be meaning Baldassare Scipione," put in the Count. "Well?"

Francesco stared, mouth agape. "You – you knew?" he bleated.

"Pooh! You are too late by an hour," said Omodei.

"Too late? Too late for what, sir?"

"For whatever is your intent, if it concern Bice and her tall captain. They are betrothed."

"Betrothed?"

"Why, yes," replied the Count, enjoying the other's plain discomfiture, for no better reason than that he neither loved nor trusted his fine nephew. "This captain of hers sought me here an hour ago upon this very matter. A fine fellow, Checco – a fine fellow and a studious. 'Twas he brought me this copy of Lucretius. A rare work, a precious work on Nature and her ways. It might interest you who lay such store by Nature."

Francesco's rage blazed up. "And do you barter your daughter for a wretched tome?" he exclaimed.

"Art a fool, Francesco," said his uncle with conviction, "and Scipione is to marry Bice. I have no more to say."

"But I have, sir."

"Then go say it elsewhere, in the name of all the devils. You have interrupted me in an engrossing passage. Go say what you have to say to your creditors. They will be glad enough to hear from you."

But Francesco was of no mind to be dismissed. "What do you know of this fellow Scipione?" he demanded.

Omodei made a gesture of weariness. "What do I know of any man?" he asked. "He is a fine soldier and a student, and when a man is both these things he is the best things that a man can be. Add to it the fact that he loves Bice and that Bice loves him – and so, God give them joy of each other."

"Ha!" laughed Francesco mirthlessly. "Ha! Ha! But who is he, whence is he? And what – what of his family?"

The question was prompted by despair, and even as he asked it, Francesco felt its weakness and futility. A plea of "family" was rarely urged on any count by the cinquecentist. Family – a toy which was new to the rest of Europe – had long since ceased to interest the average Italian of the cinquecento, who recognised in man no worth that was not personal to himself.

Add to this the consideration that the count had been reading Lucretius, and you will appreciate the contemptuous sniff with which he met the question.

"If you read Lucretius, Francesco, you would think less of family," said he.

"But I do not read Lucretius," answered Francesco, desperately pursuing his weak contention, "and the world does not read Lucretius, and so – "

"If you read Lucretius you would think less of the world."

"But I do not read him," the young man insisted.

"If you did, you would understand why I find him more interesting than yourself. So go with God, Francesco, and leave me to my old scholar."

Francesco went, discomfited. He was sick with despair and rage. He thought of seeking Amerigo again. But knew it idle. He had come to the end of peaceful propositions. To sever the relations between

Madonna Bice and this Borgia adventurer, to open a way for Amerigo, and thus serve his own interests, only cold steel remained. He turned pale at the mere thought of it. He dared not procure assassination. He was of a keen and vivid imagination which might have served him well had he but had the industry to employ it to good purpose. This imagination now chilled him, causing him to feel the strangler's rope already about his wind-pipe.

So he resolved at length upon the duello. He would so affront the captain as to leave him no choice but to issue his cartel, and if he killed Scipione in the encounter no blame could attach to one who was not the challenger. But if the captain killed him? It was a risk he must envisage, and either way, he reflected bitterly, his creditors should be appeased.

But it came to pass that late that night, as he still sat brooding upon the matter, he bethought him of something he had once read in a book of Lorenzo Valla's. Though no student by disposition, he found much in Valla to interest him, and he had a copy of that writer's works at hand.

He sought the volume in a painted coffer that stood in his chamber, and turned to the page that he had in mind – the indictment of homicide and the justifications that may exist for it.

Thus had Valla written:

There is the instance, which many yet remember, of Messer Rinaldo of Palmero, a gentleman of Tuscany, who, hearing voices in his sister's chamber late one night, did enter there to discover her in the arms of her lover, one Messer Lizio d'Asti. And Ser Rinaldo, blinded by just choler at the sight, unsheathed his iron and slew them both, that their blood might purify his house of that dishonour. And Ser Rinaldo was by the State commended and honoured for the deed.

Such homicide has ever been, from the most ancient times, and must ever be accounted just and justified. It is the inviolable right of every male to slay whomsoever hold too lightly the honour of his female kin, provided that he take the offender *in flagrante.*

Francesco set the volume down, and remained long bemused. "*In flagrante*," said the learned Valla. That was the difficulty; and without that circumstance the slaying upon such grounds was fraught with danger, for the slayer must make good by proofs his accusation.

If he could but contrive to lure Scipione to her house at dead midnight, and there, taking him unawares, speed a dagger through his heart, who would dare blame him? Though not her brother, yet Francesco stood near enough to Beatrice in kinship to claim the right to guard the honour of the Omodei.

But how – how draw Scipione to the snare?

And then the means flashed into his subtle, wicked brain. He saw a way! A monstrous, appalling plan took shape. But he never hesitated to adopt it, since it solved his problem.

He rose, an oath of satisfaction ringing through the laughter that bubbled on his lips.

Francesco's plan stood the test of the morning's reflection. Now that he had slept upon it, it pleased him even better than when it had first occurred to him. He discovered in it as many facets as a diamond, and each one as clear and brilliant as the rest.

Nothing that he could have devised could have equalled this for completeness. Borgia justice – being justice, after all – must accept the deed and must commend it. No suspicion could attach to his motives; not even though it could be shown that he had entertained a private malice for Scipione. Scipione's presence in Madonna Beatrice's chamber should be a sufficient answer to every question that suspicion could prompt or ingenuity devise.

His first impulse – an impulse of sheer vanity, while the hot glow of pride in his invention was upon him – was to seek Amerigo, dazzle him with the announcement of the amazing scheme which for his benefit he had devised. But the very vanity which prompted this, prompted upon further reflection that he should wait. First let him accomplish his design; and then announce to Amerigo not a mere plan but an achievement. How Amerigo would stare! How lost in wonder must he not be at Francesco's fertile wit!

So he matured his cruel plans, down to the minutest detail, keeping the house that day and until the second hour of night had struck. Then he called for his hat and cloak, his sword and dagger, and went forth attended by a groom to light him on his way.

He came to the door in the garden wall from which we saw Scipione emerge on the evening before last. He tried it, to find it latched on the inside; and the wall was fully ten feet high. So he bade his lackey quench his torch, and that being done he ordered the man to stand against the wall, what time Francesco used him as a ladder and mounted upon his shoulders. Standing erect he was able to throw an arm over the wall's summit. Active and sinewy, he was astride of it a moment later. Then he lowered himself to his full length on the inner side, and so dropped gently upon a bed of yielding mould.

Next, he admitted his servant, and bidding the man follow, went forward through the leafy gloom of that scented place.

He took his way through the familiar alleys, and the beacon by which he steered his course was a light gleaming from one of the windows of the mezzanine. It was the window of a room which, he knew, Beatrice affected – a sort of anteroom to her bedchamber – and it opened doorwise upon a wide balcony of granite, whence a flight of some twenty steps, guarded by a balustrade that was smothered in a luxuriance of ivy, ran down into the garden.

At the foot of this staircase Francesco halted to consider the face of the house. Save for that window, all was darkness, which meant that the household was by now abed. True he could not see the windows of the library, which faced the street. It was likely enough that his uncle would be at one of his studious vigils. But then his uncle was not lightly disturbed, and Francesco did not intend to make himself heard until his plan had reached fulfilment.

Bidding his groom await him there he went up that granite staircase to the balcony with noisy foot and clank of scabbard to herald his approach. And ere he was midway the lighted space above was widened as the curtains were flung quickly aside. The glass doors stood open, and a figure, black against the light, appeared under the lintel.

"Who comes?" he heard his cousin's voice.

"It is I, Bice," he answered promptly, and made his voice quiver, as if he were a prey to excitement. "I – Francesco." And as he gained the balcony and stood level with her: "Is your father with you?" he asked breathlessly, and added, "I come with news."

She drew back and aside to give him entrance. She eyed him in astonishment – a slender slip of womanhood, with the black hair and pale skin that was common to the Omodei.

"An odd hour this for visiting," said she. "My father is at his studies. I will fetch him."

"Did I not say that I bring news, Bice?" he cried, and the quiver in his voice became more marked. "Let your father have peace. My news concerns yourself."

"Me?" Her soft eyes regarded him with some mistrust. She knew her cousin's fame for shiftiness and guile. Her very father had schooled her in that knowledge.

"Ay, you," he answered, and flung, exhausted, into the nearest chair, breathing noisily and fanning himself with his velvet cap. "I – I have run at least a mile, to bring you word – in time," he gasped.

His well-played fatigue, his distraught air, were awakening her alarm. She blenched as she regarded him from where she stood by the window door, one slender arm uplifted, the hand grasping the curtain's edge above her head. She was all in white, in a loose robe that was open at the neck, and caught at the waist in a girdle of hammered gold with a turquoise clasp. Her ebony hair hung behind her in two heavy plaited ropes, dressed so for the night.

All was as it should be, opined Messer Francesco with satisfaction. He had judged his moment as he judged all things, he reflected complacently, with a judgment that was unerring.

She stared at him, her eyes dilating, dark glistening pools in the white beauty of her face, and held her breath what time she awaited his explanation.

But instead of explaining he continued to play upon her fears and to strain them to the very verge of breaking point.

"A cup of wine!" he panted. "A draught of water! To drink – Gesù! give me to drink!"

At last she stirred. She moved to a diminutive press of brown walnut carved with podgy cupids, that stood in a corner of that very choicely appointed chamber and into a dainty thin-stemmed beaker poured him a draught of Puglia.

"Whence do you come?" she asked, impatient for his news, and infected by some of his excitement.

"No matter whence I come," said he, taking the cup from her hands. "It is my news that matters." And avidly he gulped the wine, what time she watched him, wondering and uneasy.

"It concerns Messer Baldassare Scipione," he enlightened her, and saw her sudden start.

"What – what of him?"

His eyes narrowed now as they pondered her. "I know you and him to be betrothed," he explained. "Your father told me of it but yesterday. Hence my anxiety, my haste to bring you word of this thing that is to do." And like a thunderbolt he launched his lying message: "There is a plot to murder Captain Scipione this night."

"Gesù Maria!" she gasped, and clutched her breast, the last remnant of her mistrust of her cousin whelmed in sudden terror for her lover. Her eyes were wild, her face livid, her bosom heaved convulsively; she looked as she would faint.

"Nay, nay, courage, Bice! Courage!" he admonished her. "There is still time to save him – else had I not been here."

She made an effort to control her fears; to put them by, and summon reason to her aid. "Put why – why have you lost time in seeking me? Why did you not instantly bear your story to the podestà?" she questioned.

"To him? To Ramires?" He laughed softly and with infinite scorn. "Because the magistrate himself is in this business."

"Ramires!" she cried. "Oh, impossible!"

"Ah, wait." His tone was a thought impatient as he proceeded to offer an explanation that should render credible his bold lie. "Men who stand high in their master's favour, as does Scipione in Cesare Borgia's, are seldom loved by their fellow-servants. Ramires fears that Scipione may supplant him. Envy and jealousy are scorpion-whips to drive such men as the Podestà Ramires. They have urged him to ally himself with Scipione's other enemies, and so, tonight, the thing is to be done."

It seemed incredible. Doubts of its truth recurring, instinctive mistrust of her cousin flickered anew in Beatrice's mind. But she cast them out, bethinking her that did she heed them and were she in error, her lover's life might pay the price of these same doubts. Yet they insisted and demanded satisfaction.

She controlled her fears, and eyed her cousin, as if to pierce to the very soul and brain of him.

"Here is a very sudden and strange concern, Francesco, for a man you never loved. It would seem more natural to me to find you linked with his enemies than have you come here to warn me."

He stared at her for a moment, as if dumbfounded – as indeed he was. Then he rose with an angry stamp of exasperation.

"God give me patience!" he exclaimed. "Here's woman's logic – woman's way! You'll stand in talk and seek to plumb my motives while they cut your lover's throat. By the Host! girl, I may not have loved this fellow of your choice. But must it follow that I wish his death?"

"Yet, so much emotion for a man you do not love – "

"Hear her, O Virgin!" quoth he, and turned upon her in a blazing heat of impatience. "Is my emotion for *him*, do you say? Bah!" He snapped finger against thumb. "Let them slit his throat and be done with it, for aught I care. My concern, my emotion, is for you. Shall I see you widowed or ever you are wed? Have I no right to a concern on your behalf, Bice? But there, I see you do not trust me; and, as God lives, I know not why I should serve you, that being so."

With a gesture expressing injury and anger he pulled his cloak about him, and strode to the window. But now terror, like a hurricane, swept her after him, to clutch his arm, and to detain him.

"Nay, Franceschino, wait! I was wrong – so wrong!"

He paused, looking down, ruffled, yet long-suffering.

"Can you serve me?" she asked him breathlessly. "Is there aught you can do to save him?"

"For that purpose have I sought you," he answered, with a great dignity. "They do not strike till midnight."

"Midnight!" she gasped. "It wants but an hour."

"Time and to spare for what you have to do."

"I? What is there I can do? What power have I?" She was pleading piteously through such questions.

"The power to subtract him from his enemies before they are upon him; to get him away from his house in the Zoccolanti. Bring him here to your side, and keep him here till morning – till the danger is overpast. Then he can call his men to arms, and take measures for his safety."

She recoiled, staring at him between wonder and horror. "Keep him here – here? And till morning? Are you mad, Francesco?"

He pondered her, did this very subtle gentleman, with positive contempt. "Is this your love for him?" he asked. "At every step you raise an obstacle. And why not here? You're soon to be his wife."

A crimson flush spread slowly on her face, and was gone, leaving her paler than she had been. "Francesco," said she, in a voice that was forcedly calm, "if you desire to serve me and to save me the life of Baldassare, you may do it without putting this shame upon me. Go to him. Warn him of his peril, and bear him home with you to your own house, there to abide till morning. Go – and send me word when it is done. I shall not sleep until I hear from you."

He stood surveying her, and his expression melted from contempt to pity; a faint smile appeared at the corners of his tight-lipped, cruel mouth.

"You try my patience very sorely – by the Host you do!" said he. "I wonder what this captain finds to love in such a fool!" Then in a sudden heat he went on: "Why, every ninny sees a demi-god in the lout who quivers at her touch. Yet you – you – say you love this man;

you believe you love him, and yet you hold him in such base esteem that you can picture him fleeing in terror to take hiding in my house at a word of peril that I may speak to him. Is that your conception of Baldassare Scipione?" he demanded with scathing scorn. "Do you account the man you love so poor-spirited a cur? Why, girl, it is odds he would not believe me; and if he did, he would scorn my offer and stay to have his throat cut for his honour's sake. Such, at least, is the Baldassare Scipione whom I know – I, who do not love him."

It was all most subtly thought of, and it sank deep into Beatrice's mind, and there took root. How could she doubt the truth of an argument that revealed her lover as a hero of romance? What woman could resist the flattery of so conceiving the man she loved? Conviction overwhelmed her. Then a fresh doubt leapt up, but of another sort.

"But – but if this be so – how can I hope to lure him from his danger?"

"By not allowing him to perceive it," he answered promptly.

"How, then – " she stared at him, utterly at a loss.

He smiled, reassuringly and faintly mocking, a smile that seemed to ask what should she do without his guidance.

"I have thought of it all," he said. "You will represent the danger as threatening you – not him. You will write him three lines to say you are in grave peril and in urgent need of him, bidding him come to you upon the instant. Such a call as that he will not refuse. He will come – Mars borne upon the wings of Eros."

"That were to lie to him," said she.

"Oh, give me patience!" he cried again. "It is no lie. You *are* in danger – in danger of going mad, in danger of dying of a broken heart when they bring you word of how he perished. So bid him come," he urged her sharply, "and bid him come by the garden and that staircase. Thus he will be less in danger of being seen."

That hint of secrecy revived her erstwhile scruples. She stood now by the table, which was strewn with a half-wrought embroidery and the coloured silks that had been her materials, and she confessed her horror in her glance.

"I can't, I can't!" she wailed. "How can I, Francesco? To keep him here – here!" And shivering as she spoke, she covered her crimsoning face.

Francesco snorted. "Would you prefer that his enemies prevail?" he asked her fiercely. "Shall Baldassare Scipione be so much carrion tomorrow?" He leaned towards her, urging eagerly: "Come, come! Is this an hour for scruples. Its sands are running down. Soon it will be too late. As for your fair name – tush! your fears are idle. I will remain with you. Or, if that suffice not to quiet your scruples, your father shall be summoned to join us in this vigil."

Her face cleared. "Then all is plain. Why did you not say this earlier?" And yet she hesitated, and knit her brows whilst he fetched writing materials from the press, and thrust aside the embroidery on the table, clearing a space, that she might write. "How shall we keep him, once he comes and finds there is no danger for me?"

"Write!" he snapped. "I have thought of everything. Come, come, or he'll be butchered whilst you are asking questions."

Conquered at last, she sat down and wrote furiously:

MY BALDASSARE, – I am in danger, and in urgent need of you. Come to me instantly. The garden door is unlatched; come by the steps to my chamber.

BEATRICE.

She folded the note, tied it with some threads of crimson silk, and gave it to him. Her heart was beating as it would stifle her.

"You are sure that we shall be in time?" said she.

"No doubt," he reassured her, "though you've wasted a deal of it."

He stepped to the window, and whistled softly. At the same time, she moved in the opposite direction to the door.

"Where are you going?" he asked sharply.

"To call my father," she answered, her hand upon the latch.

"Wait!" He was so impressive, and mysterious that she obeyed him, and came slowly back to the table.

Steps pattered on the stone staircase. His groom appeared on the balcony. Francesco tossed the note to him.

"That to the Illustrious Captain Scipione at once, and make all haste," he ordered.

The man's steps pattered down again and through the garden at a run. Francesco came slowly back into the room, his face a shade paler than it had been, his manner restless, his eyes furtive.

"Your servants will be abed?" he asked, as if in idleness.

"Why, yes," she answered. "But I will rouse them when I call my father."

It was fortunate for me – more fortunate still for your fine captain – that you, at least, had not retired before I came. Will you not sit?" And he advanced a chair. "There is something I wish to tell you ere you rouse the house."

She sat, he standing behind the chair he had proffered. From under his cloak he drew a coil of slender rope, noosed with a running knot, all ready for his purpose. Quick as lightning he slipped the loop over her head, and down so that it encompassed her arms and body and the chair's tall back. He drew it tight almost in the same movement, and then, as alarmed she parted her lips to cry out, he clapped one hand to her mouth, whilst with the other he fumbled for the gag he had brought.

When all was done, and gagged and with a second cord lashing her ankles to the chair, she sat helpless and mute before him, a wild terror staring from her dark eyes, he surveyed her, smiling, well pleased with the swift adroitness wherewith he had performed his task. He crossed to the door, and locked it. Then he drew the heavy crimson curtains across the windows, and that done he sat down, flung one silken leg over the other, and surveyed her with a smile of gentle mockery.

"I am more distressed than I can say, to have been compelled to submit you to this rough usage and this discomfort. Necessity is my task-master. I will not have your father or your servants disturbed just yet. Presently I, myself, will call them. Meanwhile, dear Bice, dispel your personal alarms, for I swear to you that you shall suffer no hurt; that what I have done, I have done but as a temporary restraint."

And now he proceeded to explain. "You are to understand, dear cousin, that when I told you that there is a plot afoot to murder your fine captain, I told you not a word more than the truth. Too often has he presumed to affront me, sheltered like a coward behind the shield of Borgia justice, which would have strangled me had I slain him – though honourably – in the duello. But he was a fool for all his pains, for he might have known that Francesco degli Omodei was not the man to leave unavenged the insults of an upstart condottiero. Tonight he pays his score."

In loyalty to his friend Vitelli – his paymaster in this foul business – Francesco made no mention of his name. Besides his loyalty, he had to consider that for the fruition of his schemes Amerigo must ultimately wed Beatrice. To that end this business was but the means. Therefore Amerigo must nowise be associated here with Messer Francesco.

"Are you wondering," he resumed, "why I have chosen such a place and hour in which to do this thing? You shall learn, sweet cousin, lest you should suffer through concern for my safety when it is done.

"When this fool Scipione, hastening hither all on fire with love and rage and valour, shall cross that threshold, then he dies. Here in your chamber shall he breathe his last. What greater blessing could he ask of Fate? Such happiness is not given to every lover, though many sigh for it – in their verses.

"Do not suppose that when the thing is done I shall become a fugitive from justice." He smiled infernally, for he was cruel to the core of him. "In that hour I shall call your father, loose your bonds and rouse the house – all Urbino will I rouse, and myself, fetch the podestà to hear the tale of how, surprising your Captain Scipione here in your arms at dead midnight, I slew him for the honour of the Omodei.

"You think, perhaps, that you will deny my story? And so, no doubt, you will. But consider now," he mocked her, "who is there will believe you? You dream perhaps that my servant will tell of the note he bore at my bidding. Build not upon that. My servant I can trust for silence."

Her eyes flashed him mute hatred from out of her livid face. But Francesco was nothing daunted, nothing moved. Rather did her dumb agony spur him to further derisive explanation.

"Urbino shall acclaim me for this night's work," said he. "I may even come to figure in song and story for future ages to admire me."

Thereafter there was a spell of silence, and the cousins sat awaiting the coming of Beatrice's lover; she in a torture of fear, in a sickness of remorse for having given so little heed to the warnings of her intuition against this man of whose life she had never known a single deed of good.

He sat uneasy now, fearful of interruption. It was approaching midnight; the old scholar above stairs might bethink him to seek his bed, and ere he went might come to see that all was well with his daughter. Francesco's fears grew with every beat of his pulses. He sat livid, fretful, gnawing at his nails, his ears straining, his nerves starting at every creak that broke the midnight stillness.

Yet were his fears all idle. The old count in his library had fallen soundly asleep over the fourth book of the "*De Rerum Natura.*"

Meanwhile, Francesco's servant, a lank, loose-limbed fellow, whose name – for what it matters – was Gasparo, sped swiftly towards the Zoccolanti and the house of Scipione, on the errand that was to fetch the victim to the springe so cunningly prepared.

Had Messer Amerigo Vitelli but known of it, all had been well – from the monstrous point of view of nimble-witted Franceschino. But Messer Amerigo did not know, and thence it was to ensue that Francesco was to pay for the vanity that had bound him to silence until the thing should be accomplished.

It came about by one of those coincidences, which, meeting us at every step and weaving themselves into the warp of our intentions, alter, modify and set a pattern upon the fabric we call Life.

Messer Amerigo had been supping at the house of one Nomaglie, whose banquets outrivalled any that Lucullus ever spread. He was rolling home, flushed spiritually, and materially fired by a Vesuvian wine which he had grossly abused and some of whose sulphur had got into his veins and made him ripe for any devilry. With him came some half-score merry gentlemen of Urbino, entirely of Amerigo's kidney and similarly charged with Nomaglie's volcanic brew. The noisy party was flanked by four stalwart lackeys, bearing torches, and preceded by a boy in cloth-of-gold wearing a gilded mask in the form of a calf's head – the emblem of the Vitelli – and thrumming a lute.

Into this company blundered our friend Gasparo, to find his way blocked; for the noisy troop sprawled itself from wall to wall across the narrow street.

The servant flattened himself in a doorway to give passage to them. But they were by no means minded to give passage in their turn to him or any other whom at that hour they might chance to meet.

"Now, who may this be?" quoth Amerigo, in his sweet, mincing voice, his tongue stumbling over the consonants. "And why does he lurk there like a spy?" He stopped, and the procession halted with him – the master of these revels. "Hale him forth," he commanded.

Gasparo was instantly charged by the foremost roysterers, seized, and dragged, exceedingly scared, into mid-street before Amerigo. The latter struck a judicial attitude, its dignity a trifle marred by the leaning of his pink cap over his left eye. His podgy figure was gorgeous in rosy silk, with a line of diamond buttons running down the middle of his doublet; his hose was striped pink and white, vertically from foot to knee, horizontally thence to his trunks. He looked extremely absurd.

"So, rogue," he roared, "explain this night-walking."

"I – I am Gasparo, sir," pleaded the lackey, nor thought to explain that he was the servant of Francesco degli Omodei, conceiving in his vanity that he was as well known to Messer Amerigo as was Messer Amerigo to him.

"Oho!" crowed Vitelli. "You are Gasparo, eh?" And to the company he imparted with drunken owlishness the solemn information. "He is Gasparo. Mark that well, sirs. He is Gasparo."

And the revellers responded by linking arms and dancing furiously about the lackey and his interlocutor in a circle, howling to the renewed thrumming of the lute:

> "He is Gasparo – paro – paro!
> He is Gasparo – paro – puh!"

This gibbering, swirling human vortex frightened the poor groom out of the little sense he had received from stingy Nature. Already he foresaw an ugly ending to this frolic, imagined grim horrors to which this demoniac mummery was but the prologue.

Amerigo took him by the arm, and drew him close. "We are detaining you, you say?" quoth he. "Of course we are detaining you. You will abstain from fatuous observations of that sort. We cannot endure them. This, sir, is a company of wits."

Upon that word of his the lute thrummed again, the circular dance was resumed, the page in the golden calf's head improvised, and the others howled the chorus:

> "Oh, Gasparo – paro – paro!
> Oh, most fortunate of cits!
> Oh, Gasparo – paro – paro!
> You are fallen among wits!"

Round and round went the idiotic, howling, drunken crew, a swirl of many coloured legs, a rainbow of fluttering cloaks, weird, phantasmagoric, and – to Gasparo – wholly terrific as seen in the ruddy, fitful glare of the torches.

"You are expected, eh, Gasparo?" quoth Amerigo, when presently the dancers paused.

"Indeed, I am, sir. Let me go; let me go, I beg, Magnificent," implored the lout.

"He's expected," said Amerigo to the company, very solemnly and a trifle thickly. "This laggard lover is expected, and he wastes his time here with a parcel of drunken, bawdy midnight brawlers. Shame on thee, Gasparo." Then in Gasparo's ear, but loud enough for all to hear him: "Where does she live now, and what's her name? Is she tall or short, fat or lean, black or golden? Descant, man! Propound her virtues of the spirit and the flesh, that we decide if you shall keep this tryst. I am Amerigo Vitelli, the *arbiter foeminae* of Italy. You may have heard of me. So descant freely – as to a judge."

And now Gasparo saw light of a sudden in his trouble. He had but to mention the name of the man to whom he bore his message, and there would be an end to this baiting.

"You mistake, Messer Amerigo," said he. "You mistake, Magnificent. I am expected by the Captain Baldassare Scipione at his house yonder. I beg that you'll suffer me to go."

The leer faded slowly from Amerigo's flushed and puffy face. Some of the drunken vacuity departed from his eye, and the company, either noting or feeling the change, fell silent. Gasparo felt it too. It was as if a chill wind had blown suddenly upon him.

"What are you to Messer Scipione?" asked Amerigo, his voice now harsh. He was grown wicked of a sudden, and from mischievously ape-drunk that he had been, he was turned lion-drunk at the mention of his successful rival. His mood was now to roar and rend.

Scared back into the tremors from which he had been daring to emerge, Gasparo stammered, "I – I have a letter, Magnificent, for the captain."

Had the fool but said from whom he came instead of to whom he went, all might have been well. But, because he imagined himself known to Vitelli, he did not.

The mere mention of the letter filled Amerigo with suspicious jealousy, which in his drunken state craved satisfaction. Harshly he demanded its production. The lackey whimpered that he dared not obey; implored them anew to let him go; for he had the scent of danger breast-high by now.

Amerigo in his new mood was very short with him. "The letter!" he snarled. And then to his friends, with a wave of a fat white hand: "Obtain it me!" he commanded.

They were like hounds unleashed upon a quarry, in their eagerness for the frolic that obeying him entailed. Four of them pounced upon the unfortunate Gasparo. In the twinkling of an eye the doublet was gone from his back, ripped into four pieces; his vest followed it, similarly quartered, and lastly, his very shirt. The rent garments were flung to others to be searched.

A dagger was inserted at Gasparo's waistband, and his trunks were swiftly slashed away, he never daring to move, lest the dagger's other edge should scrape acquaintance with his flesh.

Within five seconds of their laying hands upon him, Gasparo stood as naked as upon the occasion of his first appearance in this vale of sorrow, and in Amerigo's hands was the letter which his doublet had yielded. The completion of their work of denudation had been mere wantonness.

Reckless of any consequences, Amerigo broke the threads which bound the missive, and called for light. A torch was advanced. Vitelli read, and his face grew black with rage, then lighted again with inspiration. If Beatrice was in danger, as the letter said, was not he, himself, the very man to fly to her assistance. If not, if the letter were... He checked on the notion, scowling again in an effort of thought. The blundering servant had said, he remembered, that he was expected by the captain. Then this letter... Again he checked, and very softly licked his lips and smiled.

Meanwhile the Saturnalian dance about Gasparo was resumed. The lute throbbed, and the boy improvised, whilst the others thundered after him, and awakened the street from end to end.

> "He's as rosy as a cupid,
>   This Gasparo – paro – paro;
> And his legs are sweetly crooked,
>   Oh, Gasparo – paro – puh!"

Amerigo broke through the ring. "Away, away!" he cried. Then beckoned a torchbearer. "Attend me, you," he commanded. "Gay people, a happy night! Seek your sport elsewhere. My game's afoot! Good night! Most happy night!"

And he was gone, stumbling and lurching down the street, at once lighted and supported by his torchbearer.

They watched his departure in a sudden silence of surprise; then vainly shouted to him to return.

"This will end badly," muttered one. "He is overdrunk to be let go."

"Why, then, after him!" put in another.

The procession formed up once more, the golden boy placed himself at the head, and so led them away down the street, thrumming his lute, and improvising fresh verses on the subject of Gasparo.

The lackey, shivering and whimpering in a doorway, watched their departure. Then he crept forth, and picking up the poor remains of his garments, disguised his nakedness as best he could in them. In a fury, fiercely hoping for vengeance, he went off resolutely to thunder on Messer Baldassare Scipione's door, to inform the captain of what had taken place, and of how he had been robbed of a letter from Monna Beatrice degli Omodei, which he had been bidden bring with all dispatch.

The captain listened patiently, questioned fruitlessly, swore fiercely, called for sword and hat, dispatched Gasparo to rouse the podestà, and himself set out at a run for the house of Omodei.

In Madonna Beatrice's chamber sat the cousins waiting. The man consumed by his impatience and his fears of an interruption at the eleventh hour; the girl in frozen terror, with thudding heart and heaving bosom; desperately sustained from fainting by the imperative necessity to witness whatever might come to pass; fostering – and yet afraid to foster – the hope that Francesco's diabolical plans should yet miscarry.

Abruptly and silently Francesco came to his feet, with head

slightly inclined, listening intently. He smiled cruelly. The game was won.

"Your lover comes, Beatrice," he announced, very softly.

His ears had caught the distant creak of rusty hinges, and so had hers. Her heart worked ponderously, a sickness oppressed her, and rolling noises were booming in her ears; and yet, knowing that she dared not sink into the merciful unconsciousness stealing over her like a slumber, she shook it off, and by a sheer effort of will regained her self-control.

Francesco softly crossed to her, and plucked away the gag.

"Scream now, if it will comfort you," said he. And she, knowing that to cry out would but serve to hasten her lover to his doom, was silent.

Her cousin drew away, and went to take his stand by the heavy curtains, a fine, tall figure, brave in grey and gold. He crouched a little, balanced for the spring, his long dagger gleaming in his hand.

To the ears of the twain, strained now and super-sensitive, came a snapping of twigs in the garden below. The lover approached in reckless, headlong haste. At last his step was on the staircase – the step of one whose foot is softly clad – mounting swiftly to the balcony.

Francesco, pale and something breathless, with furrowed brow and dilated nostrils, moved neither limb nor eye as he waited at his post. Had he but done so – had he but chanced to look at Beatrice in that moment he would have seen in her face that which would have given him pause.

She sat there in her bonds, her head thrust forward, her lips parted, her eyes wide. And though fear sprawled lividly across the winsome beauty of her face, yet there was something else – a certain surprise and even some relief. For Beatrice knew that the man who was climbing the staircase to meet Francesco's dagger was not her lover. In that moment, as she listened to those approaching steps, she lived but in her hearing, which had absorbed into itself the entire sentiency of her being.

Even Francesco should have known that this soft-shod, stealthy, yet uncertain footstep was not Scipione's. To herald the captain's approach there had been a firmer tread, the clink of spurs, perhaps the clank of sword.

His reason should have warned him of the thing which she had learned entirely without reasoning. But like herself, he, too, had whittled all his faculties into one sharp point, and was intent but upon that.

She would have cried out had she bethought her that hers was the power of utterance. She would have stayed Francesco's hand; for she knew not into what breast his dagger was about to plunge. But her brain was numb to all save three mighty facts which absorbed her consciousness – knowledge, surprise and infinite relief that this was not Baldassare.

The steps pattered across the balcony, and the crimson curtains bellied inwards. And in that same moment, Francesco struck; once, twice, thrice, in quick succession his poniard rose and descended through the thick velvet of the curtains into the body of the man beyond.

There came a muffled cry, a cough, a gurgling groan, and with them a frantic agitation of the curtains that told of clutching for support. Then the rod snapped above, a man hurtled forward, tripped by the draperies he had torn from their hangings and enveloped by them. Swathed in them as in a winding-sheet, he rolled at their feet, a crimson velvet bundle from which protruded two legs in pink and white silk that kicked convulsively, and then were stiff and still.

Francesco, breathing noisily in his excitement, stepped briskly across that writhing heap to cut the cords that bound Beatrice. He whipped them quickly away, and flung them behind the press.

Limp, now that the bonds supported her no longer, she huddled, half swooning in the chair. But Francesco had no time to think of her. Steps sounded in the passage, someone tried the door, then rapped impatiently, and his uncle's voice called Beatrice.

Francesco dashed the sweat from his clammy brow, strode briskly to the door, turned the key, and flung it wide.

On the threshold he came face to face with his white-haired uncle, candle in one hand, the inevitable book closed upon his forefinger in the other.

"Francesco!" he exclaimed, and frowned between anger and amazement. "What make you here at such an hour? And what is happening? Why was that door locked?"

Francesco, miraculously self-controlled by now, his face a mask of sorrowing concern, drew his uncle by the arm into the chamber, and closed the door.

The old man's eye caught that ominous red bundle on the floor, and he started forward, and perceived the absurd plump legs in their pink and white stockings. Then he looked at his daughter, who sat livid, dull-eyed, and no longer more than half conscious. Lastly he turned his blank, scared face upon his nephew.

"What does it mean?" he inquired hoarsely, a quaver in his voice, a sense of evil overcoming his usual mistrust of his nephew.

Francesco flashed a glance at Beatrice; then his grimness all deserted him. "My God!" he cried out. "How shall I tell you?" He buried his face in his hands; his shoulders heaved, and a sob escaped him.

"Francesco!" cried his uncle in tremulous appeal. "What is it? Who is that?" And he pointed to the body on the ground.

And then Francesco made pretence to control himself, and told his wicked story, told it with a cunning as surpassing as that of the tale itself, with averted eyes, in a voice stifled now by emotion, broken now by sobs. Thus did he relate how passing homeward he had seen the garden postern standing wide; wondering he had stepped into the garden, and seeing a light in the window of the chamber Beatrice was wont to inhabit, he had advanced, moved by a premonition that all was not well. Through the window he had seen them – Baldassare Scipione and Beatrice – there together. By a strange negligence, which had proved the man's just undoing, they had not bethought them to draw the curtains close. Inflamed by a kinsman's righteous indignation, he had climbed the stairs, and so surprised them. He had fallen upon Scipione and he had slain him.

Old Omodei sat, a bowed figure, hands on knees, head fallen forward, and listened to his nephew's infamous invention, entirely duped by it, convinced by the grim evidence at hand. A while after Francesco had done, he remained so, like one bereft of understanding. At last he moved; a groan escaped him, and Francesco looking furtively saw two tears trickle slowly adown his uncle's furrowed cheeks. Yet Francesco knew no pity.

Suddenly the old man stiffened. He rose, determination on his ashen face. He looked steadily and long at Beatrice, who met his glance with one that he accounted of defiance. She had heard the story. She knew that she must contradict it, knew that she held this vile Francesco in the hollow of her hand. And yet she sat spellbound, incapable of speech, frozen out of volition by an odd curiosity to see what these men would do. She was as a spectator at some play in whose movement she was nowise concerned.

The Count turned fiercely to Francesco. "Give me your dagger," he demanded, and held out his hand.

"What would you do?" cried Francesco, now alarmed.

"Complete the work that you have but half done. Wipe out the remainder of this stain. Give me your dagger."

Francesco drew away, aghast. "No, no!" he cried. "You shall not. I swear that you shall not."

"You fool!" his uncle snarled at him. "Can I let live an Omodei at whom the vulgar may point the finger of scorn? Shall I suffer her – my daughter – to be leered at for a strumpet each time she goes abroad. Come, come! Give me your – "

He checked abruptly. His mouth fell open. He hunched his shoulders, like one gathering to resist a blow.

Beatrice had found her voice at last, and used it – used it to utter a soft, scornful laugh.

The Count recovered, and the anger that had momentarily ebbed came flooding back. "You laugh!" he cried, his eyes ablaze. "You dare to laugh?"

She rose slowly. Her recovery of her faculties was complete. The immensity of her scorn blotted out fear and horror and all other things, leaving her supremely mistress of herself.

"I laugh, my father, at that poor fool and liar who has dug himself a pit as deep as death. I could almost laugh at you for very scorn of your readiness to believe him. I think, sir," she pursued, with a dignity the like of which he had never dreamed could dwell in her, "that you have lived too much with your books and too little with your daughter, else you had known better than for one instant to have given heed to this foul knave."

In that fair virgin's eyes there glowed a majesty of anger that made her father cringe and tremble. No longer he the executioner of her, but she the judge of him, and pitiless in her judgment as only the child can be to the parent who has failed in parenthood.

He leaned against the table and hung his head, a very criminal with all the feelings of a thief convicted. Mere words, after all, had robbed him of his self-respect, and Francesco was at hand to restore it him with words.

"Alas, Beatrice!" sighed her cousin. "Better would it beseem you to admit your fault in all humility, to go down upon your knees and sue for pardon, than add to all the rest this gross... Oh, sir, oh, sir," he cried to his uncle, "I have no words for it. That she should seek to hector so, while the body of her lover lies at her feet, here, to speak her shame."

"Ha!" It was a growl from her father. His eye rekindled. He threw back his old white head. "Can you explain that?" he challenged her.

"I can," said she, quite calmly. "But it would make a long story."

"Not a doubt," he rumbled savagely.

"It shall be told you later. Meanwhile, there is a shorter should suffice to brand this subtle gentleman, your nephew. That body which Francesco says shall speak my shame shall speak his villainy instead."

She crossed to the body, her glance upon Francesco who watched her in surprise. "Who do you say lies here?" she asked him, a world of disdain in her voice, almost a shadow of a smile about her pale lips.

The look, the tone went through Francesco like so much steel. He steadied himself, attempted to shake off his sudden fears, studied the pink and white legs, and was stricken dumb.

But the Count broke the momentary silence. "What serves that question? You heard him say 'your lover' – Baldassare Scipione."

She looked from one to the other, then down a moment at the bundle lying there. Stifling her repugnance she stooped quickly, and with shaking fingers pulled away the velvet folds that had formed about the dead man's head. She disclosed at last the livid face and staring eyes of Amerigo Vitelli.

"Look!" she bade them, erect now, and pointing to that face.

They looked, and Francesco all but screamed his horror. He controlled himself, and his fertile brain worked now at fever pace. How this thing had chanced he could not for the moment think, nor did he greatly care. What mattered was to save himself – to save his neck from the strangler's noose that was dangling now so close.

The Count stared, and gasped, utterly bewildered. Suddenly his voice challenged Francesco, harsh and quivering: "What say you now, Francesco?"

He looked at his uncle by an effort of will. By a still greater, he looked at Beatrice. Then he spoke. His voice trembled, his face was ghastly; but all this was as it should be. He had found his answer.

"It is strange indeed, I should have been so mistaken," said he. "Perhaps because I knew how my cousin stands towards Captain Scipione, I never dreamed that her midnight visitor could be another."

It was shrewd – infernally shrewd. For a moment it convinced the Count; for a moment it made Beatrice feel that the ground she had deemed so firm was crumbling beneath her feet. Then from the balcony a new voice spoke: "There are some folks in the garden can explain more fully."

They started round at that intruding sound, at that voice that rang with such sardonic calm. On the balcony, sharply outlined against the night's black background by the light that beat upon him from the room, stood the tall figure of Baldassare Scipione in his scarlet cloak. So absorbed had they been that his soft approach had gone unheeded.

He turned now, and made a sign into the night. From the garden, in response, came a faint clank of arms, then heavy steps rang on the staircase.

Scipione stepped forward into the room. Beatrice sped to him. He put an arm about her, in protection, and over her head confronted the bewildered Count and the now terrified Francesco who had backed away before him until he clawed the arras and could back no farther.

"There are some drunken revellers in the garden who followed their friend Vitelli, and saw him done to death but ten minutes since, as he was entering here, before he had passed those curtains. He fell into a snare that was baited for myself. You shall know more anon, sir. Meanwhile, here are the bargelli of the podestà to seek the murderer."

Six of the podestà's men clattered in, some of the revellers hanging fearfully in their wake. One there was who pushed forward into the room – a slim figure in cloth of gold and with a gilded calf's head mask upon his face. That absurd mask he tore off as he entered, and at sight of his dead master's body, Amerigo's page flung aside his lute, and poured forth twixt rage and sorrow the tale of what he had beheld. He was the witness to bring Messer Francesco degli Omodei within the clutches of the Justice of the Duke, and his neck into the strangler's noose.

Chapter 6

THE LUST OF CONQUEST

The hour of Cesare Borgia's power and glory was that of full noontide. He had made an end of the treacherous condottieri who had dared to rise against him and for a moment to hold him in check, threatening not only to arrest his conquering progress but to undo all that he had done. He had limed a springe for them at Sinigaglia, and – in the words of the Florentine Secretary, Machiavelli – he had lured them thither by the sweetness of his whistling. They came the more readily in that they mistook their roles, conceiving themselves the fowlers, and him the victim. He quickly disabused their minds on that score; and having taken them, he wrung their necks with no more compunction than had they been so many capons. Their considerable forces he partly destroyed and dispersed, partly assimilated into his own vast army, whereafter he swept southward and homeward to Rome by way of Umbria.

In Perugia his sometime captain, Gianpaolo Baglioni, one of the more fortunate rebels who had escaped him, was arming to resist him, and making big talk of the reckoning he would present to Cesare Borgia. But when from the high-perched eyrie of his ancient Etruscan stronghold, Gianpaolo caught afar the first gleam of arms in the white January sunshine, he talked no more. He packed instead, and fled discreetly, intent to reach Siena and take shelter with Petrucci.

And no sooner was he gone than Perugia – which for generations had been weary of his blood-smeared family – sent ambassadors with messages of welcome to the Duke.

Gianpaolo heard of this in Assisi, and his rage was a prodigy even for a Baglioni. He was a black-browed, powerful man, built like an ape with a long body and short legs, a fine soldier, as all the world knows, endowed with a reckless courage and a persuasive tongue that lured men to follow him. In quitting Perugia, he had listened for once to the voice of discretion, urged by the cold and calculating quality of his hatred of the Borgia, and by the hope that in alliance with Petrucci he might stir up Tuscany, and so return in force against the Duke.

But now that he had word of how cravenly – as he accounted it – his city of Perugia had not only bent her neck to the yoke of the conqueror, which was perhaps inevitable, but had further bent the knee in homage and held out her arms in welcome, he repented him fiercely of his departure, and was blinded to reason by his rage.

He was so mad as to attempt to induce Assisi to resist the advancing Duke. But the city of St Francis bade the belligerent Gianpaolo go with God ere the Duke arrived; for the Duke was already on his way, and did he find Gianpaolo there, the latter would assuredly share the fate which had visited his fellow-rebels.

Baglioni angrily took his departure, to pursue his road to Siena. But some three miles to the south of Assisi he drew rein, and lifted his eyes to the stronghold of Solignola, poised, gaunt and grey, upon a projecting crag of the Subasian hills. It was the lair of that indomitable old wolf Count Guido degli Speranzoni, whose pride was as the pride of Lucifer, whose fierceness was as the fierceness of the Baglioni – to which family he claimed kinship through his mother – whose defiance of the Pope was as the defiance of an infidel.

Gianpaolo sat his horse under the drizzling rain, and considered Solignola awhile, with pursed lips. Tonight, he reflected, Cesare would lie at Assisi, which was as ready as a strumpet for surrender. Tomorrow his envoys would wait upon the Lord of Solignola, and surely, if he knew the old warrior, Count Guido's answer would be a haughty refusal to receive the Duke.

He took his resolve. He would ride up, and seek out Speranzoni. If the Count were indeed prepared for resistance, Gianpaolo had that to say that should encourage him. If his resoluteness had not been weakened, as had most men's, by the mere approach of Cesare Borgia, then it might yet come to pass that here they should do the thing that at Sinigaglia had so grievously miscarried. Thus should his strangled comrades be avenged, and thus should Italy be rid of this scourge. Of that same scourge, as he now dubbed the Lord Cesare Borgia, he had himself but lately been one of the thongs. But Messer Gianpaolo was not subtle.

He turned to his armoured followers – a score or so of men-at-arms who remained faithful to him in this hour of general defection – and made known his intention to ride up to Solignola. Then, by a winding mountain path, he led the way thither.

As they ascended from the vast plain of Umbria, so leafless, grey and desolate under that leaden wintry sky, they perceived through a gap in the hills the cluster of little townships and hamlets, on the slopes and in the eastern valley, which formed the territory and dominion of Solignola. These lay practically without defences, and they must fall an easy prey to the Duke. But Baglioni knew that the fierce old Count was not the man to allow any such considerations to weaken his resolve to resist the Borgia, and to that resolve Gianpaolo hoped to spur him.

Dusk was descending when the little company of Perugians reached the Northern Gate of Solignola, and the hells of the Duomo were ringing the Angelus – the evening prayer in honour of the Blessed Mother of Chastity revived in Italy by the unchaste Borgia Pope. Baglioni's party clattered over the bridge spanning a chasm in the rocks in the depths of which a foaming mountain torrent, swollen and umber-tinted by the recent rains, hurled itself adown its headlong course to join the Tiber in the valley.

Having satisfied the guard, they rode forward into the city and up
the steep long street to the Rocca, regarded with awe by the burghers,
who looked upon them as the harbingers of this invasion which they
knew to be sweeping towards them from the north.

Thus they came to the mighty citadel and thudded over the
drawbridge into the great courtyard, where they were instantly
hemmed about by a swarm of men-at-arms who demanded of them
not only an account of themselves, but news as well of Cesare
Borgia's army. Gianpaolo satisfied them briefly, announced his name,
and demanded to see Count Guido at once.

The Lord of Solignola sat in council in the Sala degli Angioli – a
chamber so known from the fresco which Luini had painted on the
ceiling, representing the opening heavens and a vision of angels
beyond the parted clouds. With the Count sat Messer del Campo,
the President of the Council of Anziani, Messer Pino Paviano, the
Master of the Artificers' Guild, two gentlemen from the valley – the
Lords of Aldi and Barbero – a gentleman of Assisi – Messer Gianluca
della Pieve – and the Count's two principal officers, the Seneschal of
Solignola and the condottiero Santafiora.

They sat about a long, quadrangular oak table in the thickening
gloom, with no other light but that of the log fire that roared under
the wide cowled chimney; and with them, at the foot of the table,
facing the Count, odd member of this warlike council, sat a woman
– the Lady Panthasilea degli Speranzoni, Count Guido's daughter. In
years she was little more than a girl; in form and face she showed a
glorious maturity of womanhood; in mind and character she was a
very man. To describe her the scholarly Cerbone had already, a year
ago, made use of the term 'virago' – not in its perverted, but in its
literal and original meaning, signifying a woman who in intellect and
spirit is a man.

It was by virtue of these endowments as much as because she was
Count Guido's only child and heir, that she attended now this
council, and listened gravely to all that was urged in this matter of
the Borgia invasion. She was magnificently tall, and very regal in her
bearing and in the carriage of her glorious head. Her eyes were large,

dark and lustrous; her hair of a glowing copper; and her tint of the delicate fairness that is attributed to the daughters of the north. The rich colour of her sensitive lips told of the warm blood that flowed in her; their set and shape bore witness to her courage and her will.

Into this assembly, which rose eagerly to receive him, was ushered the Lord Gianpaolo Baglioni. He clanked into the room upon his muscular bowed legs, a sinister figure as seen in the gloom with the firelight playing ruddily upon his armour and his swarthy black-bearded face.

Count Guido advanced to embrace him and to greet him with words of very cordial welcome, which at once told the crafty Baglioni all that he most desired to know. The Count presented him to the company, and invited him to join their council, since his arrival was so timely and since, no doubt, he would be able to offer them advice of which they stood most sorely in need, that they might determine upon their course of action.

He thanked them for the honour, and dropped with a rattle of metal into the proffered chair. Count Guido called for lights, and when these were fetched they revealed the haggard air of Messer Gianpaolo which was accentuated by the splashed harness in which he came amongst them, just as he had ridden. His smouldering eye travelled round the board, and when it found the Assisian gentleman, Gianluca della Pieve, he smiled sombrely.

"Hard though I have ridden," said he, "it seems that another is before me with news of what is happening in Assisi."

Della Pieve answered him. "I arrived three hours ago, and I bore the news that Assisi has thrown up her gates to receive and harbour the invader. The Communal Palace is being prepared for him; it is expected that he will remain awhile in the city, making it a centre whence he can conduct such operations as he intends against such strongholds as may resist him."

"And is Solignola to be reckoned among these?" inquired Gianpaolo bluntly, his eyes upon Count Guido.

The old Lord of Solignola met his glance calmly, his shaven hawk face inscrutable, his almost lipless mouth tight and firm. It was a face at once handsome, strong and crafty – the face of one who never would yield lightly.

"That," he answered slowly, "is what we are assembled to determine. Have you anything to add to the information afforded us by della Pieve?"

"I have not. This gentleman has told you all that is known to me."

"None the less your coming is most timely. Our deliberations make no progress, and we do not seem likely to agree. You, perhaps, may guide us with your counsel."

"You see, Messer Baglioni," put in the Lord of Barbero – a red-faced, jovial gentleman of middle-age – "our interests are different, and we are naturally governed by our interests."

"Naturally, as you say," agreed Baglioni with imperceptible sarcasm.

"Now we of the valley – and my friend Francesco d'Aldi, there, cannot deny it – we of the valley lie open to attack; we are defenceless; the few townships that have walls at all, have not such walls as will resist bombardment. It is a fine thing for Count Guido and the folk of Solignola itself to talk of resistance. Solignola is all but impregnable. And well-provisioned and well-garrisoned as the city is, Count Guido may, if it please him, resist long enough to enforce advantageous terms. But what in the meanwhile will be our fate down yonder? Cesare Borgia will avenge upon us the stubbornness of the capital. Therefore do we urge his Excellency – and we have in this the suffrage also of the Master of the Artificers' Guild – to follow the example of Assisi and your own Perugia" (Gianpaolo winced) "and send his ambassadors to the Duke with offers of submission."

Gianpaolo shook his great head. "It is not the Duke's way to avenge upon dependencies the resistance of a capital. He is too guileful, believe me. Whom he subjects he conciliates. There will be no such fire and sword as you fear for your townships of the valley. Solignola's resistance – if she resist – will be visited upon Solignola alone. That much I can say from my knowledge gained in service with the Duke. Let me remind you of Faenza. What harm was suffered by the folk of the Val di Lamone? Why, none. The strongholds surrendered, and knew no violence, although Faenza herself resisted stubbornly."

"But to little purpose," put in Paviano – the Guildmaster – sourly.

"That," said Count Guido, "is beside the point. And Faenza had not the natural strength of Solignola."

"Yet, ultimately," protested Barbero, "surrender you must. You cannot resist an army of ten thousand men for ever."

"They cannot besiege us for ever," snapped Santafiora, the condottiero, rearing his cropped bullet-head.

Baglioni sat back in his chair, and listened to the hot debate that followed now. He was as one who has tossed down a ball into a field of players, and, having done so, watches it being flung back and forth in the course of the ensuing game.

Count Guido, too, took little part in the discussion, but listened silently, his eyes passing from speaker to speaker, his countenance a mask. Facing him his daughter was sitting forward, her elbows on the table, her chin in her cupped palms, intent upon every word that was uttered, her eyes now glowing with enthusiasm, now coldly scornful, as the argument turned for or against resistance. But it was all inconclusive, and at the end of a half-hour's wrangling they were no nearer a decision than when Gianpaolo had arrived.

It was at this stage that Count Guido turned again to the Perugian, and, profiting by a momentary silence following a vigorous plea for resistance from Santafiora, invited him to speak.

"It may be that I can help you," said Gianpaolo slowly, "for it happens that my proposal supports neither one side nor the other of the discussion to which I have listened. My suggestion concerns a middle course; and since something of the sort seems to be needed here if you are not to spend your days in talk, perhaps your courtesy will give attention to what I have to say."

The company stirred expectantly, and settled into an attentive silence. Panthasilea's eyes turned with the others upon the grim face of the speaker, and never left it whilst he was delivering his message.

"Sirs," he said, "here has been talk of resistance and of surrender. Of attack, of assuming the offensive, it seems not one of you has thought."

"To what purpose?" quoth Santafiora, scowling. "We have a bare five hundred men."

But Baglioni imperiously waved the condottiero into silence. "Hear me out before you judge me, and do not outrun me by conclusions of your own. You may know – or you may not, for Italy is full of lies upon the subject – of the business in which those gallant gentlemen, who were my friends, came by their deaths in Sinigaglia – a death which I, myself, have very narrowly escaped by the infinite mercy of God." And he crossed himself piously. "It had been planned, sirs, to take this Duke, and make an end of him. An arbalister was to have shot him as he rode into the town. But he is the fiend – the incarnate fiend. He came forewarned. *Praemonitus et praemunitus.* He turned the trap about, and took in it those who had plotted to take him. The rest you know." He leaned forward, and his blood-injected eyes ran over the assembled company. "Sirs," he concluded in a thick, concentrated voice, "that which failed at Sinigaglia might succeed in Assisi."

There was a stir, breaking the rapt silence in which he had been heard. He looked at them with challenge in his glance. "Needs more be said?" he asked.

"Ay," cried Paviano, "the how and the when, the ways and the means."

"Why that, of course. But first – " He turned to Count Guido. "Have you a mind to follow such a course; to rid Italy of this scourge at a single stroke; to save your dominions and the dominions of others from being ravished by this insatiable devourer? Destroy Cesare Borgia, and you will have destroyed the head and brain of the Pontifical forces; thus there will be an end to this conquest of the Romagna, which presently will spread into a conquest of middle Italy; for if he lives he will not rest until he is king of Tuscany. He is not easy of access, and since Sinigaglia he uses all precautions. Yet while he is resting in Assisi should be your opportunity if you have a mind to seize it."

Count Guido sat thoughtful and frowning, whilst eagerness glowed on several faces, positive fierceness of concurrence on one or two. But one dissentient there was in old del Campo.

"It is murder you are proposing," he said in tones of chill reproof.

"And what then? Shall a mere word set up a barrier for grown men?" demanded the fierce Baglioni.

"It would not for one woman that I know of," said the clear boyish voice of Madonna Panthasilea, and so drew upon herself, with those first words she had ventured to utter in that council, the gaze of all. There was a feverish light in her dark eyes, a feverish glow in her fair cheeks. Meeting their glances she addressed them: "What my Lord Gianpaolo has said is true. While Cesare Borgia lives there is no peace for middle Italy. And there is one thing, and one thing only that can save Solignola – the death of Cesare Borgia."

A roar of acclamation was the answer to those words – words uttered already by Baglioni – now that they fell from her red lips. It was her beauty and her glorious womanhood that swayed them – as men ever will be swayed even against reason, against honour and against knowledge.

But old del Campo remained untouched by the subtle magnetism of sex. He rose as the acclamations died down. He turned a calm, impassive face upon Count Guido.

"My lord," he asked, his voice ice-cold, "does this receive your countenance?"

The white face of the old Count was set and hard, as his voice was hard when, after a moment's thought, he spoke. "Upon what grounds, Messer del Campo, would you urge that it should not? for that is clearly what you would urge."

The President of the Anziani steadily met the Count's steely glance. He bowed a thought ironically. "I am answered," he said. He thrust back his chair, and stepped from the table. "Permit, my lord, and you, sirs, that I withdraw before you go further in a matter in which I will have no part."

He bowed again to all, drew his furred robes about him, and proudly left the chamber in the ensuing silence, leaving a chill behind him.

Scarce had the door closed after him than Gianpaolo was on his feet, his face pale with excitement.

"Sir Count," he cried, "that man must not leave the citadel. Our lives may hang upon it. Too many such schemes have miscarried through less than this. Cesare Borgia's spies are everywhere. They will be in Solignola now, and should del Campo utter a word of what has passed here, the Duke may hear of it tomorrow."

There was a moment's silence. Count Guido's eyes seemed to ask Gianpaolo a question.

"There is no dungeon in your castle too deep for Messer del Campo until this thing is done," said he; and he added almost under his breath: "Indeed, I doubt if there be any deep enough."

The Count turned to Santanora. "See to it," he said in a low voice, and Santanora rose and departed on his errand.

Madonna Panthasilea's face grew very white; her eyes dilated. She feared the worst for old del Campo, who had been her own and her father's faithful friend for many a year. Yet she saw the necessity for the measure, and so crushed down the womanly weakness that arose in her, and spoke no word of intercession for him.

Presently the Count solemnly addressed the company.

"Sirs," he said, "you have plainly signified your agreement with the proposal made by Messer Gianpaolo."

"A thought occurs to me," put in Francesco d'Aldi, and at once he claimed their attention. He was a scholar, a patron of the arts, a man of natural shrewdness and much worldly experience, who had dwelt much in courts and for a season had been the Orator of Solignola at the Vatican. "A doubt occurs to me as to the wisdom of my Lord Baglioni's proposal as it stands."

Angry glances, a snort or two of impatience, and a short contemptuous laugh from Baglioni, were his answers. But he fronted the disapproval calmly, and in that moment of his pause Santafiora re-entered the chamber.

"Give me your patience, sirs," said Messer Francesco, and he almost smiled. "I do not wish to bear del Campo company in his dungeon."

Santafiora smiled grimly as he resumed his seat. That and his silence told the company all that it could have asked the condottiero.

"Say on," the Count bade the Lord of Aldi. "We all know your worth, Francesco."

Messer Francesco bowed, and cleared his throat. "Messer Gianpaolo has told us what would result from the death of Cesare Borgia – enough to justify the slaying of him so far as the ultimate consequences are at issue. But we, here in Solignola, have also to consider the immediate consequences of this act; for those immediate consequences would touch ourselves."

"Sacrifice for the State's weal is the duty of the individual," said Gianpaolo harshly.

"Since Messer Gianpaolo proposes to seek safety for himself in Siena, it is easy for him to utter these beautiful sentiments," said Aldi tartly.

Some laughed, Baglioni spluttered an angry oath, and Count Guido intervened to sooth him.

"Myself," proceeded Francesco d'Aldi, "I oppose the sacrifice of the individual where it is not necessary, and in this case I hold that it is not. We are to consider that with Cesare Borgia are several condottieri who are devoted to him. Such men as Corella, Scipione, della Volpe and others would never allow his death to go unavenged. And the measure of revenge they would exact is such as no man may calmly contemplate. Solignola would cease to exist; not a town, not a hamlet would be left standing – no man, woman or child would they spare in their devastating fury. Can you envisage that, sirs?" he inquired, and was answered by gloomy looks and silence. "But I have an alternative proposal," he continued, "which should more effectively

173

meet our needs, and lead to the same result for us – for Solignola, Assisi and Perugia.

"It is that we take the Duke of Valentinois alive, and hold him as a hostage, threatening to hang him if we are beset. That should keep his condottieri in check, and meanwhile we send our envoys to the Pope. We offer his Holiness his son's life and liberty in exchange for our own lives and our own liberties, in exchange for a Bull of perpetual franchisement from the States of the Church; and to quicken his Holiness' penmanship we add a threat that if the Bull is not in our hands within a given term we will proceed to hang the Lord Cesare Borgia."

"Most shrewd!" Baglioni cried, and others echoed the applause.

"But there is a difficulty," said Francesco. "It lies in the Duke's capture."

"Indeed, yes," agreed Paviano gloomily.

"But surely by guile," urged Count Guido, "he might be lured into some – some trap."

"We should need such guile as Cesare Borgia's own," said Santafiora.

And now for a while they talked to no purpose, and first one offered a suggestion, then another; but these suggestions were all as obvious to propose as they were impossible to execute. That a half-hour was spent, and they were no nearer a solution; some indeed were beginning to despair, when Madonna Panthasilea rose slowly to her feet.

She stood at the table's end, her bands resting lightly upon the board, her tall, lithe body in its russet gown, inclining slightly forward, her bosom rising and falling, and the pallor of excitement on her face, the sparkle of excitement in her liquid eyes.

"It is most fitting," she said slowly, her voice steady and composed, "that Solignola's future mistress should be Solignola's saviour in this hour. Thus shall I prove my right to rule here when the time comes – and please God it may lie very distant yet."

The silence of utter amazement that followed her words was broken at length by her father.

"You, Panthasilea? What can you do?"

"What no man of you all could do. For here is a matter that may best be fought with woman's weapons."

Against this they protested clamorously, some in horror, some in anger, all excited, save only Baglioni, who cared not how the thing were done so that it was done.

She raised a hand for silence and obtained it.

"There is between the Borgia and me this matter of saving Solignola. That alone were matter enough to spur me. But there is more." She grew deathly white and swayed a moment with closed eyes. Then, recovering herself, continued: "Pietro Varano and I were to have wed this spring. And Pietro Varano was strangled three months ago in the market-place of Pesaro by Borgia justice. That too lies between me and the Duke of Valentinois; and vengeance should give me strength in this enterprise, which must be approached by such ways as only a woman's feet may tread."

"But the danger of it!" cried Count Guido.

"Think not of that. What danger shall I run? I am not known in Assisi, where I have not been since I was a little child. I am scarce known in Solignola itself, where I have been seen but little since my return from Mantua. And I shall be careful how I show myself in Assisi. Sirs, you must not gainsay me in this. I set my hand to the task to preserve our State's independence, to save thousands of lives. As Messer Gianpaolo has said, sacrifice for the State's weal is the duty of the individual. Yet here so much can scarcely be required."

Men muttered, and looked at her father. It was for him to speak. The Count took his head in his hands and sat in thought.

"What – what is your plan?" quoth Gianluca della Pieve thickly.

Her ready answer showed how fully already she had considered the matter. "I shall go down to Assisi, taking with me a dozen men of Santafiora's condotta, disguised as peasants and lackeys. And while Solignola defies Cesare Borgia, and so detains him in Assisi, I shall find ways to lure him into a snare, bind him hand and foot and bear him off to Siena, where Messer Gianpaolo will await me. For my purpose, Messer della Pieve, your house in Assisi will be necessary to me. You will lend it me."

"Lend it you?" quoth he in horror. "Lend it to be a mouse-trap in which you – your matchless womanhood – shall be the cheese? Is that your meaning?"

She lowered her eyes; a crimson flush overspread her face.

"Solignola," she replied, "is in danger of being conquered. In the valley thousands of women and little children are in danger of homelessness, of death and worse than death. Shall one woman hesitate" – and now she raised her eyes again and flashed them defiantly upon the company – "shall one woman hesitate to endure a little insult when at the price of it she can buy so much?"

It was her father who returned the answer that none other dared return. He uncovered a face that had become grey and haggard.

"She is right," he said, and – odd argument for an Italian of the cinquecento – "it is her sacred duty to the people she was born to rule," he informed them. "Since there offers no way by which a man's strength may prevail against Valentinois, della Pieve you will lend your house; you, Santafiora, the men that she requires."

Assisi, conquered without bloodshed, all trace of conquest sedulously removed as was the way of Cesare Borgia, was settling down to its workaday aspect which the Duke's occupation had scarcely ruffled.

Though princes perish, thrones crumble in ruin, and dynasties be supplanted, citizens must eat and live and go about their business. Thus, whilst some remained in Assisi who scowled as Cesare Borgia, Duke of Valentinois, went abroad, the greater portion bared their heads and bowed their duty to the conqueror, the great captain who had made it his life's task to reconsolidate into one powerful state these petty tyrannies of the Romagna.

The half of Cesare's army was encamped in the surrounding country. The other half, under Michele da Corella, had advanced to lay siege to Solignola, which had returned a defiant answer to Cesare's envoys when these had gone to invite Count Guido to surrender.

It was a difficult place to take, and Cesare was too wise a captain to be in haste where haste must prove expensive. Assisi afforded him pleasant quarters, and was a convenient centre for the transaction of such business as he had with Florence and Siena, and so he sat down very patiently to await the result of certain operations which he had indicated to Corella.

The chief feature of these was the preparation of a mine under the walls on the southern side of the city, almost under the very citadel itself at the point where it was flanked by the hill. Between the difficulties of access to the place, and the vigilance and continual sorties of the defenders, it became apparent at the end of a week that at the present rate of operations it would take Corella a month to effect a breach. Cesare began to consider the wisdom of opening a bombardment, deterred, however, by the difficulty there would be in effectively mounting a park of artillery upon those rocky slopes.

The matter of this obstinate but futile resistance offered by Solignola, intrigued his Highness of Valentinois, and he was assured that some explanation for it must exist that was not obvious. That explanation he sought on every hand, for the Sinigaglia affair had rendered him doubly wary and alert.

One fair morning in early February, on which the deeper golden of the sunlight told of approaching spring, Cesare rode down the steep borgo from the market-place, the centre of a brilliant group of horsemen – captains in steel, courtiers in silk, and, beside him, upon a snow-white mule, the handsome scarlet figure of Cardinal Remolino, the Papal legate *a latere*.

It was a joyous cavalcade, most of its members being as young as the young Duke himself; and gay talk and laughter leaped from them as they rode forward to visit Corella's camp under Solignola.

In the open space before the Convent of Santa Chiara their progress was arrested for a moment by a mule litter that struck across their course towards one of the streets that led to San Rufino. It was attended by two footmen, and a very elegant cavalier on a big roan horse who rode on the litter's farther side.

The Cardinal-legate was speaking to Cesare, and Cesare was allowing his eyes to stray, as do the eyes of a man not over-interested in what he is being told. They chanced to fall upon the litter, and what he saw there caught his roving glance, and held it.

The curtain had been drawn aside, and at the very moment that he looked, the cavalier was – or so it seemed to him – stooping to point him out to the lady who sat within. It was this lady's splendid beauty that now engrossed his gaze; and in that instant her eyes, large and solemn as a child's, were raised to his.

Their glances met across the little intervening space, and Cesare saw her lips part as in surprise, saw the colour perish in her cheeks, leaving them ivory white. In homage – not to the woman, but to the beauty that was hers, for like all of his race he accounted beauty the most cardinal of all the virtues – the conqueror doffed his hat, and bowed to the very withers of his horse.

The Cardinal, checked in full flow of argument, scowled at this proof of inattention, and scowled more darkly still when to reveal the full extent of it, Cesare asked him softly: "Who is that lady, do you know?"

The prelate, who had a famous eye for feminine beauty, followed Cesare's indication promptly. But in that moment the curtain fell again, thus baffling his eager glance.

Cesare, a smile on his lips, uttered a slight sigh, and then fell very pensive, intrigued by the element of abnormality, slight as it was, that the incident had offered. He had been pointed out to her, and at sight of him she had turned pale. What was the reason? He could not recollect that he had ever seen her before; and had he seen her, hers was not a face he had forgot. Why, then, did the sight of him affect her in so odd a manner? Men enough had turned pale before him, ay, and women too. But there had ever been a reason. What was the reason here?

The litter and its attendants vanished into the by-street. But still Cesare was not done with it. He turned in his saddle to an Assisian gentleman who rode behind.

"Did you mark the cavalier who accompanied that litter?" quoth he, and added the question: "Is he of Assisi?"

"Why, yes, Excellency," was the answer. "That is Messer Gianluca della Pieve."

"Della Pieve?" said Cesare, thoughtful. "That is the member of the council who was absent when the oath was taken. Ha! We should have more knowledge of this gentleman and his motives for that absence." He rose in his stirrups as his horse moved forward, and called over the heads of some others: "Scipione!"

One of the steel captains pushed forward instantly to his side.

"You saw the litter and the cavalier," said Cesare. "He is Messer Gianluca della Pieve. You will follow them, and bring me word where the lady resides, and at the same time you will bring me Messer della Pieve. Let him await my return at the Palace. Should it be necessary you will use constraint. But bring him. Away with you. Forward, sirs."

Baldassare Scipione backed away, wheeled his charger, and departed in discreet pursuit of the litter.

Cesare pushed on, his cavaliers about him; but he went thoughtful, still pondering that question: "Why did she turn pale?"

The reason, had he known it, might have flattered him. Madonna Panthasilea had come to Assisi to destroy by guile one whom she had never heard described save as an odious monster, the devastator of all Italy. She had looked to see some horror of a man, malformed, prematurely aged and ravaged by disease and the wrath of Heaven. Instead she found a youthful cavalier, resplendent of raiment, superb of shape, and beautiful of countenance beyond all men that she had ever seen. The glory of his eyes when she had found them full upon her own, seeming to grope into her very soul, had turned her faint and dizzy. Nor did she recover until the curtain fell again, and she remembered that however noble and gallant his presence, he was the enemy of her race, the man whose destruction it was her high mission to encompass as she stood pledged.

179

Reclining in her litter as it moved forward, she half closed her eyes, and smiled to herself as she remembered how avid had been his gaze. It was well.

The litter curtain was slightly lifted from without. "Madonna, we are being followed," murmured Gianluca.

Her smile grew broader, more content. The affair was speeding as it should. She said so to her cavalier.

Her smile and her words caused an anger to flare out in Gianluca – an anger that for a moment had manifested itself that night when first she had committed herself to this task, and had been smouldering since.

"Madonna," he cried in a voice that was hoarse, "this is a Delilah's work to which you are committed."

She stared at him, and paled a little to bear this brutally true description of the task; then she took refuge in haughtiness.

"You are presumptuous, sir," she told him, and so lashed him with that answer that he lost his head.

"Presumptuous enough to love you, madonna," he replied, almost fiercely, yet muttering, that her attendants should not overhear him. "That is why I abhor to see you wedded to a task so infamous; making a lure of your matchless beauty, a base – "

"Stop!" she commanded him, so sternly that he obeyed her despite himself.

She paused a moment as one who chooses words, nor looked at him again after that first imperious glance.

"You are singularly daring," she said, and her voice was pitiless. "We will forget what you have said, Messer Gianluca – all of it. As long as I am in Assisi I must continue under your roof, since my mission demands it. But I trust, sir, that you will relieve me of your attendance, thus sparing me the memory of your offence, and yourself the sight of one whom you condemn so harshly."

"Madonna," he cried, "forgive me. I meant not as you think."

"Messer della Pieve," she answered, with a little, cruel laugh of scorn, "to be frank, I care not greatly what you meant. But I beg that you will respect my wishes."

"Depend upon it that I will, madonna," he answered bitterly, "and suffer me to take my leave of you."

He let the curtain fall, and even as he did so the litter came to a halt before the portals of his house – one of the handsomest palaces in Assisi, standing by the Duomo of San Rufino.

With a white, sullen face he watched her alight, leaning upon the arm of a footman who had hastened to discharge the pleasant duty that usually was Gianluca's own; then he doffed his hat, bowed frigidly, and wheeling his horse, he rode slowly away, nursing his sorely lacerated pride, which the young Assisian mistook for injured love, just as he had mistaken for love the ambition which had caused him to lift his eyes to the future high and mighty Countess of Solignola.

It was, therefore, a very short-tempered young gentleman who found himself suddenly confronted and hailed by a tall warlike fellow on a tall horse. Messer Gianluca scowled at Cesare's captain.

"I do not know you, sir," said he.

"That misfortune I am here to amend," said the bland Scipione.

"I do not seek your acquaintance," said Gianluca still more rudely.

"You shall have it, none the less. For I have orders to force it upon you if necessary."

Now these were ugly words to one whose conscience was not clear of treason. Della Pieve's dark mood was elbowed aside by fear.

"Is this an arrest?" he asked.

Scipione laughed. "Why, no," said he. "I am sent to escort you; that is all."

"And whither, sir?"

"Now here's a catechism! To the Communal Palace, to repair your omission to wait upon his Highness of Valentinois."

Gianluca looked into the other's rugged face, and observed that it was friendly; he took courage, and made no more demur. And as they rode, he sought to draw information from Scipione, but finding the captain as close as an oyster, and mistrusting this closeness, he grew afraid again.

At the Communal Palace matters were no better. He was left to cool his heels in an antechamber for two hours and more, to await the return of the Duke who was abroad. It was in vain that he begged to be allowed to depart, vowing that he would return anon. He was desired, for only answer, to be patient; and so the conviction was forced upon him that in some sort he was a prisoner. He remembered Baglioni's words, that the Duke had spies everywhere, and he began to fear the worst. So engrossed was he with these fears that all thought of Panthasilea faded utterly from his mind – that lesser matter being supplanted by this greater.

At length, when his torture of suspense had reached a climax, and he had begun to shiver in that chilly anteroom, an usher came to inform him that the Duke awaited him. Whether it was of intent that the Duke had submitted him to this suspense, to the end that through fear his spirit might be softened as metal in the furnace, it is not possible to say. But it may well be that some such purpose this crafty Duke had sought to serve, desiring as he did to ascertain precisely what was the attitude towards himself of this puissant gentleman of Assisi who had failed to come with his brother *Anziani* to take the oath of allegiance. Certain it is that della Pieve was a very subdued and morally weakened young man when at length he was admitted to Cesare Borgia's presence.

He was ushered into the gloomy hall of the palace, which was lighted by windows set high in the wall, and decorated by a multitude of rampant lions – the Assisian emblem – frescoed in red upon a yellow ground, unpleasantly bewildering to the eye. The place was chill, for all that a wood fire was burning in the vast fireplace. About this stood a group of Cesare's captains and courtiers, talking and laughing, when Gianluca was admitted. His advent, however, was followed by a general and somewhat disconcerting silence, and he became the object of a no less disconcerting attention on the part of those same gentlemen, whilst here he caught a smile, and there a shrug, all serving to heighten his uneasiness.

He gained the middle of the chamber, and hung there pausing awkwardly for a moment. Then from the group the Duke's tall figure detached itself. His Highness was all in black, but his doublet was embroidered in arabesques of gold thread, so finely wrought that at the little distance separating them, Gianluca thought him to be wearing damascened body-armour.

Cesare advanced, his pale young face very set and grave, fingers toying with his tawny beard, eyes sad and thoughtful.

"I have waited a week to give you welcome, Messer della Pieve," said he coldly. "As I seemed in danger of having to forgo the honour, I was constrained to send for you." And he paused as if awaiting an explanation.

But della Pieve had nothing to say. His mind seemed benumbed under the Duke's steady glance, under the eyes of all those gentlemen at the room's end.

It was Cesare's aim to determine whether della Pieve's recusancy was that of active or of passive enmity. If passive, the man might go his ways; but if active, Cesare must know more of it. And meanwhile he had been gathering information.

He had ascertained that Gianluca della Pieve had quitted Assisi on the eve of his own arrival, and had returned upon the morrow of that event, bringing with him a very beautiful lady, a kinswoman of his, it was put about. That lady was lodged in his palace, and was shown a great deference by her attendants.

Such was the sum of Cesare's information. Slight in itself; most certainly too slight to have aroused the least suspicion against della Pieve, had he but come to take the oath. Viewed, however, in the light of that recusancy and in conjunction with the sudden pallor of the beauty in the litter at sight of Cesare, his Highness judged that there was matter to be proved. And now he had della Pieve's confused and guilty bearing to confirm him in that judgment.

As the Assisian offered no explanation, Cesare passed to questions.

"Although you are one of the first citizens of Assisi, you were not among the *Anziani* when the oath was taken on Sunday last," he said. "I shall rejoice to hear your motives for that absence."

"I – I was not in Assisi at the time, Magnificent," said della Pieve.

"Ay – but dare you tell us where you were?" cried Cesare sharply – and his tone was the tone of one who questions upon matters fully known to him. "I do not wonder that you hesitate to answer," he added after a moment's pause, and that completed Gianluca's assurance that his movements were already known.

"My lord," he faltered, "Count Guido was my father's friend. We owed him many favours."

Here was knowledge gained, and upon it Cesare built rapidly.

"I am not quarrelling with your visit to Solignola," he said slowly, and the stricken Gianluca never suspected that he, himself, had just afforded the first intimation of that same visit. "Nor yet am I quarrelling with your friendship for Count Guido. My displeasure is with the motives that led you to seek him."

That fresh vague random shot of Cesare's went home as had done the others. Gianluca blenched. Plainly all was known.

"My lord," he cried, "I swear before Heaven that I took no willing part in any of the measures determined at Solignola."

So! Measures had been determined at Solignola! Cesare turned it over in his mind, recalled the fact that della Pieve had gone alone and had returned accompanied by a lady – the lady of the litter, the lady who had turned pale at the sight of him that day. Undoubtedly she was from Solignola. It remained to ascertain her identity.

"How am I to believe you?" he asked.

Della Pieve clenched his hands. "I have, of course, no means of proving what I say," he admitted miserably.

"Indeed you have, sir. There is one proof you are overlooking." Cesare's voice was very cold. "It is yours to use frankness with me now, and so convince me of your honesty. Yet you are careful to tell me nothing." His eyes narrowed, and again in that tone of one who is possessed of the fullest knowledge: "Not even," he added, "in the matter of this lady whom you fetched from Solignola with you on your return."

The Assisian recoiled as if he had been struck, unable to follow
the simple method of inference by which Cesare had arrived at the
conclusion that the lady was from Solignola, never dreaming that the
Duke was but groping for information, and assured that the identity
of Panthasilea must be known to this man with as many eyes as
Argus.

He took refuge at the last in falsehood, touching the motives of
his visit to Count Guido's stronghold. "Magnificent," he began by
way of preface, "since you know so much you will understand the
rest."

"My present aim," said Cesare, "is to test your honesty."

Gianluca plunged headlong into the falsehoods he contemplated,
praying Heaven that Cesare's information might be sufficiently
limited to admit of his being believed.

"Why, is it not natural, Excellency, that being determined upon
this resistance, Count Guido should have desired to place his
daughter in safety – to remove her from the perils and discomforts
of a place besieged? In my having given her the shelter of my house,
is there anything that reflects upon my honesty towards your
Highness? I have said that my father owed great favours to Count
Guido. Could I, then, do less than I have done?"

Cesare stood surveying him, his face inscrutable. So! The lady was
Count Guido's daughter. That was valuable knowledge gained. But
that Count Guido's daughter should have come to Assisi – into
Cesare's very camp – to seek safety and shelter, was a foolish clumsy
lie. Therefore there must be some other motive for her presence,
which Gianluca found himself forced to withhold.

Thus reasoned the Duke. And having formed his sound
conclusions, he shrugged and laughed scornfully.

"Is this your honesty?" he asked. "Is it thus that you would prove
that you are not my enemy?"

"It is the truth, my lord!"

"It is a lie, I say," the Duke retorted, raising his voice for the first
time. "I am too well informed, sir, to be hoodwinked so easily." Then
dropping back to his calm, level tones: "You abuse my patience, sir,"

he said, "and you forget that there are the rack and the hoist below stairs with which I can force the truth from you if necessary."

Gianluca's manhood rebelled at the threat. He braced himself by an effort of will, and looked the Duke boldly between the eyes, sustained by the courage of the desperate.

"Neither hoist nor rack could extract another word from me," he said. "For I have no more to tell."

Cesare continued to ponder him in silence. He was not prone to needless or fruitless cruelty. And he fancied that having learned so much already, the rest might be discovered without resorting to the violence of the rack. For the moment, however, it was plain that della Pieve would say no more. He nodded slowly.

"You have no more to tell me, eh? An ambiguous phrase, sir. But I think I read its real meaning."

He turned to the group about the hearth, which included the tall captain Scipione. He beckoned the condottiero to him.

"Baldassare," said he, "take Messer della Pieve hence, and place him under arrest until I make known my pleasure. Let him be closely confined with guards you can trust to allow him to commune with none."

It was not Cesare's intention to run the risk of Panthasilea's learning that her identity was known to him; for in that case the present gain would all be wasted, and the true aim of her presence in Assisi remain undiscovered.

The matter intrigued Cesare Borgia not a little. He took counsel that night with Agabito Gherardi, his shrewd, white-faced secretary; and Agabito, though by nature a mild and kindly man, had no hesitation in recommending that the torture should be employed to squeeze the last drop of truth from Messer della Pieve.

"We may come to it in the end," said Cesare. "But the moment, I fancy, is not propitious. There was in this fellow's face this morning a look as of willingness for martyrdom, which does not augur well. I infer that he loves Count Guido's daughter, and, so, is strengthened in obstinacy. What is at the bottom of it all I cannot even guess. I swear it would baffle that crafty Florentine Secretary Machiavelli – which is as much as to say the devil himself."

And at that same hour Madonna Panthasilea degli Speranzoni was in earnest talk with one of her faithful followers from Solignola, a youth named Giovanni. Until tonight the manner of approaching her task had baffled her completely, since della Pieve had failed her in her original scheme. She had desired him to make pretence of loyalty to the Duke, and to present her as his kinswoman, Eufemia Bracci of Spoleto. But della Pieve, out of repugnance for the whole affair, had refused, and so had thwarted her.

But now that at last she had seen her man, and taken his measure as much by his brave appearance as by the very ready gallantry expressed in the obeisance to which the mere sight of her had moved him, she saw her way; and she was laying her plans for the morrow with Giovanni.

The morrow dawned fair and clear, a day that was more of April than of February. A soft wind was blowing from the south, warm and subtly fragrant, and from a cloudless, cobalt sky the sun shone genially upon the plain of Umbria, and struck fire and silver from the tumbling waters of the Tescio.

It was at the ford, almost under the very walls of Assisi, that Cesare Borgia, returning with a half-dozen gentlemen from an early morning ride to the camp under Solignola, came suddenly and unexpectedly upon Madonna Panthasilea.

She was seated upon the ground in a forlorn and dejected attitude, resting her shoulders against a grey boulder that had partly concealed her from the Duke's eyes until he was abreast of her. She was dressed in that bright russet gown in which you beheld her at her father's council; cut low in the bodice it revealed the perfection of her throat, the splendid column of her neck. Her bright hair was partly unbound, and strands of it caught the breeze and fluttered distractingly about her faintly-tinted cheeks. Her veil had fallen back and slipped down on to her shoulders.

In the meadow, at some little distance, a riderless mule was cropping the short grass.

At sight of her Cesare instantly swung himself from the saddle, and she had leisure to admire the athletic ease of the movement and the matchless grace of the man as he approached her, cap in hand, his long bronze-coloured hair gleaming in the sunlight.

At a glance he had recognised her; at a glance perceived the plight – real or pretended – in which she found herself; and, however that might be, he rejoiced in this chance to come to grips with her.

He bowed profoundly, and she found herself looking into the gentlest and most beautiful eyes that she had ever seen. The appeal to her womanhood of this very perfect manhood, this splendid youth and strength of which he was the incarnation, was instant and irresistible. A pang shot through her at the thought of her task; her first qualm beset her with that first glance of his. But it was no more than the momentary outcry of her instincts under the shock of the encounter; immediately reason's cold hand seized the reins of her will, and governed it.

"You are hurt, madonna," he murmured, in that gentle yet richly melodious voice that was one of his greatest charms. "The mischance you have suffered is very plain to see. Permit that we assist you?"

She smiled at him, and even as she smiled her mouth assumed a painful twist and grew as quickly smooth again. "It is my ankle," she complained, and put a hand to the injured limb.

"It must be bound," said he, and swiftly loosed a scarf he wore about his body.

"No, no!" she cried – a cry of real alarm, as his sharp ears detected. "My women will tend it when I reach home. It is not far."

"Believe me," he insisted, "it should be bound at once."

She crimsoned under his glance. She looked up piteously and very beautiful, and made the crimsoning do service for a blush of virgin modesty.

"I implore you not to pain me by insisting," she pleaded. And he, playing his part as she played hers, lowered his eyes in submission, and shrugged his regret at such injudicious obstinacy.

She proceeded to tell him how she came in such a plight. "My mule had crossed the ford," she said, "and was mounting the hither bank when it slipped upon those stones, came down upon its knees and threw me off."

He looked grave concern. "Ungracious beast," said he, "to cast off so fair a burden!" And he added: "You should not ride forth alone, madonna."

"It is not my custom. But on such a morning, the spring I think was in my soul, and I was athirst for freedom."

"A dangerous thirst," said he, "the quenching of which has been the death of many. You should have considered all the Borgia soldiery a-swarm about the countryside."

"What should I fear from them?" she asked him, bewitchingly innocent, her eyes wide. "You, yourself, are one – are you not? Must I then fear you?"

"Ah, madonna," he cried, " 'tis you fill me with fear."

"I?" quoth she, lips parting in a half-smile.

"Fear for this same freedom which you seem to prize, and which I prize no less. What man can account himself free who has met your glance? What man can be other than a slave thereafter?"

She laughed lightly as she turned aside that thrust in the high lines. "Why, here's a courtier," said she. "And I deemed you but a soldier."

"I am a courtier here, madonna," he said, bowing low before her. "Elsewhere I am the Duke."

He watched the pretty play of feigned surprise upon her face; the simulated sudden confusion. "The Duke – you!"

"Your slave," said he.

"My lord, I have been blind – very blind. It had been better had I been as dumb. What must you deem me?"

He looked at her, and sighed. "Life is so short! I should not find it long enough to tell you."

She flushed again under his burning gaze; for despite suspicion and all else he found her – as all men must – very good to see; and his admiration showed clearly in his glance.

"We are forgetting my poor foot, my lord," she reminded him. "And I detain you. Perhaps one of your gentlemen will come to my assistance."

"Nay, in this office I will not be supplanted. But one of them shall fetch your mule." He turned, and sharply gave an order which sent his gentlemen all spurring towards the grazing beast. "Can you rise with help?" he asked her.

"I think I could."

He stooped, and crooked his arm. But she drew back. "Highness!" she murmured in confusion, "It were too much honour! By your leave, I will await one of your gentlemen."

"Not one of them shall have my leave to help you," he said, laughing, and again, insistently, he thrust his arm upon her notice.

"From such masterful ways – how can I defend myself?" said she, and taking his arm she rose painfully on her one sound foot; then lost her balance, and fell heavily against him with a little cry.

His arm flashed round her waist to steady her. Her hair lay an instant against his cheek; the sweet fragrance of her filled his brain. She murmured piteous excuses. He smiled, silent, and held her so until the mule was brought. Then, without a word, he lifted her in his arms as though she had been a child, and set her in the saddle. And the strength of him amazed her, as it had amazed many another to more hurtful purpose.

One covert but very searching glance he bestowed upon the mule's knees. As he had expected, they were smooth and glossy, and showed no slightest hurt or stain. It left him no doubt that her ankle was in like case, and with a little smile he turned and vaulted lightly into his own saddle. Then, coming beside her, he took the bridle of her mule in his right hand, and called to one of his gentlemen to protect her on the other flank.

"Thus, madonna, you will be safe," he assured her. "And now – forward!"

They went down the short incline to the water, and splashed across the ford, and so rode forward into Assisi. As they went, the Duke talked lightly, and she responded with a ready tongue and many a sidelong glance of admiration for his person and of pleasure in the flattering homage of his words, which was not wholly feigned. As they were entering the town, he asked her whither did she desire them to conduct her.

"To the house of my kinsman, Messer Gianluca della Pieve, by San Rufino."

Her kinsman! Here, considered Cesare, was more deception. How did she propose to call herself, he wondered; and bluntly asked her.

Her reply came readily. "I am Eufemia Bracci of Spoleto, your Highness' devoted subject."

He made no answer to Eufemia Bracci of Spoleto. But he smiled fondly upon her, such a sweet, guileless smile as assured her that Gianpaolo Baglioni had by much overrated his acuteness.

At the door of della Pieve's house he took his leave of her. And at the last moment, and purely out of malice, he promised to send his own physician Torella to attend her; and he dissembled his amusement and his perception of the sudden fear that leaped for a moment to her eyes. She implored him not to think of it, assured him that a day's rest would mend her foot, and she was obviously relieved that he took her word for this, and did not insist.

He rode away bemused, and once back at the Communale he sent for Agabito Gherardi and told him what had passed,

"And so, Agabito," he concluded, "the Lady Panthasilea degli Speranzoni is here in Assisi, calling herself Eufemia Bracci of Spoleto, the kinswoman of della Pieve. She has thrust herself upon my notice, and sought to enlist my interest and ensnare my senses. Can you read me this riddle?"

Agabito's round white face was contemptuously placid. "It is extremely simple," said he. "She is the bait in a trap that has been set for you."

"That, Agabito, is what I have been telling you. What I desire to know is the nature of the trap itself. Can you hazard me a guess?"

"The matter is too serious for guessing," replied the secretary, unmoved. "If I might venture to advise you, Highness, it is that you go armed abroad and with all precaution, and that you do not adventure yourself within the doors of the Palazzo Pieve save with an ample escort."

Cesare opened his black doublet to show Agabito the gleam of the steel mesh he wore beneath. "Armed I am," said he. "But for the rest of your advice – " he shrugged. "There is a way of handling these traps so that they close upon those who set them. There was such a trap prepared for a man in Sinigaglia, not so long ago. But you know that story."

"In that case, my lord, you had precise knowledge of what was intended."

Cesare looked at the other, smiling cruelly. "Knowledge which the torture wrung from Messer Ramiro de Lorqua," he said. "Bid them prepare a hoist in the hall below, tonight; and let the executioner and his assistants be summoned to await my pleasure."

Agabito departed, and the Duke turned his mind to other matters. That evening he sat late at supper with his gentlemen, and when he dismissed them it was to closet himself with Agabito and his clerks and keep them at work upon despatches for Rome and Florence until far into the night.

Towards midnight he turned to Agabito to inquire had all been made ready for the examination of della Pieve; and then, even as the secretary was answering him, the door was opened and a servant entered quickly.

"What now?" demanded Cesare, frowning.

"Soldiers from the camp under Solignola, Magnificent, with a prisoner."

He raised his brows, surprised. "Admit them," he said. And a youth in peasant garb and cross-gartered leggings, his hands pinioned behind him, was led in between two men-at-arms. With them came a young officer of Corella's, whom Cesare instantly addressed.

"What is this?"

The officer saluted. "We took this man, Magnificent, less than an hour ago, upon the slopes under Solignola. He had eluded our sentries and was through our lines, and but that in the dark he loosed a boulder, and so drew our attention, he had gained the city. We found him to be the bearer of a letter written in cipher. But Don Michele was unable to induce him to say whence this letter or for whom."

He handed Cesare a small square of paper the seal of which had already been broken. The Duke took it, ran his eye over the array of baffling ciphers, examined the seal, and finally bore the paper to his nose and sniffed it. Very faintly he caught a fragrance that reminded him of a woman in a bright russet gown; just such a fragrance had he inhaled that morning during those brief moments in which she had lain in simulated helplessness against his breast.

He advanced towards the travestied messenger, his solemn eyes upon the man's calm intrepid face.

"At what hour," he asked quietly, "did Madonna Panthasilea degli Speranzoni despatch you with this letter?"

The man's countenance changed upon the instant. Its calm was swept away by a consternation amounting to fear. He recoiled a step, and stared wide-eyed at this Duke, who watched him with such awful impassiveness.

"Men speak the truth of you!" he cried at last, carried away by his excited feelings.

"Rarely, my friend – believe me, very rarely." And the Duke smiled wistfully. "But what have you heard?"

"That you have made a compact with the devil."

Cesare nodded. "It is as true as most things that are said of me. Take him away," he bade the officer. "Let him be confined in strictest solitude." Then to the youth: "You have nothing to fear," he said. "You shall come by no harm, and your detention shall not exceed a week at most."

The youth was led out in tears – tears for the mistress whom he served, persuaded that from this terrific Duke nothing was concealed.

Cesare tossed the note to Agabito. "Transcribe it for me," he said shortly.

"It is in cipher," said Agabito, bewildered at the order.

"But the key has been obligingly supplied. The last word is composed of eleven numerals and of these the second, sixth and last are the same. Assume that word to be 'Panthasilea'. It will simplify your task."

Agabito said no more, but bent, quill in hand, over the letter, whilst Cesare – a long scarlet figure in a furred robe that descended to his ankles – thoughtfully paced the chamber.

Soon the secretary rose, and handed Cesare the transcription.

I engaged his attention at last this morning, and I have made an excellent beginning. Within a few days now I count upon an opportunity to carry out the business. I am prepared. But I shall proceed slowly, risking nothing by precipitancy. – PANTHASILEA.

Cesare read, and held the paper in a candle flame, reducing it to ashes. "It tells no more than we already knew. But that much it confirms. Mend the seal of the original, and let means be found to convey it to Count Guido. Let one of my men replace the original messenger, then let him pretend that he is wounded, and so induce some rustic with a promise of good payment from Count Guido to bear the letter to Solignola.

"And let Corella be advised that he is to see to it that he captures no more messengers at present. Thus he will find it easier to complete the mine; for as long as the folk of Solignola depend upon my defeat here in Assisi and believe it to be progressing, they are not likely to be as vigilant as if they had but their own efforts to depend upon. And now for Messer della Pieve. Let him be sent for."

The Assisian gentleman had been confined in no dungeon. He was comfortably lodged in one of the chambers of the palace; his bed and board were such as befitted a gentleman of his station; and his gaolers used him with all deference. Therefore it is no matter for marvel that he slept soundly on the night in question.

From that sleep he was rudely roused to find four men-at-arms in his chamber, looking grim and fantastic in the light of the single smoky torch that was held aloft by one of them.

"You are to come with us," said the man whose heavy hand still rested upon Gianluca's shoulder.

Della Pieve sat up in alarm, blinking but wide-awake, his heart beating tumultuously.

"What is it?" he demanded in a quavering voice. "Whither must I go?"

"With us, sir," was all the answer he received – the man who answered him obeying to the letter the orders he had received.

The poor gentleman looked fearfully from one to another of those bearded faces, gloomy and mysterious in the shadows of their steel morions. Then, resigning himself, he flung back the covers, and stepped from the bed.

A soldier cast a mantle over his shoulders, and said: "Come."

"But my clothes? Am I not to dress?"

"There is not the need, sir. Come."

Frozen now with fear, assured that his last hour had struck, Gianluca permitted them to conduct him barefoot as he was along chill passages, down a dark staircase and into the very hall where yesterday he had been given audience by the Duke.

Into this was he now ushered, and so into a scene that Cesare had carefully prepared with the object of torturing the man's soul – a merciful object, after all, since thus he hoped to avoid the maiming of his body.

Ranged against the wall, midway up the chamber, stood a table draped in black. At this sat the black figure of the questioner, gowned and cowled like a monk. He was flanked by a clerk on either hand, and before each of these were paper, ink-horns and quills. On the table stood two candle-branches, each bearing a half-dozen candles. There was no other light in that great vaulted chamber, so that the greater portion of it remained mysteriously in shadow.

On the hearth at the room's far end stood an iron tripod supporting a brazier in which the charcoal was glowing brightly. Thrust into the heart of this fire Gianluca observed with a shudder some wooden-handled implements to be heating.

Across the chamber, facing the questioner's table, grey ropes, like the filaments of some gigantic cobweb, dangled from pulleys that were scarcely visible in the upper gloom of the groined ceiling – the torture of the hoist. By these ropes stood two men in leathern vests, their muscular, hairy arms bared to the shoulder. A third man, similarly dressed, stood in the foreground making knots in a length of whipcord.

In mid-chamber – the one spot of colour in all that hideous greyness – stood Cesare Borgia in his long scarlet gown, thumbs hooked into his silken girdle, a scarlet cap upon his head. His eyes were indefinitely sad and wistful as they rested now upon Gianluca.

The young Assisian stood there and looked about him in dread fascination. He knew now to what purpose he had been awakened and dragged from his bed. He fought for air for a moment; the beating of his heart was stifling him. He reeled, and was steadied by the leathern-clad arm of one of the soldiers.

No word had been spoken, and the silence entered into alliance with the chill breath of the place, with the gloom and with the horror of preparations indistinctly revealed, to make the scene appear to Gianluca as some horrific nightmare. Then at a sign from Cesare, the executioner's assistants advanced, almost silent-footed, to receive the patient from the soldiers. These surrendered him and clattered out.

Gianluca was led forward to the table, and stood there between his two fearsome guards to face the questioner.

From the depths of the cowl a cold voice spoke, and to Gianluca it seemed to ring and boom through the vaulted place.

"Messer Gianluca della Pieve," said the voice, "you are guilty of having conspired with Count Guido degli Speranzoni, Tyrant of Solignola, against the High and Mighty Lord Cesare Borgia, Duke of Valentinois and Romagna; and of having prepared here in Assisi a pitfall for this same High and Mighty Lord. Thereby you have deserved death. But worse than death have you deserved when it is considered that his highness is Gonfalonier of Holy Church, that the battles he fights are the battles of Holy See. Therefore have you sinned not only against the Duke's Magnificence, but against God and His Earthly Vicar, our Holy Father the Pope. Yet since the Church has said: '*Nolo mortem peccatoris, sed ut magis convertatur et vivat,*' his Highness in our Holy Father's name desires to spare you so that you make frank and full confession of your sin."

The booming voice ceased; yet echoes of it still reverberated through the tortured brain of Gianluca. He stood there, swaying, feebly considering his course. He hung his head.

"Look behind you," the voice bade him, "and behold for yourself that we do not lack the means to unseal your lips should you prove obstinate."

But Gianluca did not look. He did not need to look. He shivered; but still said no word.

The questioner made a sign. One of the executioners whipped the cloak from Gianluca's shoulders, and left that poor gentleman standing in his shirt. He felt himself seized by strong – cruelly strong – hands. They turned him about, and dragged him across the room towards the hoist. Midway he hung back, throwing his entire weight upon their arms to check them.

"No, no!" he pleaded through ashen lips.

Suddenly the Duke spoke. "Wait!" he said and, stepping forward, barred their way. He waved his hand, and the executioners fell back, leaving Gianluca alone with his Highness in mid-apartment.

"Messer della Pieve," said Cesare gently, and he placed a hand upon the Assisian's shoulder, "consider what you do; consider what is before you. I do not think the questioner has made that clear enough. You have seen the hoist at work; you have perhaps seen it wrench a man's shoulders from their sockets." And his steely fingers tightened about the shoulder that he held, until it seemed to Gianluca that a thousand threads of fire were coursing down his arm. He gasped in pain, and the Duke's grip at once relaxed. Cesare smiled – a smile of tender, infinite pity.

"Consider by that how little you are fitted to endure the cord. Be assured that you will speak in the end. And what do you think would follow? Your release? Indeed, no. If once the cords of the hoist have grappled you, you become the property of the law; and when the law has made you speak, it will silence you for ever. Consider that. From the agonies of a broken body your release lies through the hangman's hands. Consider that you are young – that life has much to offer you, and consider above all that your silence will profit no one, your speech betray no one that is not betrayed already – that your obstinacy will lead you to sacrifice yourself for no useful purpose."

Gianluca's eyes looked piteously at the Duke from out of his ashen face.

"If – if I could believe that!" he murmured.

"It is easy to convince you, and in convincing you of that I shall convince you also of my own disinterestedness in seeking to save you even now.

"Learn, then, that Madonna Panthasilea degli Speranzoni has already spread her net for me; that today she thrust herself upon my notice; that tonight she sent a letter to her father informing him of this good beginning and that within a week she looks to accomplish her treacherous work and take me in her toils.

"Knowing so much already, am I likely to fall a victim to this thing they plan? Can anything that you may add be of so much moment that you should suffer torture and death sooner than reveal it?"

Gianluca shivered. "What do you desire to know?" he asked. "What can I add? You seem already to know all – more even than do I. Or is it," he added in sudden apprehension, "that you seek my evidence to use it against this lady?"

"Already have I all the evidence I need, were such my aim. There is the letter which she wrote her father. That alone would doom her did I desire it. No, no. All that I seek to learn from you is the precise nature of this trap that has been prepared. You will see that in telling me that you can no longer do any hurt to Count Guido or his daughter."

"Why – if that is all – "

"That is all," said Cesare. "A little thing. And there stands the horrible alternative awaiting you. Could I be more generous? Speak, and you may return to bed; I shall hold you a prisoner for caution's sake until Solignola falls. Then you may go your ways in perfect freedom. I pledge you my word for that. Be silent, and – " He waved a hand to the grey cords of the hoist, and shrugged.

That was the end of della Pieve's silence. He saw clearly that no purpose could be served by persisting in it; that he would but sacrifice himself in vain – and this for a woman who had deemed his love presumptuous and had used him with so little mercy, So he told the Duke the little thing his Highness sought to know – that his abduction was the purpose of the conspiracy, the aim for which Madonna Panthasilea was in Assisi.

Towards noon upon the morrow a very dainty page in the Duke's livery came to della Pieve's house bearing a scented letter in Cesare's own hand, wherein his Highness like the humblest suitor, craved permission to come in person and receive news of Madonna Eufemia Bracci.

Panthasilea's eyes sparkled as she read. Her plans were speeding marvellously. Fortune for once was arrayed against this Cesare Borgia whose proverbial luck had caused him to be dubbed *Filius Fortunae*.

The permission his Highness sought she very readily accorded, and so it fell out that the Borgia came in person some few hours later. Leaving his splendid cavalcade to await him in the little square, he went alone into her house.

He came magnificently arrayed, as a suitor should. His doublet was of cloth of gold; milk-white one silken hose, sky-blue the other, and the girdle and carriages of his sword were ablaze with jewels worth many a principality.

He found her in a chamber whose window doors opened upon the topmost of the garden's several terraces, and it was a room that was a worthy setting for so rare a gem. Eastern carpets were spread upon the mosaic floor, rich tapestries arrayed the walls; books and a lute stood upon an ebony table that was inlaid with ivory figures. By the fireplace two of her women were at work upon the embroidering of an altar-cloth, whilst madonna, herself, reclined upon a low couch of Eastern pattern. A subtle fragrance hung upon the air – the bitter-sweet of lilac essences, a trace of which he had yesternight detected in the intercepted letter.

Upon his entrance she made as if to rise; but in that he checked her. With sweet concern he forbade the effort, and swiftly crossed the room to stay her by force if need be; whereupon she sank back, smiling.

She was all in white, coiffed in a golden net from which a sapphire, large as a bean, hung upon her brow.

One of her women hastened to approach a low chair of antique design, whose feet, carved in the form of the lion's paw, were of solid silver. He sat, and solicitously inquired how fared madonna's ankle, to receive her assurance that by tomorrow it should bear her weight again.

Their interview was brief, perforce, and flavoured by hints from him of the deep regard he had conceived for her; it was confined to pretty play of courtly speeches, a game of fence at which Madonna Eufemia Bracci of Spoleto showed herself no novice.

And yet, tightly strung to her task though she was, she feasted her eyes upon the rare grace and beauty of his resplendent presence, nor repelled the dangerous rapture which his haunting eyes and soft melodious voice aroused in her.

When at length he departed, he left her very thoughtful.

On the morrow he returned, and again upon the following day; and ever did the cavalcade await him in the square below. The game began to interest him beyond all his expectations. This thrusting of his head into the lion's maw afforded him sensations such as he had never yet experienced; this hunting the hunters, this befooling the befoolers, was no new thing to him, but never had he engaged upon it under circumstances more entertaining.

On the occasion of his third visit he found her alone, her women having been dismissed before his entrance. Wondering what fresh move in the game might this portend, he dropped upon one knee to thank her for the signal favour of it, and bore her fragrant hand to his devout lips. But her face was very grave, and for the first time she surprised him.

"My lord," she said, "you mistake me. I have dismissed my women because I had that to say to you which you must prefer that I say without witnesses. My lord, you must visit me no more."

For once in his life he was so astonished that he permitted his countenance to reflect his feelings. Yet she mistook for chagrin the sudden change she saw there.

"I must visit you no more, madonna!" he cried, and his accents confirmed her impression. "How have I offended? Tell me, that on my knees, here at your feet, I may atone."

Gently she shook her head, gazing down upon him with a tender sadness. "How should you have offended, my lord? Rise, I implore you."

"Not until I know my sin." And his eyes were the eyes of the humblest suppliant at a shrine.

"You have not sinned, my lord. It is – " She bit her lip; a gentle colour warmed her cheek. "It is that I – I must think of my good name. Oh, have patience with me, Highness. You will make me the talk of this scandal-mongering town if daily your escort is seen awaiting you below whilst you come to visit me."

At last he understood the fiendish subtlety at work within that lovely head. "And is that all?" he cried. "Is there no other reason – none?"

"What other reason should there be?" she murmured, eyes averted.

"Why, then, it is soon remedied. In future I will come alone."

She pondered a moment, and gently shook her head. "Best not, my lord. Indeed, that were worse. You would be seen to enter. And coming thus – oh, what would folks not say?"

He sprang up, and boldly put an arm about her. She suffered it, but he felt the shudder that ran through her. "Does it matter – what they say?" quoth he.

"Not – not to you, my lord. But me – consider me. What is a maid's fair name once it is blown upon by scandal?"

"There – there is a back way – by your garden. Thus none would see me. Give me the key, Eufemia."

Under lowered lids he watched her face, saw what he looked for, and released her. Inwardly he smiled. He was the very prince of amorous boobies, of love-lorn fools – the most obliging numskull that ever dashed into a trap prepared for him. So was she thinking, not a doubt, in a mental glow at the subtleties of her poor strategy.

She stood trembling before him. "My lord, I – I – dare not."

So much fencing began to nauseate him; the daring of it amounted to folly and moved him to some contempt. He grew cold upon the instant.

"So be it, then," said he. "I will not come again."

He reduced her now to terror. He saw the quick alarm that leapt to her dark eyes. He admired her swift recovery of a situation that was slipping from her grasp.

"My lord, you are angry with me." She hid her face on his shoulder. "You shall have the key," she murmured.

He departed with it, persuaded that she was the most callous, heartless traitress that had ever drawn the breath of life. He might have thought differently had he seen her as she sat there after his departure, weeping bitterly and reviling herself most cruelly. And yet that night she wrote to her father to tell him that all was speeding excellently, and that the end was near.

And Solignola, lulled more and more by these messages and by the desultory manner in which the siege was being conducted, kept but indifferent watch. They heard at times the blows of picks under the southern wall of the citadel, and they knew that Corella's men were at work there. But they no longer sallied to disperse them, deeming it but an idle waste of life now that another and more effective method of checkmate was all but in their grasp.

The following afternoon was well advanced when Cesare Borgia tapped upon the window doors of the room in which it was Panthasilea's custom to receive him. He found her alone; and there was some confusion in her manner of receiving him now that he came in secret, as a lover avowed. But he was that day the very incarnation of discretion.

They talked of many things that afternoon, and presently their talk drifting by the way of the verse of Aquilano to the writings of Sperulo, who had followed Cesare's banner as a soldier, the Duke fell into reminiscences. He spoke of himself for once, and of his task in Italy and his high aims; and as he talked, her erstwhile wonder at the difference betwixt what she found in him and what she had looked for, arose again. He was, she had been told, a man compounded of craft and ambition; harsh, unscrupulous, terrible to foe and friend alike; a man devoid of heart, and therefore pitiless. She found him so gentle, courtly, and joyous, and of so rare a sweetness of thought and speech that she was forced to ask herself, might not envy of his great achievements and his strength be the true source of the hatred in which he was held by those upon whom he warred.

A tall-necked Venetian flagon of sweet Puglia wine stood that afternoon upon the table, having been left there by her women; and, moved by an impulse she could scarce explain, she poured a cup for him when towards dusk he rose to take his leave. He came to stand beside her by the table whilst she brimmed the goblet, and when she would have filled another for herself, he covered the vessel with his hands.

It was as if some of the passion latent in him, at which, as if despite him, his ardent glance had hinted none too seldom, leaped of a sudden forth.

"Nay, nay," said he, his great eyes full upon her, their glancing seeming to envelop her, and hold her as in a spell. "One cup for us twain, I do beseech you, lady, unworthy though I be. Pledge me, and leave on the wine the fragrance of your lips ere I pledge you in my turn. And if I reel not hence ecstatically, divinely drunk, why, then I am a clod of earth."

She demurred a little, but his will made sport with hers as does the breeze in autumn with the leaf; and he watched her the while for all the hot passion that seemed to film his eyes. For he was acquainted with drugged wines, and such pretty artifices, and had no fancy for unnecessary risks in this game that he was playing.

But this wine was innocent. She drank, and handed him the cup. He bent his knee to receive it, and drained it, kneeling, his eyes upon her face.

Thereafter he took his leave of her, and she stood at the window looking after his departing figure as it descended the garden and was merged at last into the thickening gloom. Then she shivered, a sob broke from her quivering lips, and she sank limp into a chair, again as yesterday to fall a-weeping for no reason in the world that was apparent.

And again that night she wrote to the Count, her father, that all was going better than she could have dared to hope, and that within three days she looked to place in the hands of those who waited that which should enable them to purchase the emancipation of Solignola.

He came again upon the morrow, and upon the morrow of that again; and now Count Guido's daughter entered upon a season of sore experiences. In Cesare's absence she ripened her plans for his ultimate capture; in his presence she was all numb, fascinated by him, filled with horror and self-loathing at her task, the very creature of his will.

At last was reached that fateful evening that had been settled for the Judas deed. He came at nightfall, as she had begged him – urging her request as an added precaution against scandal – and he found her awaiting him in the gloom, no other light in the chamber save that of the logs that blazed upon the hearth. He took her hand and bore it to his lips. It was ice-cold and trembled in the clasp of his as trembled all her body now. He scanned her face and saw that it was drawn, for all that its pallor was dissembled by the ruddy firelight. He saw that she could not bear his gaze, and so concluded – as already he had suspected – that the snare was to be sprung tonight.

"Eufemia!" he cried. "My Eufemia, how cold you are!"

She shivered at the endearment, at the soft caress of his voice, the pleading ardour of his eyes. "It – it is very chill," she faltered. "The wind is in the north."

He turned from her and crossed again to the windows, her glance following him. He drew the heavy curtains close, and shut out what little daylight yet lingered in the sky.

"So," he said, "it will be more snug within."

He was dressed from head to foot in the warm red-brown of leaves in autumn; and as he stood there against the dark background of the curtains, the red light of the logs, playing over the smooth velvet of his doublet and the shimmering silk of his hose, turned him into a man of flame; and of shifting liquid fire seemed the girdle of gold scales that clasped his waist.

Tall, majestic, and magnificently lithe and graceful, he seemed to her now the very embodiment of perfect manhood. More than man he seemed in the fantastic, ardent panoply he borrowed from the firelight.

He moved, and fire glowed and shot, quivered, vanished and gleamed again along his scaly girdle. He took her hands and drew her down beside him on the Eastern settle, out of the firelight's direct range, yet so that her face remained illumined.

She submitted despite herself. All her instincts cried out against this dangerous propinquity, thus in the flame-lit gloom.

"I – I will call for lights," she faltered, but made no attempt to rise or to disengage the hand he held.

"Let be," he answered gently. "There is light enough, and I have not long to stay."

"Ah?" she breathed the question and felt her heart-beats quickening.

"But a moment; and I am more grieved since it is my last evening here with you."

He noted the guilty start, the sudden spasm of fear that rippled across her face, the quivering half-stifled voice in which she asked: "But why?"

"I am the slave of harsh necessity," he explained.

205

"Work awaits me. Tomorrow at dawn we deliver the final assault which is to carry Solignola."

Here was news for her. It seemed that not an hour too soon had she resolved to act.

"You – are certain that it will be final?" she questioned, intrigued by his assurance, eager to know more.

He smiled with confidence. "You shall judge," said he. "There is a weakness in the walls to the south under the hill, spied out from the commencement by Corella. Since then we have spent the time in mining at that spot; and there has been during these last days an odd lack of vigilence on the part of Count Guido's followers. Solignola seems as a town lulled by some false hope. This has served us well. Our preparations are complete. At dawn we fire the mine, and enter through the breach."

"So that I shall see you no more," said she, feeling that something she must say. And then, whether urged to make-believe or by sheer femininity, she continued: "Will you ever think again, I wonder, when you pass on to further conquests, of poor Eufemia Bracci and her loneliness in Spoleto?"

He leaned towards her, his head thrust forward; and his eyes, glowing in the half-light, looked deeply into hers, so deeply that she grew afraid, thinking he must see the truth in the very soul of her. Then he rose, and moved away a step or two until he stood in the full glow of the fire, one velvet-shod foot on the andiron. Outside the window he had heard the gravel crunch. Someone was moving there. Her men, no doubt.

He stood awhile like a man deep in thought, and she watched him with something in her face that he would have found baffling had he seen it. Her right hand was playing fretfully about her throat and heaving bosom, betraying by its piteous movements the stifling feeling that oppressed her.

Suddenly he turned to her. "Shall I come back to you, my Eufemia?" he asked in a hushed but very ardent voice. "Would you have it so?" And he flung out his arms to her.

Her glance upraised met his own, and her senses reeled under those imperious eyes instinct with a passion that seemed to enwrap her as in a mesh of fire. Suddenly she began to weep.

"My lord, my dear lord!" she sobbed.

She rose slowly, and stood there swaying, a poor broken thing whelmed by a sudden longing for the shelter of those outstretched arms, yet horribly afraid, with a mysterious fear, and filled too with self-loathing for the treachery she had plotted. Once it had seemed to her that she did a noble and a glorious thing. Now of a sudden, in the very hour of accomplishment, she saw it vile beyond all vileness.

"Eufemia, come!" he bade her.

"Ah, no, no," she cried, and hid her burning face in her trembling hands.

He advanced, and touched her. "Eufemia!" The appeal in his voice was a seduction irresistible.

"Say — say that you love me," she pleaded piteously, urged to demand it by her last remaining shred of self-respect — for in all their communion hitherto not one word of love had he included in the homage he had paid her.

He laughed softly. "That is a bombardment with which any clown may win a citadel," said he. "I ask a free surrender."

His arms went round her as she fell sobbing on his breast, willing and unwilling, between gladness and terror. She was crushed against him; his lips were scorching hers. Her sobs were stifled. If to her eyes he had seemed a thing of flame a moment since, to her senses now he was live fire — a fire that seared its way through every vein and nerve of her, leaving ecstatic torture in its wake.

Thus they clung; and the leaping firelight made one single and gigantic shadow of them upon wall and ceiling.

Then he gently disengaged the arms that had locked themselves about his neck, and gently put her from him.

"And now, farewell," he said. "I leave my soul with you. My body must elsewhere."

Rafael Sabatini

At that, remembering her men who waited in the garden, her terror rose about her like a flood. She clutched his breast. "No, no!" she cried hoarsely, eyes wide in horror.

"Why, what is this?" he protested, smiling; and so sobered her.

"My lord," she panted, controlling herself as best she could. "Ah, not yet, my lord!"

She was mad now. She knew not what she said, nor cared. Her only aim was to keep him there – to keep him there. He must not be taken, Her men must be dismissed. She must tell him. How, she knew. not; but she must confess; she must warn him, that he might save himself. So ran her thoughts in a chaotic turbulence.

"I know not when I may see you next. You ride at dawn. Cesare, give me an hour – a little hour."

She sank down, still clutching the furred edge of his doublet. "Sit here beside me awhile. There is something – something I must say before you go."

Obediently he sank down beside her. His left arm went round her and again he drew her close. "Say on, sweet lady," he murmured, "or be silent at your pleasure. Since you bid me stay, that is enough for me. I stay, though Solignola remain unconquered for tomorrow."

But in surrendering to his clasp once more, her courage left her; it oozed away, leaving her no words in which to say the thing she longed to say. A sweet languor enthralled her as she lay against his breast.

Time sped. The logs hissed and cackled, and the play of firelight gradually diminished. The flames lessened and died down, and under a white crust of ash the timbers settled to a blood-red glow that lighted but a little space and left black shadow all about the lovers.

At long length, with a sigh, the young Duke gently rose, and moved into the little lighted space.

"The hour is sped – and more," said he.

From the shadows a sigh answered his own, followed by the hiss of a quickly indrawn breath. "You must not leave me yet," she said. "A moment – give me a moment more."

He stooped, took up the iron, and quickened the smouldering fire, thrusting into the heart of it a half-burned log or two that had escaped consumption. Flames licked out once more; and now he could discern her huddled there, chin in palms, her face gleaming ghostly white in the surrounding gloom.

"You love me?" she cried. "Say that you love me, Cesare. You have not said it yet."

"Does it still need words?" he asked, and she accounted that caress of his voice sufficient answer.

She hid her face in her hands and fell a-sobbing. "Oh, I am vile! Vile!"

"What are you saying, sweet?"

"It is time that you knew," she said, with an effort at control. "A while ago you might have heard steps out yonder had you listened. There are assassins in the garden, awaiting you, brought here by my contriving."

He did not stir, but continued to look down upon her, and in the firelight she saw that he smiled; and it flashed upon her that so great was his faith in her, he could not believe this thing she told him – conceived, perhaps, that she was jesting.

"It is true," she cried, her hands working spasmodically. "I was sent hither to lure you into capture that you may be held as a hostage for the safety of Solignola."

He seemed slightly to shake his head, his smile enduring still.

"All this being so, why do you tell me?"

"Why? Why?" she cried, her eyes dilating in her white face. "Do you not see? Because I love you, Cesare, and can no longer do the thing I came to do."

Still there was no change in his demeanour, save that his smile grew sweeter and more wistful. She was prepared for horror, for anger or for loathing from him; but for nothing so terrible as this calm, fond smile. She watched it, drawing back in fascinating horror, as she would not have drawn back from his poniard had he made shift to kill her for her treachery. Sick and faint she reclined there, uttering no word.

Then, smiling still, Cesare took a taper from the over-mantel, and thrust it into the flame.

"Do not make a light!" she pleaded piteously; and, seeing that he did not heed her, she hid her scarlet face in her hands.

He held the flame of the taper to each of a cluster of candles in the branch that stood upon the table. In the mellow light he surveyed her a moment in silence – smiling still. Then he took up his cloak, and flung it about him. Without another word he stepped towards the window.

It was clear to her that he was going; going without word of reproach or comment; and the contempt of it smote her cruelly.

"Have you nothing to say?" she wailed.

"Nothing," he answered, pausing, one hand already upon the curtains.

Under the spur of pain, under the unbearable lash of his contempt, a sudden mad revulsion stirred within her.

"The men are still there," she reminded him, a fierce menace in her tone.

His answer seemed to shatter her wits. "So, too, are mine, Panthasilea degli Speranzoni."

Crouching, she stared at him, and a deathly pallor slowly overspread a face that shame and anger had so lately warmed. "You knew?" she breathed.

"From the hour I met you," answered he.

"Then – then – why –?" she faltered brokenly, leaving her sentence for his quick wit's completing.

At last he raised his voice, and it rang like stricken bronze.

"The lust of conquest," he answered, smiling fiercely. "Should I, who have brought a dozen states to heel, fail to reduce me Count Guido's daughter? I set myself to win this duel against you and your woman's arts, and your confession, when it came, should be the admission that I was conqueror in your heart and soul as I am conqueror elsewhere."

Then he dropped back into his habitual, level tones. "For the rest," he said, "such was their confidence in you up there in Solignola that they relaxed their vigilance and afforded me the time I needed to prepare the mine. That purpose, too, I had to serve."

The curtain-rings clashed, as he bared the windows.

She struggled to her feet, one hand to her brow, the other to her heart.

"And I, my lord?" she asked in a strangled voice. "What fate do you reserve for me?"

He considered her in the golden light. "Lady," said he, "I leave you the memories of this hour."

He unlatched the window doors, and thrust them wide. A moment he stood listening, then drew a silver whistle, and blew shrilly upon it.

Instantly the garden was astir with scurrying men who had lain ambushed. Across the terrace one came bounding towards him.

"Amedeo," he said, "you will make prisoners what men are lurking here."

One last glance he cast at the white crouching figure behind him, then passed into the darkness, and without haste departed.

At dawn the mine was fired, and through the breach Solignola was carried by assault, and Cesare the conqueror sat in the citadel of the Speranzoni.

Chapter 7

THE PASQUINADE

The lute strings throbbed under the touch of the fair-haired stripling in green and gold. His fresh young voice was singing Messer Francesco Petrarca's madrigal:

> *"Non al suo amante piu Diana piacque*
> *Quando, per tal ventura, tutta ignuda*
> *La vide in mezzo delle gelide acque;"*

At this point, and inspired perhaps by the poet's words, Cardinal Farnese – that handsome voluptuary – leaned over the Princess of Squillace, sighing furiously and whispering things which none might overhear.

The scene was the spacious Pontifical Chamber of the Vatican – the Sala dei Pontefici – with its wide semicircular colonnade overlooking the beautiful gardens of the Belvedere, and its wonderfully frescoed ceiling where panels recording the deeds of popes hung amid others depicting the gods of pagan fable. There was Jupiter wielding his thunderbolts; there Apollo driving the chariot of the Sun; there Venus and her team of doves, Diana and her nymphs, Ceres and her wheat sheaves; and there Mercury in his winged cap, and Mars in all the panoply of battle. Inter-wrought were the signs of the Zodiac and the emblems of the seasons.

The time was early autumn, when cooler breezes begin to waft away the pestilential humours that overhang the plain of Rome during the sweltering period of Sol in Leo.

A vast concourse thronged the noble apartment – an ever shifting kaleidoscope of gorgeous human fragments – the purple of prelates, the grey steel of soldiers, the silks of rustling courtiers of both sexes, as many-hued as the rainbow itself, and here and there the sober black of clerks and of ambassadors.

At the chamber's farthest end, on a low dais, sat the imposing figure of Roderigo Borgia, Ruler of the World, Father of Fathers, under the title of Alexander VI. He was robed in the pontifical white, the white house-cap upon his great head. Although in his seventy-second year, he retained a vigour that was miraculous, and seemed a man still in his very prime. There was a fire in the dark, Spanish eyes – eyes that still retained much of that erstwhile dangerous magnetism whereof Gasparino da Verano wrote so eloquently some years ago – a ring in the rich voice and an upright carriage in the tall, full figure that argued much youth still lingering in this amazing septuagenarian.

Near him, on the stools upon which the Teutonic Master of Ceremonies had, with his own hands, placed cushions covered with cloth of gold, sat the lovely, golden-haired Lucrezia Borgia, and the no less lovely, no less golden Giulia Farnese, named by her contemporaries Giulia La Bella.

Lucrezia, in a stomacher stiff with gold brocade and so encrusted with gems of every colour as to lend her a splendour almost barbaric, watched the scene before her and listened to the boy's song with a rapt expression in her blue eyes, her fan of ostrich plumes moving slowly in her jewelled fingers. She was in her twenty-second year, divorced of one husband and widowed of the other yet preserving a singular and very winsome childishness of air.

In the corner of the room, on the far right hand of the dais, her brother Giuffredo, Prince of Squillace, a slim, graceful, pale-faced youth, stood gnawing his lip, his brows contracted in a frown as he watched his Aragonese wife, who, in the distance, was shamelessly wantoning with Farnese.

A certain bold beauty was this Donna Sancia's endowment, despite the sallowness of her skin, a tint that was emphasised by the ruddiness of her henna-dyed hair. She was something fleshy, with full red lips and large liquid eyes of deepest brown, low-lidded and languorous, which of themselves betrayed her wanton nature and justified her husband's constant torture of jealousy.

But with all this our concern is slight. It is no more than the setting of another tragi-comedy of jealousy that was being played that afternoon in the Sala dei Pontefici.

Over by the colonnade, Beltrame Severino, a tall, black-browed gentleman of Naples, was leaning against one of the pillars, apparently concerned with the singing-boy and the company in the chamber, in reality straining his jealous ears to catch what was passing between a youth and a maid who stood apart from the rest, in the loggia that overlooked the gardens.

The youth was one Messer Angelo d'Asti, a fair-headed son of Lombardy, who had come to Rome to seek his fortune, and was installed as secretary to the Cardinal Sforza-Riario. He had a lively wit, and he was a scholar and something of a poet; and the Cardinal, his master, who, to a desire to be known as a patron of the arts, added an undeniable taste for letters, treasured him the more on that account.

Let the Cardinal Sforza-Riario love him to a surfeit for his verses. With that, Beltrame, his rival, had no concern. What plagued the lithe and passionate Neapolitan was Lavinia Fregosi's interest in those same verses and in their author. For, indeed, this progress of Angelo's in Lavinia's regard was growing so marked that Beltrame accounted it high time to be up and doing if he would be saved the pain of submitting to defeat.

As he leaned now against his pillar, urged by his jealousy to play the eavesdropper, he caught some such words as:

"...in my garden tomorrow...afternoon...an hour before the Angelus..."

The rest he missed. But what he caught was sufficient to lead him to conclude that she was giving an assignation to this Lombard poetaster – it was thus, with a man's nice judgment of his rival, that Beltrame dubbed Messer Angelo.

He narrowed his eyes. If Messer Angelo thought that tomorrow afternoon, an hour before the Angelus, he was to enjoy the felicity of undisturbed communion with Madonna Lavinia, he was sowing disappointment for himself. Beltrame would see to that. He was your dog-in-the-manger type of lover, who would allow to no other what he might not himself enjoy.

As the boy's song came to an end, and a murmur of applause rolled through the room, the twain came forward through the pillars, and so upon the Neapolitan. The latter attempted to greet Lavinia with a smile and Angelo with a scowl at one and the same time; finding the performance impossible, he was feeling foolish and therefore increasingly angry, when, suddenly, a diversion was created.

A brisk step rang through the chamber, to the martial jingle of spurs. Men were falling back and a way was opening of itself before some new-comer, who must be of importance to command so much by his mere presence. A curious silence, too, was creeping over all.

Beltrame turned, and craned his neck. Down the middle of the long room, looking neither to right nor to left, and taking no account of the profound bows that greeted his advance, came the tall figure of the Duke of Valentinois. He was dressed in black, booted and armed, and he strode the length of the Pontifical Chamber as if it were a drill ground. His face was white, an angry fire glowed in his eyes, and his brows were drawn together. In his right hand he carried a sheet of parchment.

Arrived before the dais, he bent his knee to the Pope, who had watched the unusual character of his son's advent with a look that plainly reflected his surprise.

"We have been expecting you," said Alexander, speaking with the slight lisp peculiar to him; and he added, "but not thus."

I have had that to do which has delayed me, Holiness," replied the Duke as he rose. "The lampoonists are at work again. It is not enough that I deprived the last of these obscene slanderers of his tongue and his right hand that he might never utter or pen another ribaldry. Already he has an imitator – a poet this time." He sneered. "And not a doubt but that unless we make an example of him he will not lack a following."

He held out the parchment that he carried, unfolded and smoothed it with an angry hand. "This was attached to the plinth of the statue of Pasquino. Half Rome had been to see it and to laugh over it before news reached me, and I sent Corella to tear it down and fetch it me. Read it, Holiness."

Alexander took the parchment. His face had reflected none of Cesare's anger whilst the latter was announcing the cause of it. It remained smooth now that he read, until at last it broke into creases of amusement.

"Do you smile, Holiness?" quoth Cesare in the angry tone that he alone dared use to the father who at once loved and feared him.

Alexander laughed outright. "Why, what is here to fret you so?" he asked. He handed the parchment to Lucrezia, inviting her to read. But no sooner had her fingers closed over it than Cesare snatched it impatiently away from her, and left her staring.

"By your leave – no," he said. "Enough have laughed already." And he looked with meaning at the Pope. Here at least he had expected sympathy and an indignation responsive to his own; instead of which he had found but amusement.

"Come," said the Holy Father soothingly, "the thing is witty, and it has none of the more usual lewdness; nor yet is it so gross an exaggeration of the truth, when all is said." And he rubbed his great nose reflectively.

"Your indifference is comprehensible, Holiness," said Cesare. "The thing does not touch yourself."

"Pshaw!" said the Pope with a broad gesture. "What if it did? Am I the man to waste heat upon anonymous pasquinaders? My child, the great shall never lack defamers. It is the price of greatness in a mean world. Be thankful that it has pleased God to make you worth defaming. As for the earthworms that pen ribaldries – why, if their lampoons are witty, relish them; if merely stupid, ignore them."

"You may be as patient as you please, Holiness. Patience becomes your sovereign station." He seemed, never so faintly, to sneer. "As for myself – I am resolved to stamp out this passion for lampoons. Slander shall be driven down into its lair of filth and mud, and choked there by my justice. Let me but find the author of this pasquinade, and, I swear to God," he went on, raising his voice and shaking his clenched hand at the ceiling, "that I will hang him though he be a prince – temporal or spiritual."

The Pope shook his great head, and smiled tolerantly upon all this heat.

"Let us pray, then," he lisped, "that you do not find him. The writer of those verses gives much promise."

"He does, Holiness. He gives great promise of a sudden death from suffocation."

The Pope's smile wavered nothing in its benignity. "You should follow my own ensample, Cesare, of contempt for these scribblers."

"I do, Holiness. The bargelli have my orders to make diligent search for this rhymer. When they have found him you shall see me express my contempt for him. This ribaldry shall end."

He knelt again, kissed the ring on the hand the Pope extended, and upon that withdrew as he had come, white-faced and angry to an extent that was most rarely shown by him.

"You do not seem at ease, Angelo," murmured Beltrame in his rival's ear.

Angelo turned to face the speaker fully. He had paled a little during Cesare's angry speech, and Beltrame observing this had thereafter watched him, actuated by a suspicion that was born of hope and founded upon a knowledge of Angelo's leaning towards satirical verse and of his attitude towards the family of the Pontiff.

This inimical and satirical attitude of Angelo's towards the Borgias in general and Cesare in particular was natural in a Milanese, and it had of late been fostered in his employment by Cardinal Sforza-Riario, whose house had suffered so rudely at Cesare's hands. It was, indeed, Angelo's too-fluent pen which, in the interval of singing the thousand beauties of Lavinia Fregosi, had composed that bitter pasquinade wherein was ridiculed – somewhat late in the day, it is true – Cesare Borgia's transition from the Cardinalitial purple to the steel and leather of a condottiero.

That Beltrame should comment upon his slight agitation was disturbing now to Angelo. He very readily assumed that the Neapolitan's suspicions were not only definite, but founded upon some evidence of which he must have become possessed. That it was evidence of any value Angelo could scarcely suppose; and so he set himself to dissemble and explain his obvious perturbation.

He laughed and shrugged, as one who throws off some feeling that has weighed upon him. "Why, yes," he admitted. "I am ever ill at ease when Valentinois is present. He affects me so. I cannot explain it. A natural antipathy, perhaps. Have you never experienced it, Beltrame?"

Beltrame sneered. "Not I. Perhaps I have an easier conscience."

"Oh, the conscience of a saint, I am sure, Beltrame," said Angelo, and finding that Lavinia had meanwhile moved away on her brother's arm, he turned to follow, for Marco Fregosi was his friend.

Beltrame too had been his friend until just lately. Until they became rivals for the affections of Lavinia, they had been deeply attached and all but inseparable. Orestes and Pylades men had dubbed them. It was to Angelo a source of secret sorrow – the one cloud in the bright heaven of his hopes – that of their friendship no more than the ashes remained. He would have mended matters had it been possible. But Beltrame made it daily more impossible; grew daily more and more hostile, until Angelo realised that it was time to be wary of the man who once had loved him but who did not so much as trouble now to dissemble his hatred.

By a grey old sundial, creeper-clad, on a lawn green as an emerald and smooth as velvet, in a luxurious garden on the Banchi Vecchi by old Tiber, stood on the morrow's afternoon Lavinia and her two suitors.

Beltrame's unexpected coming had been a source of deep vexation to Angelo – though it might instead have been a source of joy had he but known how much Lavinia shared that same vexation. As it was he could but do his best to dissemble it, and maintain a smiling front.

The child – she was little more – leaned a smooth white elbow on the grey old stone, a mischievous, bewitching smile revealed her dazzling teeth in which was caught by the stem a blood-red rose, one of the last roses of the year. Her great black eyes were now veiled demurely under half-lowered lids and curved sweep of lashes, now raised distractingly to the enamoured glances of one or the other of her swains.

And they, each dissembling his annoyance at the other's presence, each revealing the joy he found in her, little dreamed what trouble lay for them in the heart of that crimson rose she flaunted, nor how one of them must pay the forfeit of his life for its possession.

Beltrame, on the spoor of his suspicions, and hoping to dash the other's easy assurance, and steady flow of talk and laughter – all of which provoked him, since he felt himself out-matched by it – dragged in an allusion to the pasquinade that had so angered Cesare Borgia.

But Angelo laughed. "He is like that," he said to Lavinia, in apology for the Neapolitan. "The skull in the cave of the anchorite – a perpetual reminder of things best forgotten."

"I can understand that you should account them so," said Beltrame darkly.

"Why, then," returned Angelo, "knowing my wishes, it will be the easier for you to respect them."

And then Lavinia, to create a diversion from this talk which was not plain to her, but which seemed laden with much menace, playfully smote Angelo's cheek with that rose of hers, saying that she did it to punish his excessive pertness.

"Such punishment," said he, "is an encouragement to wickedness." And as he spoke his hands closed over the rose, and his eyes smiled hardily upon the lady of his adoration, with never a thought or care for his rival's presence.

Beltrame flushed darkly under his tan, and his brows came together as he looked on.

"You'll crush the flower!" she cried, and more concern could not have laden her voice and glance had it been his heart that was in danger of being crushed.

"You can show pity for the flower, madonna, who have none for me."

"Out of pity, then, I relinquish it," said she, and letting the stem slip through her fingers, she left the rose in his enfolding hands.

"Pity for me, or for the rose?" he asked, his blue eyes very ardent.

"For which you will – for both," she laughed, and shyly dropped her eyes.

"Ay, madonna," snapped Beltrame. "Give him your pity. I do not grudge him that. He needs it."

She stared at the Neapolitan's brooding face, alarmed an instant; then, dissembling this, she laughed. "Why, Ser Beltrame, are you angry – and for the matter of a rose? There are still many in the garden."

"In the garden, yes. But the one I coveted, the one I begged of you but a moment since – that one is gone," he reproached her.

"And I am to blame if Ser Angelo is rude and violent?" quoth she, striving to keep the matter in the realm of jest. "You were witness that I did not give him the flower. He took it without permission; seized it with ruthless force."

Beltrame smiled, as smiles the loser in the act of paying; and the gall in his soul fermented, but was repressed for the time, to bubble forth, the more violent for its repression, an hour or so thereafter when he was alone with Angelo.

They had departed together from Lavinia's garden, and together they made their way in the twilight through the Rione di Ponte. Side by side they went; Beltrame moody and thoughtful; Angelo with smiling eyes and the lilt of a song on his lips, with new words which his mind was setting to it as they paced along.

Suddenly Beltrame spoke; his voice harsh and grating.

"Touching that rose, Angelo," he began.

" 'Twas culled in Paradise," breathed Angelo softly, and he inhaled its fragrance in an ecstasy.

"I covet it," said the other viciously.

"Ah! Who would not?" smiled the poet. And he quoted, with modifications to suit his own case, a sonnet of Petrarca's:

> "Cupid's right hand did open my left side,
> And planted in my heart a crimson rose."

" 'A laurel green' the poet has it," Beltrame corrected him.

"Petrarca, yes. But I – "

The Neapolitan's right hand fell heavily on Angelo's shoulder, and stayed him.

"We'll keep to the master's words, by your leave, dear Angelo," he laughed; and his laugh was evil and unpleasant. Angelo stared at him, the smile of ecstasy fading from his lips. "I'll play at Cupid," explained Beltrame, with a sneer, "and here's my laurel for the purpose." He tapped his sword-hilt, nodding darkly. "It shall be red anon, as a compromise to your own poetic fancy."

Horror filled Angelo, but no fear. "Beltrame," he said solemnly, "I have loved you."

"There is a green stretch that I know of close at hand, behind the Braschi. It is as smooth and green as – as the turf in Madonna Lavinia's garden. A sweet spot to die in. Shall it be there?"

Anger rose in Angelo's soul, and in the rising waxed hot and passionate as the Neapolitan's own. That this man who had been his friend should now seek his life for very jealousy, and where it could nothing profit him, incensed him by its mean unreasonableness.

"Why, since that is your mood," he answered, "it shall be where you will. But first, Beltrame – "

"Come, then," the Neapolitan bade him, harshly interrupting the appeal he guessed was on the point of following. Then he laughed his evil laugh again. " 'Angel' are you named; an angel does Monna Lavinia account you. It is high time I made an angel of you in earnest."

"And just as surely as you are a devil, just so surely shall you sup in hell this night," returned Angelo as he strode on beside the other.

But as they went the poet's eyes grew troubled. His spurt of anger spent, the folly of the thing appalled him. He must attempt to avert it.

"Beltrame," he questioned, by way of opening a discussion, "what is your sudden quarrel with me?"

"Madonna Lavinia loves you. I saw it in her eyes today. I love Lavinia. Needs more be said?"

"Why, no, indeed," said the poet, and his eyes grew dreamy again, his lips assumed a wistful smile. "If that contents you there is no doubt that it contents me. My thanks, Beltrame."

"For what?" quoth Beltrame with suspicion.

"For having seen what you saw, and for having told me of it. I lacked the certainty. It will make a sweet thought to die on, if God wills that I should die. Have you no fear, Beltrame?"

"Fear?" snorted the stalwart Neapolitan.

"Men say the gods love a lover."

"Not a doubt but they'll love you well enough to take you to their bosom."

On that they crossed the street, and skirting the Braschi Palace, they descended a narrow lane where the shadows made night, to emerge again into the twilight of an open square. And as they went Angelo's poetic soul, not to be restrained even by the matter that impended, suggested an opening line for a sonnet on a lover dying. He muttered it aloud to test its rhythm and gather inspiration to continue.

"What do you say?" asked Beltrame over his shoulder. He was a pace or two in front, as became the more eager of the twain.

"I am but muttering a verse," said Angelo quietly: " 'There's a sweet visage, sweet can render death.' Can you give me an unusual rhyme for death?"

"I'll give you the thing itself if you'll but have patience," growled Beltrame. "Come. This is the place."

They had penetrated a belt of acacias set about a stretch of smooth, green turf. Peace reigned there. The place was utterly deserted, and the trees made an effective screen in case anyone should come whilst they were at their bloody work.

Suddenly the Angelus bell boomed on the lethargic evening air. They paused, and bared their heads, and though murder was in the soul of one of them, he offered three Aves up to heaven. The bell ceased.

"Now," said Beltrame, casting his hat upon the grass, and untrussing the points of his doublet with swift, eager fingers.

Angelo started as from a reverie, and proceeded, more leisurely, to make ready. A moment he stood, holding the rose to his lips, breathing the fragrance of it; he was loath to put it down; yet he needed both his hands, one for his sword, the other for his dagger; for Beltrame awaited him, doubly armed. At last he solved the difficulty, and set the stem of the flower between his teeth.

If God willed that he should die that evening, at least her first love token should be with him in his last moments; its perfume – fond emblem of her soul – should sweeten for him his last breath on earth.

Beltrame saw him coming, the rose between his lips and lacking the wit to sound a poet's fancies, he deemed it an act of mockery, a thing done derisive and exultantly. He paled a shade. He looked furtively around. They were alone. A deadly smile flickered on his lips as he raised his weapons, and fell on guard.

He was a gentleman trained in arms, was this Beltrame; and easy, he thought, should be to him the slaughter of a scribbling poet, a man versed in no weapon but the goose-quill. Yet his certainty of victory was based on an even surer measure of precaution; his valour sprang from another advantage – an advantage that made him no better than a murderer, as you shall learn.

Sword and dagger met dagger and sword; parted, met again, circled, flashed, struck fire, were locked an instant, and once more were parted. For some five minutes they fought on. The sweat gathered on Beltrame's brow, and he breathed a prayer of thanks to a heaven that surely did not heed him, for the secret advantage that was his; without that it would almost seem that this scrivener must prove his better.

They fell back to breathe a moment, each welcoming the brief respite, for each was winded by the fierce vigour of the onslaught. Then they engaged once more, and Angelo knew in his heart that he was Beltrame's master. But that he held his hand, Angelo might have slain his adversary a score of times had the latter had a score of lives to lose. But he was gentle – as gentle as he was skilled – and he could not seek the life of the man who had been his friend. Instead he sought Beltrame's sword arm. If he could drive a foot or so of steel through it, there would be an end to the encounter; and by the time the wound was healed he would see to it that their difference was healed also; he would reason with this hot-headed Beltrame during the season of his convalescence, and seek to induce him out of his murderous jealousy.

Suddenly Beltrame's point came like a snake at Angelo's throat. Angelo was no more than in time to turn the thrust aside, and the viciousness that could aim so at a vital spot, stirred his anger anew; it also awoke him to a sense of his own danger. Unless he disabled Beltrame soon, his life would pay the price of his generosity. Beltrame was the stronger and was showing less fatigue; unless he went in soon, he might not go in at all. Since he could not reach the arm, he would take Beltrame there, high up in the right breast, above the lung, where little damage could be done, thus:

He parried a sharp thrust delivered rather high, and on the binding of the blade went in and up with a stroke that he had learnt from the famous Costanzo of Milan, who had been his preceptor in the art of swordsmanship.

His point went home unwarded; but instead of sinking through unresisting flesh, it struck something that jarred and numbed his arm; and on the stroke his rapier snapped, and he was left with a hilt and a stump of steel.

Beltrame laughed, and Angelo understood. The Neapolitan wore a shirt of mail – one of those meshes so much in fashion then, so fine that your two hands might encompass and conceal it, and yet so finely tempered as to be proof against the stoutest stroke of sword or dagger.

The poet twisted the rose to a corner of his mouth, that he might have freedom to speak, what time with his dagger and the stump that remained him, he made the best defence he could against the other's furious charge.

"Coward!" he cried in a fury of reproach. "Oh, craven hound! Assassin! Ah... Gesù!"

Beltrame's sword had found him. A second he stood shuddering, his lips twisted, his eyes surprised. Then he hurtled forward, and lay prone on the turf, horribly still, his teeth clenched fast over the stem of his red rose. Beltrame stood over him, sword embrued to the hilt, a mocking, cruel smile on his swarthy face.

Then the murderer dropped on one knee, and laid hands on Angelo to turn him over. He had killed him for the rose. He would take it now. But in the very act of setting hands upon his victim, he paused. Sounds reached him from beyond the trees, over by the Braschi Palace.

"Down there!" he heard a voice shouting in the distance; and footsteps came beating quickly on the stones.

He understood. Some one attracted by the clash of blades had spied on them and had run for the bargelli.

Swift and silent as a lizard, Beltrame darted to the dark pile of doffed garments. He snatched up his doublet, sword, belt and scabbard; he never waited to don them, but tucking them under his arm and clapping hat on head, he was gone from that open space of lawn thanking Heaven for the thickening dusk that lent him cover as he ran.

In a dark alley not twenty paces from the square he paused, laid down his bundle, and carefully wiped and sheathed his weapons. Then he donned his doublet, girded on his belt, straightened his hat, and sauntered boldly back, adown the alley.

At the mouth of it he was suddenly confronted by three of the bargelli. A lanthorn was raised and flashed on his patrician garments. An officer stepped forward briskly.

"Whence are you, sir?" he asked.

"From Piazza Navona," answered Beltrame without hesitation.

"This way?" And the officer pointed up the alley.

"Why, yes. This way."

One of the bargelli laughed. The officer stepped closer to Beltrame, and bade the lanthorn-bearer hold the light in the gentleman's face.

"This alley, sir, has but one entrance – this. Now, sir, again whence are you?"

Confused, Beltrame sought shelter in bluster. He would not be interrogated. Was not a gentleman free to walk where he listed? Let them beware how they incommoded him. He was Messer Beltrame Severino.

The officer increased in courtesy but diminished nothing in his firmness.

"A man has been done to death down there," he informed Beltrame, "and you would be well advised to return full answers to my questions, unless you prefer to go before the Ruota."

Beltrame bade him go to the devil. Whereupon the men laid hands upon him, and the officer made bold to examine his weapons. Despite his precautions, Beltrame grew afraid, for he had wiped them in the dark.

The officer looked along the sword, then peered under the quillons of the hilt. What he saw there caused him to touch the spot with his finger, and then examine this.

"Wet blood," said he, and added curtly to his men, "Bring him with you."

They carried him off that he might tell what story he pleased to the president of the Ruota, and explain his wanderings in that blind alley by the Braschi.

Now it happened that the hole that Beltrame made in Angelo d'Asti's fair body was not large enough for the escape of so great a soul. Yet might it have proved so but for another thing that happened. As they were bearing him away from the scene of the combat, wondering who he might be, and whither they should carry him, the group was met by Marco Fregosi – Madonna Lavinia's brother, and Angelo's good friend.

At sight of Angelo's face, Marco made the bearers pause, and demanded to know what had befallen. Then, upon finding that the poet's life was not yet extinct, he ordered them to carry him to his villa on Banchi Vecchi – the house which Angelo had left but an hour or so ago.

They nursed him back to health and wholeness. The beautiful Lavinia in a passion of solicitude tended him herself. Could she have done less? For you are to know that they brought him in with the red rose still tight between his teeth, and she had recognised her love token. If anything had still been wanting to complete Angelo's conquest of her virgin heart, that thing he now afforded.

It was nine days before he opened his eyes to reason and understanding, his danger overpast; life and happiness awaiting him. They told him he was at the Villa Fregosi, and the very announcement did as much to complete his recovery as their tender efforts had done to bring it thus far.

On the morrow he saw Lavinia at last. Her brother brought her to him, and seeing him awake again her eyes filled with tears, as sweet as those had been bitter with which she had watered his pillow and her own – though he knew it not, nor dreamed it – during the first days of sojourn with them, when his vital fire seemed on the point of extinction.

It was on the occasion of this visit that Marco asked him for the details of what had happened, the story of how he had come by his

227

hurt, expressing at the same time his own suspicions that it was Beltrame who had all but slain him.

"Ay," answered Angelo wistfully, "Beltrame it was – the coward! He wore a mesh of steel in secret, and forced me into a combat that must end in murder."

"And upon what grounds did you quarrel?" was Marco's next question, heedless of his sister's heightening distress.

"We fought for a rose; this." He bore his hand half-way to his lips; then, bethinking him, he smiled, and dropped it back upon the coverlet.

"I have kept it for you," said Lavinia through her tears.

The light of a great joy leaped to the poet's eyes to answer her; a flush mounted to his pale brow.

"You fought for a rose?" quoth Marco, frowning. "I hardly understand."

"You wouldn't," said Angelo. " 'Twas a rose of Paradise."

Marco looked grave. "Lavinia," said he, rising gently, "I think perhaps we had better leave him. His mind is wandering again."

"No, no," laughed Angelo, and his tone was reassuring. "Tell me – what of Beltrame?"

"He is dead," said Marco.

"Dead?" And for all that he had suffered at Beltrame's hands, for all that Beltrame had sought his life, there was distress in Angelo's voice and in the glance he bent upon Marco. "How came he to die?"

"By the will and pleasure of the Lord Cesare Borgia. He was hanged."

"And I think he deserved it, Angelo," said Lavinia. "He deserved it for his attempt to murder you, if not for the thing for which they punished him."

"For what else, then, did he suffer?"

"Do you remember," she said, "that afternoon at the Vatican?"

"Yes," he answered, mystified.

"And how the Duke of Valentinois came in, so very angry, and told of the verses that had been found that day upon the statue of Pasquino, and how his bargelli were seeking for the author?"

"Yes, yes. But what has this to do with Beltrame?"

"He was the author," said Marco.

"Beltrame?"

"It was proved so. It fell out thus," Marco related. "It was his attempt to murder you that destroyed him. He was found near the Braschi a few moments after the bargelli had discovered you. There was blood on his sword, and so they carried him before the Tribunal of the Ruota, which began his examination with the usual formality of having him searched. In his pocket was found the original of those very verses, with all the erasures and emendations and substitutions that a writer makes in perfecting his work. He denied all knowledge of them; told, I know not what preposterous lies. But they put him to the question. At the third hoist he confessed."

"Confessed?" quoth Angelo, his eyes dilating.

"Ay; the torture drew it from him. He may perhaps have thought they would not go the length of hanging him, or else, that since you were doubtless dead, they would hang him in any case, and so that he might at least avoid further agonies by confessing and being done with it. Cesare Borgia is tired of pasquinades, and wished to make an ensample. And so they hanged him next morning beside the statue of Pasquino."

Angelo sank back on his pillows, and stared at the ceiling for some moments.

"He was undoubtedly a coward," said he at length, smiling bitterly, "and he met a coward's fate. He deserved to die. And yet he was not the author of that pasquinade."

"Not the author? How do you know?"

"Because – Are we alone? Because," said Angelo softly, "it was I who wrote it."

"You, Angelo?" cried brother and sister in a breath. Angelo's eyes were wandering round the room, reflecting the bewilderment that filled his soul. Suddenly they paused, fastening upon a garment of shot silk that was thrown across a chair.

"What is that?" he asked abruptly, pointing.

"That? Your doublet," answered Marco. "They fetched it with you from the Braschi, when you were wounded."

Angelo sank back again, and he smiled never so faintly.

"That makes it clear," he said. "Beltrame took the wrong doublet in the dark. The verses were in my pocket."

Lavinia's hand stole over Angelo's where it lay upon the coverlet. He raised his eyes to hers. "We owe him much – to this Beltrame," he said slowly. "I could have known no peace while they were hunting the author of that pasquinade. He has satisfied the hunters, and so removed the danger of discovery from me. That is something. But I owe him more, do I not, Lavinia?"

"Why, what else do you owe him?" inquired Marco.

"This brother of yours is a very dull fellow, Lavinia," said Angelo, smiling as the blessed smile.

Rafael Sabatini

Captain Blood

Captain Blood is the much-loved story of a physician and gentleman turned pirate.

Peter Blood, wrongfully accused and sentenced to death, narrowly escapes his fate and finds himself in the company of buccaneers. Embarking on his new life with remarkable skill and bravery, Blood becomes the 'Robin Hood' of the Spanish seas. This is swashbuckling adventure at its best.

The Gates of Doom

'Depend above all on Pauncefort', announced King James, 'his loyalty is dependable as steel. He is with us body and soul and to the last penny of his fortune.' So when Pauncefort does indeed face bankruptcy after the collapse of the South Sea Company, the king's supreme confidence now seems rather foolish. And as Pauncefort's thoughts turn to gambling, moneylenders and even marriage to recover his debts, will he be able to remain true to the end? And what part will his friend and confidante, Captain Gaynor, play in his destiny?

'A clever story, well and amusingly told' – *The Times*

RAFAEL SABATINI

THE LOST KING

The Lost King tells the story of Louis XVII – the French royal who officially died at the age of ten but, as legend has it, escaped to foreign lands where he lived to an old age. Sabatini breathes life into these age-old myths, creating a story of passion, revenge and betrayal. He tells of how the young child escaped to Switzerland from where he plotted his triumphant return to claim the throne of France.

'…the hypnotic spell of a novel which for sheer suspense, deserves to be ranked with Sabatini's best' – *New York Times*

SCARAMOUCHE

When a young cleric is wrongfully killed, his friend, Andre Louis, vows to avenge his death. Louis' mission takes him to the very heart of the French Revolution where he finds the only way to survive is to assume a new identity. And so is born Scaramouche – a brave and remarkable hero of the finest order and a classic and much-loved tale of the greatest swashbuckling tradition.

'Mr Sabatini's novel of the French Revolution has all the colour and lively incident which we expect in his work' – *Observer*

Rafael Sabatini

The Sea Hawk

Sir Oliver, a typical English gentleman, is accused of murder, kidnapped off the Cornish coast, and dragged into life as a Barbary corsair. However Sir Oliver rises to the challenge and proves a worthy hero for this much-admired novel. Religious conflict, melodrama, romance and intrigue combine to create a masterly and highly successful story, perhaps best known for its many film adaptations.

The Shame of Motley

The Court of Pesaro has a certain fool – one Lazzaro Biancomonte of Biancomonte. *The Shame of Motley* is Lazzaro's story, presented with all the vivid colour and dramatic characterisation that has become Sabatini's hallmark.

'Mr Sabatini could not be conventional or commonplace if he tried'
– *Standard*

Printed in Great Britain
by Amazon

23747905R00136